A Christmas Present

A Christmas Present

Holiday Stories by

Loretta Chase
Judith E. French
Lisa Kleypas

And a Special Preview of
AFTER INNOCENCE
by Brenda Joyce

AVON BOOKS ◆ NEW YORK

A CHRISTMAS PRESENT is an original publication of Avon Books. These stories have never appeared together in book form. Any similarity to actual persons or events is purely coincidental.

"Falling Stars" by Loretta Chase originally appeared in *Avon Books Presents: A Christmas Collection*; "Gifts of the Heart" by Judith E. French originally appeared in *Avon Books Presents: Under the Mistletoe*; "Surrender" by Lisa Kleypas originally appeared in *Avon Books Presents: Christmas Love Stories*.

AVON BOOKS
A division of
The Hearst Corporation
1350 Avenue of the Americas
New York, New York 10019

Falling Stars

Loretta Chase

1

Wiltshire, England,
11 December 1818

I F A MAN COULD SLEEP THROUGH THE RACKET OF early morning London, Marcus Greyson told himself, he could certainly sleep through the noise of lively children. He pulled the pillow over his head, but he could hear it all the same: shrill voices and the thumping of little feet up and down the corridors. Even in the intervals of silence, he was waiting, braced for the next outburst of shrieks and thumps.

With an oath, he flung the pillow aside and dragged himself out of bed. He had slept only three hours. That, evidently, was all the sleep he was going to get. A glance at the window told him morning was well advanced—a winter morn so crisply bright it made his eyes ache.

Despite his grogginess, Marcus washed and dressed quickly, while his mind ran over a dozen possible excuses he could give his elder brother and sister-in-law for turning up in the dead of night.

Julius and Penelope probably still weren't aware he was here.

They had all been asleep when he'd come. He had simply let himself in with his own key, and gone up to the room they always kept ready for him. While they'd be delighted Marcus had changed his mind about spending Christmas at Greymarch, they were sure to wonder about his bizarre traveling schedule.

He gave his thick mane of tawny hair the usual slapdash brushing, and pulled on his coat. Since he didn't have a reasonable explanation, he might as well give an unreasonable one, so ludicrous they'd be too busy laughing to ask any more.

He opened the door and stepped into the hall just as a matched pair of fair-haired little girls came barreling round the corner. One neatly dodged and shot past. The other tripped over his foot.

Marcus caught her before she hit the floor and briskly set her back on her feet. As he met her dazed blue stare, he inhaled sharply. He knew those eyes . . . no, it was impossible.

"Delia! Livy!" came a feminine voice from the stairway.

His head swung toward the sound.

"Yes, Mama," the little girl called out. "We're just going to the schoolroom." Flashing Marcus a grin, she darted down the hall.

"Not before we have a discussion, young ladies."

Even while his mind denied, disbelieved, his senses recognized, and stirred.

The voice's owner came round the corner, then stopped dead.

All else stopped, too—his heart and breath—as

though they'd collided physically. The impact sent him reeling into the past.

He had met her in summer, but hers was winter's beauty. Her hair was pale sunlight framing the snowy purity of her skin, and there was winter, too, in her eyes, clear, ice-blue. Christina.

He regained his breath and managed a bow. "Mrs. Travers."

"Mr. . . . Greyson." The fingers of her left hand curled and uncurled against the grey woolen gown. No wedding ring. When had Arthur Travers died? Some two or three years ago?

"I was not . . ." Her full mouth formed a tight smile. "I was unaware you were here. Penelope said—that is, no one mentioned your arrival."

That low voice with its trace of huskiness . . . so like a caress . . . He pulled his wandering mind back.

"They couldn't have known," he said. "I arrived late last night. A spur-of-the-moment decision." His heart was beating too fast—because he was taken aback, Marcus told himself. He knew she and Penny still corresponded, but from all he'd heard, Christina hadn't left Cumbria since she was married. He hadn't been told she'd be here, and couldn't possibly have expected it.

He backed away a step. She did, too.

"How . . . pleased Julius will be," she said. "And Penelope. And of course, the boys. They've boasted of their uncle to the twins."

"The little girls," he said tautly. "Yours, obviously."

She nodded. "Delia and Livy." Her ice blue gaze melted a fraction. "Seven years old last month. And dreadful hoydens, as you've probably noticed. I hope their noise didn't wake you."

Seven years old. That seemed impossible. But it had been ten years since he'd last seen her, and she'd married soon thereafter—a mere three months thereafter, he recalled, with a sting of bitterness that startled him. He retreated another pace.

"The children didn't disturb me at all," he lied. "I was just going down to breakfast."

"Then I mustn't keep you."

She moved past him, a breath of scent teasing in her wake. Lavender.

He'd known many other women who wore lavender. The scent should have conjured up recent memories. Instead, as he stood in the hall listening to her light step fade, the scene opening up in his mind rose from a decade ago.

It had been late May, a fortnight before Julius's wedding, and the first group of houseguests had arrived. Julius was taking them on a tour of Greymarch, and he'd nagged Marcus into going along.

Though acutely aware of Penny's beautiful friend, Marcus had kept his distance. He detested prim and proper Society, and above all loathed its featherbrained misses, with their virginal white gowns and twittering voices and mincing, mannered ways. The males weren't much better: a lot of complacent hypocrites among whom not a single original thought could be found.

While the guests explored the old gatehouse—the Greysons' Picturesque Ruin, Julius called it—Marcus had gritted his teeth and kept his mouth shut; resolved for Julius's sake to endure boredom and frustration in silence. Marcus had been leaning against a fir tree, softly whistling the melody of a bawdy song, when Penny's friend had shyly approached.

"What is the song?" Christina had asked in that foggy, beckoning voice.

He had carefully avoided looking at her, because he'd seen what happened to other men who did. In less than twenty-four hours, this eighteen-year-old girl with her platinum hair and silver-blue eyes had effortlessly turned every unattached male at Greymarch into a dithering imbecile.

Marcus had looked at the gatehouse, the rocks, the trees, and the blue, cloudless sky—anywhere but at her—while he answered acidly that the melody was beneath the notice of good little girls because its composer wasn't anyone *genteel* like Haydn or even Rossini.

"Oh," she'd said. Only that, and she was just backing away—as he'd believed he wanted—when the spring breeze carried the lavender scent to his nostrils. It had swirled into his brain—and, dizzy, he'd looked down and watched her face slowly turning to profile, her eyes downcast so that the long lashes almost brushed her cheek. He'd watched her soft mouth turn downward ever so slightly, then saw his hand reaching to touch her muslin sleeve, while he heard his voice gentling as he said, "Shall I whistle Rossini instead?"

She had turned back, lifting doubtful blue eyes to his. Then, in the space from one heartbeat to the next, the moment of her silver-blue gaze sweeping up to meet his, he'd tumbled headlong into love . . . and two weeks later, into heartbreak.

Marcus recoiled from the memory as though it had been a physical blow. The present swung back sharply into focus.

Christina Travers was nothing to him, he told himself as he headed for the stairs. He'd scarcely thought of her in years. Young men fell in love every day, and had their hearts broken, or else they got their hearts' desire and wed. Some lived happily ever after—as Julius had—but more often they existed with their wives in a state of stultifying boredom or endless quarrel.

Christina had wed wealth and comfort—as she'd been reared to do, Marcus was well aware. According to gossip, she'd lived in virtual seclusion in the Lake District ever since, while he'd spent seven of the last ten years abroad. Had he encountered her in the interim, today's meeting wouldn't have disconcerted him. His strong physical reaction and his mind's reversion to the past were confused responses to the unexpected . . . and to her beauty, of course. He wouldn't have imagined she could grow more lovely.

Naturally he wouldn't. The last time he'd seen her, he had been a callow youth of four-and-twenty who believed Christina was the most beautiful girl in all the world. He'd believed a great many foolish things, once

Having seen the children settled in the schoolroom under Miss Finch's competent tutelage, a shaken Christina went to the sitting room to write a letter to her great-aunt Georgiana. She took up a sheet of paper, dipped her pen into the inkwell, then had to wipe the pen and put it down because she couldn't keep her hands—or her thoughts—steady. She studied her uncooperative hands in dismay, as though they belonged to a stranger. A short while ago, in the hall, she had felt like a stranger to herself. She had behaved like a tongue-tied schoolgirl—like the weak-minded young miss she'd been a decade before—frantically babbling small talk while she turned hot and cold by turns under Marcus Greyson's intent, gold-glinting stare. Worst of all, she had snatched at the first excuse to run away.

Rising from the desk, Christina moved to the window. Below her, Greymarch's formal gardens lay tranquil, their winter barrenness softened by the deep emerald of evergreen shrubs. To her right, the branches of leafless oaks etched dark webs against the vibrant blue of the sky. To her left, well beyond the winding stream, ancient fir trees blocked her view of the old gatehouse.

She didn't need to see it to remember, though.

It had been two weeks before Penny's wedding. Christina hadn't seen Penny in several months, but they'd corresponded. Julius Greyson turned out to be just as Penny had described in her letters: tall, dark, handsome, gracious, witty, and obviously in love with his bride-to-be. That much Christina managed to digest before she was introduced to his brother.

She saw a bronze god: thick, tawny hair streaked with gold, a sculpted, sun-burnished countenance, and intent, amber-flecked green eyes that lit to gold when he glanced down at her and muttered some barely polite greeting. Marcus Greyson was the most beautiful man she'd ever seen. He was also, at first, the least amiable. Bored, his impatience palpable, he couldn't be bothered to say another word to her during the subsequent tour of Greymarch.

As far as he was concerned, she didn't exist. As far as she was concerned, no one existed but him. To approach a gentleman she didn't know—who evidently preferred to know nobody—was unthinkable. To keep away was impossible. And so, when the group paused at the gatehouse, she'd walked— shaking in her half-boots—across the clearing and up to him, and said the first inane thing that came into her head.

He'd snapped at her quite rudely, which no one had ever done in all her eighteen years, and which should have sent her scurrying back to the safety of her well-mannered acquaintances. But he'd leaned against a fir tree, and there was the cool tang of evergreens about her, and some other scent—tansy and cloves, she'd guessed—emanating from him. There was something else as well—strange and different and dark—and this had slowed her retreat. When he'd touched her sleeve, she'd looked up into his eyes. He'd smiled, and she had too, helplessly, because she'd found the welcome she wanted.

His eyes had not been welcoming this morning. His handsome countenance had hardened to stone the moment he saw her, and the only emotion she'd discerned in those changeable eyes was annoyance.

Well, the surprise hadn't been altogether agreeable for her, either.

Turning from the window and a view that stirred unwanted ghosts from the past, she tried to consider the situation rationally and fairly. His annoyance very likely had nothing to do with her—or, more

precisely, with the Christina of the past. He'd surely forgotten most, if not all, of what had happened.
After all, she had been merely one in an endless
stream of infatuated females.

If he was vexed to find her here, that could easily
be because he'd expected to spend a quiet Christmas
with his family. Now there were twice as many children as he'd expected—which meant twenty times
the racket—and a widowed friend of Penny's he'd
have to make polite conversation with.

She wasn't exactly delighted about making polite
conversation with him, either, Christina thought
defensively. But that was ridiculous, she chided
herself in the next instant. She was far too mature
to hold a grudge for ten long years.

All the same, she couldn't help remembering.
She saw clearly in her mind's eye his letter with
its black, lashing script, each word sharp as the
sting of a whip. At the time she had believed her
shattered heart would never recover.

So the young generally feel when they first
experience betrayal, the mature Christina told
herself. The fact was, he'd done her a favor in
destroying her illusions. She bore no grudge. She
simply hadn't forgotten the painful lesson he had
taught her. She had nothing to fear from him. He
couldn't hurt her again. She was no longer a naive
eighteen-year-old girl.

As soon as they were released from the schoolroom, Kit and Robin hunted their uncle down, and
formally introduced him to their new playmates.
Within a very few minutes, Marcus discovered
that Livy was quiet and reflective, while Delia

was bolder and restless. It was Livy who ran to seek their mama's permission to play out of doors with Mr. Greyson, while Delia was already racing for her coat and mittens. She was first at the door, shoving a ridiculously frilly bonnet onto her head, and heedlessly pulling her mittens on backward.

Marcus crouched down before her. "May I help?" he asked politely.

At her nod, he straightened the mittens, then proceeded to tie the bonnet ribbons.

"Your eyes are two colors," she told him. "There is green and little gold speckles. Did fairies do that?"

"They might have done."

"It is very pretty. I wish I had fairy gold in my eyes."

He stood up and pulled on his gloves. "You have fairy silver," he said. "Like a blue sky with silver dust. It is much, much prettier."

"A blue sky with silver dust." She considered. "And Livy, too, then. And Mama."

"Yes."

"Yes," she repeated with a satisfied nod. She took his hand, and looked up at him, and smiled.

This was merely a child's smile of trusting innocence, and a child's tiny, mittened hand clasping his own. There was nothing in it to disturb or surprise him. He was disturbed nevertheless, because he felt the small gesture too deeply, as though it pricked some sensitive place in his heart, some old wound.

He looked away from the girl's innocent, up-turned face and the too-familiar silver-blue eyes, and the troubling sensation passed. Marcus told himself his mind was addled, that was all, and he was oversensitive from lack of sleep.

Christina was in the sitting room, embroidering a handkerchief while she listened to Penelope fret over arrangements for the following night's Yuletide ball.

"I can't think what's to be done." Pushing back from her cluttered writing desk, Penny folded her hands over her just-noticeably swollen belly. "I can hardly tell Miss Nichols to keep away. And it's no use hoping she'll break an ankle. When she learns Marcus is here, she'll come, even if she must be carried on a litter."

"I take it Miss Nichols has set her cap at Mr. Greyson." Christina jammed the needle through the fabric with rather more force than necessary.

"She'd set her hounds on him if she could. Since she can't, she'll plague him to death."

"She's a near neighbor," Christina said. "You could hardly *not* invite her, even if you'd known he was coming. Besides, he may not object to her interest." She felt a tweak of something nastily like jealousy. She glared at the knot she'd just made. "I expect she's grown quite lovely. She was a beautiful child when I first—when I last saw her, at your wedding."

Penelope turned a bit in her chair. "We weren't much more than children ourselves. Was that the last time you saw Marcus?"

Christina nodded stiffly.

"Then you find him much changed, I daresay."

"I should hope so," came a masculine voice from the doorway. "I should hate to appear a callow youth when I'm teetering on the brink of senility."

At the sound of his voice, Christina's heart gave a quick, foolish leap, just as it used to do whenever he came near. She set her jaw and resolutely turned her head toward the door.

Marcus leaned against the frame, his eyes dark and unreadable in the shadow of the doorway. He had changed little physically. He had been tall, lean-muscled, and strong ten years ago. Maturity had added a fraction more breadth to his shoulders, to his hard chest . . . but she'd noticed all that earlier, she chided herself. She didn't have to take *measurements*, for heaven's sake. She dragged her gaze away.

He had made his own way in the world—alone, she reflected, while she listened to Penny tease him for eavesdropping. People had mistrusted him once, because Marcus Greyson made his own rules, respected no authority, no boundaries set by others. But in the time since she'd known him, he'd dared and risked and won, stunning the world with the magnitude of his success. He now possessed both wealth and power, and it showed.

That didn't altogether explain why, as he eased his six-foot frame away from the doorway, he seemed to fill the room, or why her senses should bristle and quicken at his slightest motion.

She felt his knowing green-gold eyes upon her, a swiftly assessing glance, come and gone in seconds. Yet her flesh prickled and heated under it, as though under his hands, and she felt she'd been unclothed . . . and teased . . . and abandoned.

She yanked her needle through the linen.

He stopped a moment to look over Penny's shoulder at the untidy heap of paper, and teased her about preparing for a party as Wellington might a war campaign. Penny laughed and made some joking answer.

Then he moved toward Christina. She felt a frantic fluttering within, and a memory rose that sent a mortifying heat rushing up her neck.

The day after she'd first spoken to him, Marcus had found her alone in this sitting room. She'd been daydreaming out a window.

She'd heard him come up behind her, but hadn't moved. She'd felt the same inner flutter then, and a confusing warmth, and the same mingled anxiety and anticipation. He'd stood behind her, not uttering a word. She'd held her breath, waiting, wondering what would happen next, all the while terrified someone would come—and hoping someone would. Then she'd felt his breath, a whisper against her neck that sent a warm tingle down her spine, all the way to her toes. "I just want to be near you," he'd said, his voice so low it was a wonder she'd heard it past the frantic beating of her heart.

Her idiotic heart was growing frantic now, as he paused mere inches from her chair. What she felt was a perfectly sensible anxiety, she told herself. If he was still annoyed about finding her here, he could make her stay uncomfortable. And she must stay. Her house let for the next twelvemonth, Great-Aunt Georgiana gone to Scotland, Christina was trapped at Greymarch until the New Year.

At the moment she felt trapped in her chair by the tall masculine body looming over her.

"I've come to ask if you'd paint with us, Mrs. Travers."

His rich baritone came from directly above her bowed head. She was staring at his gleaming boots, a handsbreadth from her grey kid shoes. She didn't want to look up until she had collected her rapidly disintegrating composure. He had already made her blush once, and she would rather hang than do it again—like the awkward schoolgirl she'd been all those years ago.

"I beg your pardon?" There was an infuriatingly childish wobble in her voice. She stabbed her needle into the handkerchief.

"We've decided to paint dragons. Delia and Livy said you're an expert dragon painter."

"Oh. I . . . well, that is very kind, but . . ." Oh, wonderful—stammering, too, like a tongue-tied adolescent.

"Also, Delia will not wear her smock, which Livy says she must do," he went on. "Which places me in an awkward predicament."

Christina raised her head quickly, but not quickly enough to avoid the lean, muscled length of male between the boots and the glint of gold in his eyes. Was that amusement she saw—or mockery?

"Good heavens, Marcus," Penny exclaimed, "could you not leave it to a nursery maid?"

"Not before I'd ascertained the facts," he answered. "For all I knew, the child might have a terror of smocks. Children do take unaccountable aversions, I'm told. Since she's been otherwise perfectly agreeable, I concluded I had stumbled upon a strongly-rooted aversion."

Christina found her voice. "It *is* an aversion," she said. "But not to smocks in general—only Livy's in particular, which are starched."

"There, I knew it must be significant," Marcus triumphantly told his sister-in-law. He turned back to Christina. "Starch, is it? She only said it was horrid, and she wouldn't wear it."

"Nor will she." Christina rose. "I never thought to explain it to the maid. I'll go find one of Delia's smocks—unstarched—and—"

"And one for yourself," he prompted. "You don't want to spoil your gown with dragon paint."

Yes, one for herself, of course. He'd come only because he wanted her to take the children off his hands. Firmly crushing a twinge of disappointment, she hurried out to find the dratted smocks.

Marcus had meant to leave the children in Christina's care, and get away where he could put his thoughts back into order—for the angelic-looking twins had disordered them to an alarming degree.

He'd discovered that looking after little girls was nothing like minding rough-and-tumble little boys. Christina had called her daughters hoydens, but they seemed to Marcus the most fragile of china dolls. Out of doors, he found himself worrying that they weren't dressed warmly enough, then that they were overwarm, and would take a chill in consequence. Every game seemed too rough; all the places he'd taken for granted as perfectly safe for children abruptly became fraught with perils.

Aware his anxieties were absurd, he'd refrained from acting upon them and, as one would expect, no tragedy had occurred, not even a scraped knee. He'd spent the whole time on the edge of panic, all the same.

When they were safely indoors at last, he'd hardly begun to relax before Delia threw the fit about the smock, setting off all the ridiculous alarms again.

He'd given up and gone for their mama—and stumbled into other, worse difficulties.

He was thrown off-balance in the sitting room because Christina had blushed when he'd spoken to her, and the blush had drawn him too near. The scent of lavender wafted about her, and while he watched the faint pink steal slowly up her neck, the ghost of a long-banished memory had stolen upon him.

Once, in that same room, he'd wanted to touch his mouth to her flushed neck, but hadn't dared, only stood and let her scent steal into his blood and make him desperate.

Despite all efforts to banish it, the recollection still hung in his mind. The blush was long gone, and she seemed cool enough at present, her attention on her painting. Marcus sat the length of the playroom table away, his nephews diligently working on either side, but he couldn't concentrate.

The room was cozy and warm. From time to time the lavender scent stole toward him, then vanished. If it would only make up its mind and do one or the other, linger or go, he might make up his mind, too, and settle to his work or depart. But her scent continued to beckon and withdraw, leaving him uncertain and restless.

As he looked up for the hundredth time, he found Delia studying him, so gravely that he couldn't help but smile. She answered with an impish grin. Then she slid down from her chair and scampered to his side, where she stood on tiptoe, balancing herself with one hand on his arm while she tried to peer over the table at his painting.

Marcus picked her up and sat her on his lap. It never occurred to him to ask if that was where she wished to be. The action was reflexive. It must have been correct, for Delia settled there, perfectly at home, and offered to help. Even to a seven-year-old it was obvious he wasn't making satisfactory progress.

"I shall rinse the brush for you," she said, "and help you pick the colors."

Livy took umbrage at this. "You don't know the right colors. Your dragon is pink and blue."

"Perhaps Mr. Greyson *likes* pink and blue dragons," Christina said. "If he doesn't, he is perfectly capable of telling your sister so. Mind what you're doing, Livy. Your dragon's tail is about to go off the paper and onto the table."

Livy frowned. "I've spoiled it." Ignoring her mother's reassuring murmur, the child scrambled down from her chair, snatched up the painting, and trotted to Marcus.

"It's spoiled," she told him, her countenance dejected as she held up the painting. "Delia made me spoil it."

"I did not," said Delia.

"It's not spoiled," Christina said, "and you are not to plague Mr. Greyson."

"It's just broken," said six-year-old Robin.

"Uncle Marcus will fix it," his brother consoled, patting Livy on the head with all the condescending superiority of his eight years.

"You have to fix it yourself," said Delia. "I'm helping him with his dragon."

Marcus heard a faint, choked sound, suspiciously like laughter, from the other end of the table. But when he glanced that way, Christina's countenance was sober.

"You made me spoil it," Livy accused her sister. "You were whispering secrets to Mr. Greyson and telling wrong colors."

Another smothered chuckle. This time, he discerned a twitch at the corner of Christina's mouth. That was all. No reproach for the girls, no assistance to him in parlaying a truce.

Marcus took the painting from Livy and studied it. "It isn't spoiled at all, but different and interesting. It looks to me as though your dragon has a strange and mysterious kink in his tail."

Livy edged closer and, putting her hand on his, lowered the painting to her eye level for scrutiny. "What is a kink?" she asked. "Is it pretty?"

The little hand on his told Marcus what the matter was: if Delia sat on his lap, Livy must, too. "Come, I'll show you," he said. He shifted Delia onto one knee, and took Livy up on the other. Hostilities ceased.

Taking up his brush, he finished the dragon's tail, making it curl up and around in the space Livy had left for the sky.

Delia grew restive. "Now her dragon is more beautiful than mine," she complained.

"No, it can't be," he said. "I'm sure your dragon is quite handsome."

Delia shook her head. "It isn't. Mine is horrid."

"Since you have promoted Mr. Greyson to chief artist, we shall let him judge." There was an edge to the mama's voice and a flush on her countenance as she held up Delia's painting for Marcus's perusal. He wondered whether she was vexed, and with whom.

"It is very fine," said Marcus, his gaze moving from the painting to the mama. He remembered that delicate tint: a whisper of pink upon alabaster. The first time he'd dared to take her hand in his, she'd colored like this, but she hadn't pulled away. He'd held her small, gloved hand as carefully as though it had been the most fragile of eggshells, and died of happiness during that too-brief moment. Then they'd heard the others coming, and he'd had to break away and pretend he'd only just that instant accidently encountered Christina in the garden.

She wore no gloves now. Her hands were slim and elegant, smooth and white and soft.

He wrenched his mind elsewhere, to Delia, who tugged at his coat sleeve, asking him to make a kink for her.

"Perhaps Mama would be so kind as to pass Delia's painting this way," he said tightly.

She rose instead, and brought it to him, then lingered to watch while he gave Delia's dragon strange and mysterious pink and blue claws in lieu of a kinky tail.

He wanted to get away.

He found the little girls adorable and their fondness for him touching. He didn't mind their negligible weight or the tiny kid shoes absently kicking at his shins. It wasn't on their account he wanted to bolt, or even entirely on account of their mother, standing a few inches from his shoulder.

Marcus wanted to get away from himself, to disengage from the flesh-and-blood Marcus, because that flesh and blood was responding quite on its own, as though his body belonged to someone else.

He was painfully aware of Christina's nearness and of her too-familiar scent and warmth, and of long-buried longings stirring to life.

When he added a whirl of smoke above Delia's dragon's head, Christina's voice with its trace of huskiness came from above his shoulder: "Now you must give Livy smoke, too, Mr. Greyson. Then I would advise you to add no more adornments. Otherwise the rivalry will go on endlessly, I promise you."

It was a mama's voice, wise in the ways of her offspring. Yet Marcus could hear its distant echo from long ago: *I promise you, I'll be there. I promise.*

He had waited all those long, miserable hours . . . and she never came.

He set his jaw, and painted smoke for Livy's dragon, and promised himself that ghosts or no ghosts, no woman, however beautiful, would make such a fool of him again. That, beyond doubt, had ended a long time ago.

At tea, Julius and Marcus argued about Greece, so hotly that Christina was sure they'd come to blows. Her tension must have been evident, because Penny edged closer on the sofa and patted her hand. "They won't kill each other," she said. "It's simply that Marcus doesn't believe it's a proper discussion unless everyone loses his temper. In that, you see, he hasn't changed at all."

She had to raise her voice to be heard above the men. Even so, the brothers had been so furiously involved in their debate that Christina was startled when Marcus abruptly turned toward the two women.

"I don't believe it's a proper discussion," he said, "when one's opponent is incapable of comprehending the simplest facts. I'm obliged to raise my voice in hopes of getting some small piece of information into my brother's thick skull."

"You won't persuade me it's in our government's interest to support the cause of anarchists," said Julius. "Only look what came of revolution in France."

"Only look at the American colonies," Marcus retorted. "Which is ridiculous to ask of you, since you've never ventured farther west than Falmouth."

"It's ridiculous to insist that a man can't make reasonable judgments about any circumstance he hasn't personally witnessed. Even our foreign ministers—"

"Perceive the world as someone else has told them they must. They believe whatever their teachers told them, or whichever ignorant blockhead has designated himself an authority."

No, Marcus hadn't changed in this, Christina thought. It was partly his radical views, but more his tactless, often insulting way of expressing them, that a decade ago had made him unwelcome at most social gatherings and alienated virtually all his peers.

"You're frowning, Mrs. Travers," Marcus said. "You take exception to my opinion."

His expression was mocking. She wondered if he thought a mere female was incapable of possessing an opinion, let alone disagreeing with that of a male. "I certainly don't agree that the two revolutions arose from the same circumstances, or had the same result," she said.

"Both chose to overthrow what they perceived as tyranny."

"That appears to be the only parallel," she said. "The French beheaded their monarch and most of their aristocracy. The Americans merely severed a *relationship*. It was England that made a war of it."

His dark eyebrows lifted. "Indeed. England, in your view, was rather like a lover the Americans had tired of."

"If I pursue that curious analogy," she said evenly, "I might say that the Americans found their lover's demands *unreasonable*."

She discerned what might be a flicker of surprise in the gold-glinting eyes, and then, more clearly, a flash of anger. She felt a small, fierce stab of satisfaction. He had started it. If he'd thought he could hurt her with the oblique reference to the past, if he thought she would shrink away and blush, he had another think coming.

"And I might say the mistress was *capricious*," he returned.

She met his challenging stare straight on. "You might, but you don't believe that. Your sympathies are with the Americans. You're merely playing devil's advocate, Mr. Greyson. You baited Julius, and now you're baiting me."

"Certainly. He baits everyone," said Julius, moving to the tea table. "There is nothing he likes better than a great, noisy row. Come, Marcus, stop up your mouth with a sandwich, and stop staring at

Christina as though she's sprouted another head."

Marcus opened his mouth, then shut it, and Christina felt a prickle of annoyance with Julius. The argument had hardly begun, and he had smoothly squelched it. No doubt Julius thought she couldn't defend herself. He, too, had another think coming.

Marcus silently approached the tea table, but made no move to take anything. He looked at the tea tray, then at her. *Look,* however, was too passive a word to convey what he did. He had a way of taking possession with a glance and fastening all one's consciousness on him.

Christina tried to think of something to say to Penny, some excuse to divert her attention elsewhere. But her brain refused to consider anything but the man opposite.

Marcus did not sit up properly in his chair with his feet neatly planted upon the carpet, but leaned back, his long legs bridging the space between them, one boot crossed comfortably over the other just a few inches from her feet. Christina was rivetingly aware of the dark wool stretched taut over his muscular limbs and of the smoke from the fire clinging to his garments. There was also the scent, faint as an elusive memory, of tansy and cloves.

She darted a sharp glance at his politely blank countenance. His eyes, she found, were neither blank nor polite. They were intent, assessing. In this way, she reflected, he must have countless times sized up business rivals, not to mention women. The scrutiny was disquieting—as he meant it to be, she thought crossly. It was as deliberate as the way he manipulated the physical awareness. He enjoyed putting others off-balance. He was obnoxiously good at it, even better than he'd been ten years ago. Practice makes perfect, she thought. She wanted to strike him. He had no business playing this stupid, silent game with her.

"I think you've grown . . . taller since the last time I saw you," he said reflectively. "That was—when was it?—years ago, anyhow. What were you then—sixteen, seventeen?"

"Eighteen," she said. "A year younger than Penny." She turned to Penny for confirmation, and was startled to find that her friend had left the sofa and was on the other side of the room, talking to Julius. Christina calmly turned back to Marcus. He was wearing a faint, amused smile.

"But you are quite right regarding my height," she said. "I did grow another half-inch. How keenly observant you are."

Twin sparks lit his eyes. "I did not mean a mere half-inch. I must have confused you with some other girl. There were a great many of them, as I recall."

"Ah, well, you mustn't mind the error," Christina answered in tones laden with compassion. "Failure of memory is common with advancing age—it cannot be helped."

His expression remained cool, but for the muscle that jumped in his jaw, before he answered, "That's one frailty you obviously don't suffer. Your memory is keen indeed. You recall not only how old you were, but your exact height."

She wanted very much to fling the teapot at his smug face. Instead she smiled. "Not long after Penny's wedding, I was measured for my own bridal gown. I can't imagine any woman forgetting what size and age she was when she was wed."

She felt his withdrawal an instant before his long legs pulled back and his posture straightened. "Yes, of course," he said tightly. "I had altogether forgotten."

Christina had started it, Marcus told himself as he jammed the diamond stickpin into his neckcloth. She had sat upon the sofa looking cool and detached and superior, listening to Penny speak of him as though he were an ill-mannered child. But Christina had also finished it, he admitted as he turned from the looking glass.

He had only wanted to fluster her, make her blush, obtain some hint that she remembered something, anything. Instead, she had found and pierced a tender spot that shouldn't have existed: a mere three months after tossing him aside, she'd wed; it had taken Marcus three times as many months to recover. The reminder had hurt. It shouldn't have, but it had.

A great deal was happening that shouldn't.

He had spent more than an hour dressing for dinner, when it should have taken a quarter of that time. He'd just spent a full twenty minutes choosing the stickpin—as though she cared a straw what he wore, as though he gave a damn whether or not he met her standards of elegance.

Giving his cuffs an unnecessary tug, he headed for the door, then paused, his fingers inches from the handle, when he heard Christina's and Penny's voices in the hall outside.

He didn't emerge from his room until the voices

faded. Then he headed for his nephews' room, and spent a quarter hour there telling riddles and jokes, instead of offering his customary "good night" from the threshold.

He owed them the attention, he told himself as he left the room. He'd focused too much on the twins all day, and children were sensitive to such unintentional slights—as the girls' behavior in the playroom had demonstrated.

He was positive he'd done nothing—certainly not deliberately—to win the girls' affection, let alone lure them to him in the playroom. They'd simply come ... as their mama had done once, long ago.

Then, he had believed that she, too, felt the current between them, and the sense of inevitability as their gazes locked. Gad, what a moonstruck young fool he'd been. Obviously all that had drawn her was curiosity or vanity. He had kept away, when other men couldn't; naturally, this had intrigued her.

What her children saw in him was even less significant. Children took likings and aversions for reasons adults could rarely fathom. Delia liked him as she liked pink and blue dragons; Livy, as she liked starch in her smocks. This sensible adult reflection brought a twinge of sadness.

Marcus paused at the head of the stairs. He really should bid the girls good night as well. One must be even-handed, after all, though they were the children of a stranger.

He was heading toward the guest wing even as he thought it. Halfway down the hall, he felt misgivings, and his steps slowed. But soft light streamed into the hall from their open door, beckoning his reluctant feet on.

He reached the door and looked in. Though a candle was lit, they were buried under the bed-clothes.

He felt the stab of sadness again, and quarreled with it, for the two little girls were simply asleep, as they should be. He spoke anyway, his voice just a whisper: "Good night, my dears."

Two flaxen heads popped up from the bed-clothes.

"Oh, you *have* come," Delia exclaimed. "I *told* you," she chided her sister.

"You did not," said Livy. "You said *maybe*. I said *maybe*, too."

He shouldn't feel so very gratified, but he did, and all the adult common sense in the world couldn't keep Marcus from entering the room and savoring their quarrelsome welcome.

"I hope you didn't stay awake on my account," he said, though he rather hoped they had.

Their blonde heads bobbed up and down.

"Oh, dear," he said. "That will never do. Next time, I shall have to dress more quickly. It took me much longer than it should have, I'm afraid."

"Mama takes hours," Delia said. "There's all the things for underneath, and then the things on top of them."

"Yes," said Livy. "There's the chemise, and the corset, and the stockings and the petticoat and—"

"Ladies' garments can be very complicated," Marcus hastily interjected while he tried to banish the seductive vision Livy had evoked. "Though a gentleman's are much simpler, he must contend with his neckcloth, which is not very easy to tie properly."

Livy gravely considered the neckcloth. "You have a star," she said. "I like stars."

She meant the diamond stickpin. It was too gaudy, he decided, too demanding of attention. Someone might think he was trying to impress . . . someone.

"It's not a star," Delia told her sister. "It's a diamond."

"A *star*," said Livy.

"A *diamond*." Delia drove her elbow into Livy's arm.

"Do you know what I think?" Marcus put in before the disagreement could escalate into violence. "Maybe stars are diamonds with which angels adorn the heavens. Maybe sometimes they drop them, and they fall all the way to the earth."

Twin blue gazes swung abruptly back to him.

"Oh, yes," said Delia. "The ones in the sky do fall sometimes. We saw it, didn't we?" she asked her sister. "Last night we saw one fall."

"You *promised* not to tell," Livy reproached.

"He won't tell Mama."

They lifted pleading countenances to him.

"You won't tell, will you?" Delia asked. "It was very late, and we went to the window."

"When you were supposed to be sleeping?" he whispered conspiratorially.

They nodded guiltily.

Marcus crossed the room to the window and looked out. "It's very pretty, isn't it? Dark and quiet and magical. When I was a little boy, sometimes I woke very late in the night, and couldn't fall asleep again right away. I would climb onto the window seat and look at the stars, and imagine things. If I tell on you, I suppose I must tell on me, too. Otherwise, it wouldn't be fair, would it?"

The blonde heads shook back and forth.

"Well, I can't possibly bear to tell on myself. It's a special secret."

The sisters looked at each other.

"It was very, very late," Delia said.

"I counted twelve chimes," said Livy.

"Then we saw the star fall, over there." Delia's small finger pointed eastward.

Marcus felt a tingle at the back of his neck.

That was the direction he'd come last night. At the stroke of midnight, he had left the comforts of Marlborough's Castle Inn and climbed back onto his carriage, to continue the remaining thirty-odd miles to Greymarch. He couldn't explain that sudden decision any more than he could the one that had driven him from London in the first place. There seemed to be a great deal lately that he couldn't explain. A long, long time ago, he would have believed the falling star explained everything.

As a child, he had truly believed angels looked after the stars, and after him as well; and when they dropped a star, it was to send him a special message. Even as a young man—for he'd been a dreamer, as idealists generally are—he'd half-believed still.

During the fortnight preceding Julius's wedding, the clear night skies had been filled with star showers. On one such night, a week after Christina's arrival, she had slipped out to the garden to meet him. She was warm, flushed with dancing, and one cornsilk tendril had slipped from its pin to dangle at her ear. He'd brushed it back with his thumb, and she'd shivered. Then, out of the corner of his eye, he'd caught the flash of a star, torn from its moorings, taking fire as it plummeted to earth. The fiery journey would consume it, he knew—as love would consume him.

If it was a warning, it came too late. He was already bending close to brush his mouth against her ear, and trembling at his own daring. She trembled, too, but that was all. She didn't push him away as he'd feared. And so he took courage and wrapped his arms about her and, whispering love, touched his lips to her silken cheek. Then he breathed her name, and brought his mouth to hers . . . and died of happiness and lived of it, in that first sweet, stolen kiss.

The chime of the hall clock yanked him back to the present, and to the pair of fair-haired angels gazing innocently at him. "I'd better say good night," he said, "or I shall be very late for dinner."

Christina wore the diamond pendant Arthur had given her on their first anniversary, and wished she hadn't. The cold stone burnt her flesh. There were moments when she could almost believe this was because it had caught fire from the one flashing opposite in Marcus's neckcloth. There were other moments when she suspected the heat came from elsewhere: the smoldering gaze that slid from time to time to the pendant dangling between her breasts, and seemed to brand her deeper each time.

It was the gown, she told herself. It was too *risqué*. Yet it wasn't, either, for countless other gowns were cut as low or lower, and thoroughly respectable women wore them. Fashionable gowns were part of her new-won freedom, part of the pact she'd made with herself during the last months of mourning. She'd kept that pact and assumed control of her life, extricating her children, her home, her activities, and her wardrobe from the suffocating grasp of her sisters-in-law.

The struggle had been long and painful. She was entitled to enjoy her victory and her freedom.

She wished she'd worn a shawl.

She wished she were not so conscious of the man opposite. Every time he looked her way—as he must, when they conversed—the vast dining room grew correspondingly smaller and hotter, while her throat constricted and her muscles tensed another degree. By the time dessert was served, she was taut as an overwound watch spring, ticking off the seconds until she and Penny could withdraw and leave the men to their port.

When Penny finally did signal that it was time to leave, Christina sprang up from her chair like a jack-in-the-box.

She had just stepped over the threshold and was drawing a breath of relief when she heard Marcus's voice behind her: "You are *not* going to make me sit and swill that awful stuff, Julius. I never could abide port, any more than I could the tiresome rite of exchanging the same bawdy stories our ancestors told each other six centuries ago."

"What you could never abide," said Julius, "was keeping away from the ladies."

"Which is only logical," came the light answer, very close behind Christina now. "They're infinitely more aesthetic than a room full of drunken men."

He'd moved quietly, and far more quickly than she, Christina discovered, because he was at her side even as he uttered the last words.

"What enigmatic name, I wonder, have the *modistes* given the color of your gown?" he asked, dropping his voice. "I should call it russet, but that isn't fanciful enough. *Terre d'Inde*, perhaps."

"I believe she called it brick red," Christina said.

"I remember you always in white," he said. "White muslin. Silk makes . . . a different sound." His voice dropped lower still. "Another sort of . . . whisper."

As slowly and reluctantly as he uttered the words, her gaze moved up to his. Their eyes caught and held a heartbeat too long, while the corridor grew darker and hazier, thick with shades of the past.

They broke free in the same instant, turning from each other and instinctively quickening their pace. As if they both sensed that some dangerous abyss had opened in the hallway, they hastened for the safety of the drawing room.

Two cornsilk braids formed a thick coronet about Christina's head, the severe style softened by a few wavy tendrils framing her pale countenance. No plumes or lace, ribbons, or jewels adorned the simple coiffure, only the shimmering threads of goldfire where the candlelight played. It lit the silver dust in her eyes as well.

The rest was fire and ice: the graceful arch of her neck, the snowy smoothness of slender shoulders, and the swelling curves, blindingly white against the vivid russet of her silk gown. A diamond pendant shot fire sparks, as though the flesh it touched set it aflame. Marcus dragged his gaze away for what must be the thousandth time this night, and tried to attend to the story Christina was reading aloud. Of all books, she'd chosen *Frankenstein*, as though this day had not been gothic enough.

Whenever Marcus came near her, the memories rose like ghosts, palpable as her scent. When she moved, the whispering silk beckoned him nearer, and he was mortified to find that it was as hard to keep away now as it had been ten years ago.

Then, he'd almost envied the men he generally despised, because they, unlike the black sheep of the Greyson family, might woo her openly. He, on the other hand, hardly dared look at her, because to look was to long for, and he hadn't yet developed the skill of disguising his feelings. If anyone guessed those feelings, they would snatch her up and take her away, far from his corrupting influence.

Ten years ago, he'd been hemmed in by others' disapproval of his character. At present, he had to hem himself in, because he didn't approve of what he felt. He shouldn't be so obsessed with her.

He was too tired to cope with this, Marcus decided. He should just go to bed. Now. Christina was turning the page, and he was just opening his mouth to excuse himself when a servant entered and, with an apologetic bow to the company, hastened to Penny.

The footman said something in a low voice. Penny put down her knitting and rose.

"Well, this is not convenient," she said, "but tomorrow would be less so, and one must be grateful for that, at least. Julius, you must order the carriage brought round. Sally Turnbull's first has decided to make his debut this night," she explained, "and the midwife cannot be found."

Her husband frowned. "For heaven's sake, Penny, there are scores of women in the village—"

"She is young and frightened, and she's asked for me."

"You can't go in your condition, especially on such a cold night—"

"My condition, indeed. Your mother was eight months gone with Marcus when she helped a neighbor in a similar case." Penny moved to the door. "I'll fetch what I need, and I'll expect to find the carriage waiting when I'm ready to leave."

Christina put down the book. "I'd better come with you," she said as she stood up.

"Certainly not," Penny said. "What if one of the children wakes with a nightmare? You won't wish to leave Marcus alone to tend to a frightened child. He became distraught over a smock, recollect."

She left, and a grumbling Julius after her.

Christina sank back onto the sofa.

The room grew oppressively still. Marcus took up a poker and stirred up the fire.

"I wonder who—or what—has made off with the midwife," he said into the taut silence. "Frankenstein's monster, undoubtedly. Poor, confused fellow. He probably mistook old Mrs. Hobbes for his mama."

"I didn't realize you knew the story," she said. "You should have said so, Mr. Greyson. I could have read something else. How bored you must have been."

"I wasn't bored." He turned to her. "You have a most expressive reading voice. Because I was familiar with the tale, even the most harmless passages became fraught with foreboding, and gave me gooseflesh."

"Delia and Livy have ghoulish tastes, I'm afraid. They like nothing better than stories that frighten them out of their wits. And Mama must tell the tale in a creepy, bloodcurdling voice, of course."

"Ghosts and goblins?" Marcus's eyes widened. "I can't believe it of those delicate little girls."

"I believe it is a rebellion of sorts," she said. "Their activities were strictly circumscribed by others. There was a great deal not permitted. These last two years we seem to be making up for it."

She looked up then. "At present, the twins' manners aren't all they should be, as you saw in the playroom. On the other hand, two years ago they were so timid they wouldn't have dared speak to you. I did not want to undo their progress. I had rather they be a bit overbold than . . . stifled."

"Certainly," he said, stifling his own surprise. "Children aren't adults in miniature. As to manners—ah, well, I'm no judge, for mine were always dreadful, deliberately so, and still are, though I've polished the roughest edges. I saw nothing objectionable in your daughters' behavior." He managed a smile. "On the contrary, it swelled my vanity to be fought over."

She picked up the book again, and straightened the marker. "I assumed you were capable of expressing your disapproval—or simply leaving—if they annoyed you. I thought they must deal with the consequences of their behavior, for

Mama will not always be there to make everything
as they wish it."

"A life lesson," he said.

"Perhaps." The corners of her soft mouth turned
up a very little bit. "Although their aunts would
be appalled at what would appear to be a lesson
in vying for a gentleman's attention."

"Oh, yes. Aunts." He moved a step closer.
"Travers had four unwed elder sisters, I recollect.
I suppose you were a great comfort to one another after . . . after your loss. I was sorry to hear of
Travers's passing," he said dutifully. "It must have
been a great shock to you. You'd known each other
from childhood, hadn't you?"

She nodded, laying the book aside. "He had never
been strong. His sisters had reared him, and they
were accustomed to pampering him. They coddled
me, too, and the children. I'm sure the ladies meant
well, but they were—oh, I can't think how to say
it without sounding horribly ungrateful—but they
were narrow. Their world was small, their views—
It wasn't what—" She shook her head. "Once Arthur
was gone, I found I couldn't live that way any
longer," she went on hurriedly. "He left me well-
fixed, as all the world knows. I bought another
house, and simply left. The aunts descended upon
that house and tried to convince me that grief had
disordered my wits. And so I've fled again. After the
New Year, the girls and I depart with my great-aunt
Georgiana for the Continent."

He wasn't sure what he had expected to hear. He
knew only that this wasn't it: hearing her complain
of a *narrow*, conventional life, hearing her speak
of rebellion. There was no female in England less

likely to rebel against *anything* than Christina. Or
so he'd thought. But then, she'd surprised him earlier, too.

"You've changed," he said, moving another step
nearer, "a great deal."

"Most people change after ten years."

"Have I?" he asked. "Do you agree with Penny
that I'm much changed?"

She nodded. "You're more confident. You always
were outwardly, but now you are inwardly as well.
As you should be," she quickly added. "You've
accomplished a great deal, I understand."

He dropped into the chair opposite. "Oh, yes, of
course. I got enormously rich. That makes a great
difference. Those who shut their doors to me years
ago can't open them fast enough now. This last year
and a half in London has been an education."

"You didn't *get* rich," she corrected. "From what
I've heard, you worked hard for every farthing, and
took tremendous risks. Those shipping ventures in
Greece, for instance—"

"It would seem you've followed my progress
very closely," he said.

Despite what he was discovering about her, he
still half-expected her to blush. She didn't. There
was a quick flash in her eyes before they chilled to
cool blue blanks.

"Penny's letters are devoted to the doings of the
Greyson family," she said. "You, however, seem to
be her favorite topic, which isn't surprising, for you
seem to be a never-ending source of sensational stories. She's devoted whole pages to your financial
enterprises, and even more ink to your amorous
ones. You'll find me, therefore, well-versed in the

Greek ventures, as well as in the height, coloring, wardrobe, and disposition of your last mistress."

He sat bolt upright. "How the devil can Penny pretend to know of any such thing, when she only comes to London for two months out of the twelve?"

"You can't expect to be so much in the public eye and not have your activities noticed," she said. "The gossips, naturally, pass their observations on to your sister-in-law."

"And she passes them on to you." He felt terribly exposed, which was ridiculous. He'd done nothing to be ashamed of. Nevertheless, Marcus felt like a boy called to account for some misdeed.

"Evidently she believes you an *interested* party," he said. "Which would seem altogether odd—unless, of course, she'd somehow learned of what passed between us long ago."

Her chin went up. "You hadn't used to be so roundabout. Are you implying that I told her?"

"It's nothing to me if you did," he said. "Girls generally boast of their conquests, just as men do."

"Then perhaps you'll allow me to wonder whether *you* boasted to Julius. That would also account for their believing me an *interested* party."

"I never told a soul," he snapped. "Men don't usually boast of being played for fools."

"I *never* played you for a fool, Marcus Greyson." Her eyes were flashing now, blue fire. "And I can't believe a grown man of four-and-thirty could believe such a stupid thing."

"Stupid?" He clenched his fists.

"I was eighteen years old. It was the first time I'd been out of my little village, my first time in anything like Society. What in heaven's name could I have known of such games? Where could I have learned them?"

"Women are *born* knowing that game."

"Then I must have been born wrong, because I didn't."

"Then what were you about?" he demanded. "You were as good as engaged to Travers—practically since birth, I was told—yet you let me—"

"Indeed—and what were *you* about?"

He couldn't find the answer. He knew he had one, because he always did. Argument was as natural to him as breathing. But the retort he needed was stuck somewhere, and while he tried desperately to locate it, his eyes were busy too. They were taking in the blue sparks in her eyes and the flush of anger in her smooth cheeks—and its faint sister flush below, where her bosom rose and fell with her quickened breathing . . . where the diamond quivered, flashing fire.

Her slim white hand moved to shield her breasts from his stare. Ineffectually.

"I don't remember." His voice was foggy, dazed. Tearing his gaze away, Marcus shook his head. "I can't believe we're arguing about that episode after all these years. I can't believe *you* are arguing. I can't believe you're wearing that gown. How can you possibly expect me to argue intelligently? Gad, how is a man to think at all?" He got up and poked at the fire again, then stood and glared at it.

"According to report," came her low, taut voice, "your last mistress wore considerably more revealing attire. I don't see why you must take issue with mine—or blame your illogic on it."

Marcus swung round. "I don't see why you must keep plaguing me about my mistress. Or why you must continue this wrangling."

She folded her hands in her lap. "I see. I'm to hold my tongue and let you say whatever you like. That isn't in the least fair."

"It's not fair of you to pick a quarrel when you're wearing a provocative red silk gown."

"Don't make it sound as though I wore it deliberately to provoke you!"

"You wore it to provoke *somebody*—and Julius is already taken!" He stormed back to the sofa. "And you've got that great, gaudy diamond stuck between your breasts, winking at me."

"It's no gaudier than yours," she said. "And yours winks, too."

"You're not obliged to look."

"Neither are you."

They looked, nevertheless, not at diamonds, but at each other. Blue fire clashed with gold, making the space between them crackle. He could almost hear it. He certainly could feel it, crackling inside him, the current he remembered, the inexorable pull . . . to disaster.

He stepped back a pace, his heart racing. "We sound like a pair of children. The instant the grownups depart, we break out in a row."

"We could hardly have this particular row before others," she said.

"We shouldn't have had it at all." He raked his fingers through his hair. "I really am beginning to feel—" He bit back the "haunted" in the nick of time. "I don't feel quite myself," he carefully amended. "I'm tired and out of sorts. And it's absurd to blame my ill-temper on gowns or diamonds or . . . Well, you do look very beautiful, but that's hardly your fault. I just seem to have difficulty . . . digesting—that is, one can't expect you to wear modest white muslin frocks forever, and this is far more . . . aesthetic."

"Thank you," she said.

"I should also have realized that you would grow out of your timidity and learn to speak your mind," he went on, feeling as though he were picking his way through a field of nettles. "It is . . . refreshing . . . quite . . . stimulating."

"I daresay *you* find it so," she said. "However, I feel as though I've been battling a tempest. You give no quarter, do you? You say whatever comes into your head, and all the common rules of politeness, of what one may and may not say—" She made a sweeping gesture. "Gone."

"It's more interesting that way," he said. "*You* are vastly more interesting when you're vexed than when you're cool and proper and polite. For instance, I'd no idea you could be so obstinate. Or that you were so fascinated with the *demimonde*. The first time you mentioned my mistress, I nearly dropped into a faint. I'm shocked at you, Christina."

She did not appear to notice the use of her Christian name. "Until now, I've succeeded in shocking only four very unworldly middle-aged women," she said. "Perhaps I'm better prepared for Paris than I thought."

He glimpsed an escape route from this uncomfortable exchange and hastily took it. "No Englishman or woman can possibly be prepared for Paris,"

he said. "The Parisians are not French, but a breed
apart. They are—" He shrugged. "I needn't tell you.
You'll see for yourself."

"Not the Paris *you've* seen," she said. "I wish you
would tell me about it."

When Julius and Penny returned, Marcus and
Christina were still in the drawing room, talking.
After an hour or more of Paris, they'd returned
to discussing the plight of the Greeks. They were
debating the pros and cons of various diplomat-
ic strategies the British government might pursue
when their hosts entered with the news that Sally,
after some initial difficulty, had given birth to a
healthy, noisy, little boy.

"You shouldn't have waited up, all the same,"
Julius reproved his brother. "It's past three o'clock,
and in a few hours the house will erupt into chaos. You may be able to sleep through the racket,
but Christina will be awakened at dawn's crack
by overexcited children. By nightfall she'll be too
tired to dance at the Yuletide ball. In consequence
of which, several gentlemen are sure to blow their
brains out. Really, you're most inconsiderate."

"It isn't his fault," Christina said before Marcus
could retort on his brother. "I nagged him to tell
me about Paris, then Greece, until he's hoarse from
talking. Moreover, the twins will never think of
waking me. They'll be too busy interfering with
the party preparations and being tripped over by
servants."

"And I shall ask the gentlemen to step outside
to shoot themselves or hang themselves or whatever their disappointment moves them to do," said

Marcus. "We can easily collect the corpses next morning."

"There, it's all settled." Penny patted her husband's cheek. "What a fuss you make over nothing, Julius. Come to bed."

Marcus kept by Christina as they trailed upstairs after the other couple, but he didn't say a word. He continued on with her, walking to the guest wing, although his room was in the wing opposite. She should have pointed this out to him, and meant to, but she couldn't find the right words. Every imagined sentence seemed to attach too much significance to what was surely no more than absent-mindedness. Marcus had said before that he was weary, and he did appear lost in thought at present.

When they reached her door, she paused. "Thank you for giving me your company." Her voice was carefully polite. "You were generous to indulge my curiosity, and very patient with my ignorance."

"One could hardly expect you to know what most of your government doesn't. You at least ask intelligent questions. And your mind is open to new ideas."

The servants had left two candles lit in the hall. In the flickering light it was hard to read his face. The troubled expression she discerned might simply be shadows.

"I like to learn," she said. "I told you my life had been narrow."

"Yes, you did. I'd thought . . ." He looked away. "But you mean to make up for that, I see. It'll be good for you to go abroad, and good for your little girls. I'm . . . I'm glad your great-aunt goes with you. She is Julius's godmother, you may recall."

"Yes, I remember." If her parents, rather than her great-aunt, had chaperoned her ten years ago, there would have been no stolen moments with Marcus Greyson in sitting rooms or gardens or woodland paths.

"She'll be an excellent traveling companion," Marcus said. "She's highly knowledgeable and far more liberal minded than most of her generation. Equally important, she'll see that no one takes advantage of you. Innkeepers and shopkeepers, I mean. And guides. The Continent is a net of perils for the unwary."

He shook his head. "But I'm keeping you from your rest." He moved to open the door for her.

His coat sleeve brushed her arm, a breath of a touch, soft wool against her skin. For one pulsing moment they stood frozen, and the air between them warmed and thickened. Christina felt the way she had earlier when their gazes had locked: as though they were teetering on the brink of a precipice. She was afraid that if he gave the smallest tug, she would fall . . . and he was bending toward her. But he drew back quickly, almost in the same breath.

He clasped his hands behind his back. "Good night," he said.

"Good night," she said.

Then he turned and swiftly walked away.

The following day, while the two women dealt with the last minute frenzy of preparation for the ball, Marcus and Julius gathered greenery outdoors, with the dubious assistance of four rambunctious children. The girls were supposed to supervise only, according to Marcus's stern orders. They couldn't seem to do so, however, without inspecting every evergreen branch and pricking their fingers on holly. Then they must tumble about in the cart with the boys and crush their fancy bonnets and lose their mittens—and generally turn themselves into dirty little frights, as Marcus unchivalrously told them.

"What will your mama say?" he asked as he was wrestling Delia's hideously fussy bonnet back into place for the hundredth time.

"Off with those dirty things and into the bath!" she shrieked.

Livy giggled, which made Delia giggle, too, and the boys mocked them, squealing like pigs. Delia instantly dashed off in pursuit of Kit, while Livy went after his brother. The bonnets tumbled askew again, and mittens dropped into the dirt. By the time they returned to the house, all four children looked as though they'd spent the last month mucking out the stables.

Leaving Julius and the boys to carry the greenery to the ballroom, Marcus planted Livy on the antique porter's chair by the door and began tugging off her boots. Delia, as might be expected, couldn't wait for assistance. She was sitting on the cold floor wrestling with her muddy footwear when Christina entered the vestibule.

"Good heavens, where did these little ragamuffins come from?" she asked, her voice laced with amusement.

"A gypsy," Marcus answered. "He gave me these disorderly creatures in trade for Delia and Livy."

"No, no! It's *us*, Mama," Delia cried. "He didn't give us away."

"I'm sure he wishes he did." She shook her head. "I suppose you've been driving Mr. Greyson out of his wits."

"Oh, no, we were *helping* him," said Livy. She fixed an earnest blue gaze upon Marcus. "We *did* help, didn't we?"

"Certainly," he said. "I never could have found such lovely boughs without you." After carefully setting the right boot down next to its mate, he rose and turned to Christina. "I'm afraid we've lost a red mitten. I'm told a squirrel made off with it. Also, our bonnets are . . ." He gestured helplessly at the soiled, mangled bonnets. "I believe the only solution is to burn them. I *am* sorry. I should have—"

"Nonsense," Christina said briskly. "We've plenty more. Heaps of them, just waiting to be destroyed." She stepped nearer to add in a low voice, "The aunts, you know. Unfortunate tastes in millinery, yet they will keep sending the silly things."

"I did wonder," he said, reflexively lowering his own voice to the same conspiratorial pitch. "You're not at all fussy in your own attire, yet the hats were awash in ribbons and ruffles."

Her blue eyes sparkled. "They are ghastly, aren't they? I dread the arrival of those packages, because the instant the girls don their finery, I want to break out in whoops. One of these days I'm sure to strangle, trying *not* to."

"Mama, you're telling secrets," Delia reproached. She bolted upright and grabbed her mother's hand. "Tell *me*."

"Me, too," said Livy, scrambling down from the

chair. She tugged at Marcus's cuff. "Tell me what she said, Mr. Greyson."

He scooped Livy up on one arm, then held out his other for Delia. With a grin, she released her mother, and let herself be taken up as well.

"Really, Marcus, you mustn't," Christina protested. "They're too big to be carried."

He headed down the hall, obliging her to follow. "I can hardly let them run about the cold floor in their stocking feet."

"They're not nearly as delicate as they appear, I assure you."

Ignoring her, he proceeded up the stairs.

"Tell us the secret," said Delia.

He shook his head.

"*Please*," her sister coaxed. "We won't tell anybody."

"Neither will I," he said. "I'm a very good secret keeper. I shan't tell your mama's, just as I shan't tell *yours*."

Christina, mounting the stairs beside him, looked up sharply. "Oh, they've been telling secrets, have they?"

"Just one," he said. "But my lips are sealed."

"Very well," she said. "We shall simply have to pry one of your own out of you, to make it even."

The twins looked at Marcus, then at each other, and giggled.

"I see," said their mama. "He's already told you one, has he? Then I shall have to extract a secret all by myself. *A deep, dark one*," she added in the same hollow tones she'd used when she read *Frankenstein*.

Marcus knew the ominous voice was for the

twins' benefit. His flesh prickled all the same. The girls loved it, of course and, snuggling closer, expressed their hopes that his secret would be quite ghastly and horrible.

He tried to convince himself he had no dark secrets to be extracted, thus no reason to feel anxious. His life, as Christina had remarked the night before, was open to public view, mistresses and commercial endeavors alike.

Until the last two days, the outward life comfortably represented the inner man. Now there was friction. He felt it when the twins talked to him or pulled at his coat sleeves or merely looked at him. He felt an inward tug of affection—natural enough, for they *were* darlings. He didn't mind that at all. What he minded were the other feelings. Old dreams and hopes rose like sad ghosts: the girl he'd wanted to marry ten years ago, the children he'd imagined, the family of his own to care for, and for whom he'd wanted to conquer the world . . . until he'd come to his senses and realized that empire building left no room for domesticity. Until now, he'd experienced no regrets. Now, he held another man's children and ached with a sense of loss.

They might have been yours, the ghosts mourned.

And that, Marcus supposed, was one horrible secret.

Christina frowned at her reflection in the mirror. "I must have ordered this gown with Paris in mind," she told Penny. "It doesn't seem altogether suitable for a country house fete."

"It's perfectly suitable," said Penny. "Your figure is excellent. I can't think of any reason to hide it."

"I can. I don't wish to be viewed as a dashing young widow. People are too quick to believe that when we put aside our mourning, we leave our morals behind as well."

Provocative, Marcus had said last night. The remark still stung, though Christina knew it was unjust and had argued accordingly. She tugged at the low-cut bodice.

"Do leave it be," her friend said. "If I believed it immodest, I'd say so. It's no more revealing than what you wore last night, and even Julius—who can be a trifle pompous at times—approved. He said it was about time you stopped dressing like a vicar's wife." Penny studied the open jewelry box. "You must wear diamonds, of course. That simple pendant you wore last night was—"

"Objected to," Christina said.

Penny looked up, her eyebrows raised. "Was it, indeed? I can only conclude it was Marcus who raised the objection. On what grounds, I wonder?"

"He said it was . . . distracting. And my gown was *provocative,*" Christina answered crossly.

Penny laughed. "Marcus does have a disconcerting habit of saying whatever is on his mind."

"I shouldn't have told you." Christina moved away from the mirror. "But the matter has been plaguing me. Which is ridiculous. He was only goading me, picking a quarrel, which you say he always does, with everybody. But he never used to—"

She turned her attention to selecting earrings. "It was a sore spot, that's all. Arthur's sisters didn't approve of the wardrobe I selected after I left off my mourning clothes. They tried to make me feel like a tart."

"Don't tell me about the aunts, Christina. I know all about the tiresome creatures." Penny stepped closer. "I'd much rather hear what else you and Marcus quarreled about . . . as you never *used* to do."

"That isn't what I said—meant." She snatched up the pendant. "I hardly knew—*know* him." She fumbled with the clasp.

"Let me." Penny took the necklace from her. "You're trembling."

"I'm chilled. I should have worn a warmer gown."

"You'll feel warmer shortly," Penny said as she deftly fastened the necklace. "The gentlemen will swarm about you and strive their utmost to raise your temperature. Marcus will have to fight his way through the throng if he wishes to take exception to your attire. And your other beaux, naturally, will leap to your defense. The evening promises to be most exciting."

"I don't wánt any beaux," Christina said, pulling on her gloves. "But everyone will think I'm . . . I'm looking out for a man—because of this dratted gown."

"You're just nervous, because you haven't been in company—frivolous company, that is—in eons. But we'll stop and visit the boys, and let them admise us, then get more of the same from the girls. After the children are done telling us how pretty we are, we shall be prepared to face the rest of the world with sublime assurance."

When Marcus stopped to bid his nephews good night, the two women were leaving.

"A topaz," said Penny, studying his stickpin with what Marcus felt was a far too knowing expression. "It matches your eyes."

"It was supposed to match my waistcoat," he said stiffly. "It was also supposed to be subtle. According to Beau Brummel, a gentleman's attire shouldn't call attention to itself."

"I didn't know you were a devotee of Brummel's," said Penny. "I thought you employed a valet to worry about your clothes, since you couldn't be bothered."

"Since my valet is still in London, I'm obliged to be bothered."

At the moment, Marcus was a great deal more than bothered. Christina was wearing a sapphire silk gown. The style was severely simple, bare of ruffles and furbelows, shorn of anything that might distract one from the sensuous curves it enfolded. She might as well be naked, he thought. It was all the same to him—or rather, to the mindless flesh and blood Marcus, whose muscles tightened painfully, whose fingers curled helplessly into his palms.

The other Marcus—the rational, civilized one—coolly answered several more teasing comments from Penny and dutifully complimented the ladies. He promised to join them downstairs very soon, certainly before the guests began arriving, and kept his face utterly expressionless as he watched them walk away.

Then he entered the boys' bedchamber and tried to calm down.

That took more than twenty minutes, which he filled with a story about Aegean pirates. And now he would be late for the party, because he still needed to say good night to the twins, as he'd promised earlier.

He hurried down the hall, round the corner, then stopped short. Two blonde heads poked out of the doorway. Two little faces were looking expectantly his way and lighting up with smiles. Something inside him lit up, too, and made him feel enormously pleased with himself as he continued toward them. He endeavored, however, to appear stern.

"Shouldn't you be in bed?" he asked, with a reproachful glance at the naked toes peeping out from under their flannel nightdresses.

They both nodded.

"Why aren't you, then?"

"We were waiting for you," said Delia, taking his hand.

"To say good night," said Livy, taking the other.

"Indeed. Without your robes, without your slippers, standing in a draughty doorway. If your mama finds out—"

"We won't tell," said Delia. "Will you?"

"You are little minxes," he said. He snatched them up and carried them to their bed. Then he simply let go and dropped them, which they found hilarious and delightful. So much so that they demanded he do it again.

"No. It's not playtime. It's time to sleep," he said. "Under the bedclothes with you."

After they had crawled into their respective places, he pulled the blankets up over them.

"Will you tell us a story?" Livy asked.

"A ghastly, horrible one?" her sister amplified. "Mama told one, but it wasn't horrible at all."

"It was too short," Livy said. "Mama had to hurry."

"As I ought to," he said. "The grownups are having a party, remember. It would be very impolite of me to be late—which I shall be, if I stay to tell you a story."

They thought this over. "You mustn't be late," Livy said at last.

"Will you dance with Mama?" her twin asked.

"Yes, of course. I shall dance with all the ladies who let me."

"Mama will let you," said Delia.

"She likes to dance," said Livy.

"I'm glad to hear it." Marcus neatly tucked them in.

Livy elbowed Delia, who elbowed back harder. Before Marcus could remonstrate, the latter said, "Livy wants to kiss you good night."

He told himself the request wasn't significant. They were affectionate children who liked him, that was all. He bent and politely presented his cheek to Livy. Her lips touched it, light as an angel's wing.

"Me, too," said Delia. She gave him a hug, along with a noisy smack.

He felt the tug again as well as the sadness, stronger than before.

They weren't his. He wished they were. Wished it fiercely.

He straightened, and forced a smile. "Good night and happy dreams, my little angels."

To Christina the ballroom seemed thick with ghosts. The men swarmed about her just as Penny had predicted, and just as they'd done ten years ago. The compliments now were warmer, the flirtations bolder. Otherwise it was all the same because, like the young girl of the past, she scarcely heard a word, only answered automatically, while all her consciousness fixed on the one man who kept away.

That also was just as he'd done all those years ago, even though the barriers of the old days no longer existed. Christina was no longer a green girl, and he was no longer a social outcast.

She answered her dance partner's compliments and witticisms while she wondered why Marcus was avoiding her. They had managed to get along so well last night—after that short, nerve-wracking row—and today, too. But not altogether well, she silently amended. The past remained like some galvanic current, pulsing under the surface of everything they said and did. There was tension, and she couldn't believe she was the only one who felt it.

The dance ended. The next, she knew, would be a waltz. She looked toward the windows where Marcus stood gazing into the darkness. He was not very far away. She could see the gold glints the candlelight made in his tawny hair. On a summer day long ago, a timidly conventional girl had crossed a distance like this.

She collected her courage and moved quickly, before she could think twice, and didn't pause until she stood three feet from his black-clad back.

"Marcus," she said.

Stiffening, he turned to her.

"Won't you dance with me?" she asked.

* * *

Marcus looked at her—all of her: the shatteringly beautiful face with its pale gold halo, the gown, vividly blue against the snowy purity of her skin, and the sinuous curves it clung to and caressed. He thought, *What's the use?*

He also thought, *No, not again.*

He said, his voice strained, "I don't think that would be wise."

"Oh," she said. Her lashes lowered, her mouth turned down a fraction, and she was turning away.

His heart ached, his fool heart, and his fool hand wanted to touch her, bring her back. He kept his hands by his sides. "I mean yes," he said hoarsely. "Of course I mean yes."

Of course, he thought, as her blue gaze swept up to his. Of course he wanted her. How could he help it? How could he let her turn away?

The music started up. Last night, he had scarcely touched her, yet he'd felt the jolt and the current pulsing between them. But last night he'd been tired and vulnerable, he told himself.

He brought his hand to her waist . . . and the shock of contact darted through his nerve endings. She gave a tiny gasp, and stiffened . . . shocked, too.

"Too late now," he said under his breath. One overwarm gloved hand firmly clasping her waist, the other tingling against her gloved palm, he whirled her into the dance.

It seemed as though every eye in the ballroom was fixed on them. And why not? This was the first waltz of the evening, and he of all men had won the privilege of partnering her. How shocked they'd all be if they knew Christina Travers had broken the rules and asked *him*.

"Why did you ask me?" he said.

"Because you forgot to ask *me*."

"I see. Every other man in the place has fallen victim to your snares. Now your conquest is complete."

He spun her into a turn that brought her thigh against his and made the silk gown ripple about his legs. He thought of soft thighs pressing against his and of the rustle of sheets. His breath quickened and his grip of her waist tightened.

"Marcus," she gasped.

He looked down. Her face was pink. "What is it?"

"You are driving the whalebone into my back."

"Whalebone?"

"My *stays*," she hissed, flushing more deeply.

Of all things, she had to remind him of her undergarments. Reluctantly he eased his hold. "What the devil do you want with a corset? You scarcely even dressed."

He gazed down at the creamy expanse of bosom offered to his view—and that of every other male in the ballroom. "By my calculations, you took three hours, only to come out half-naked."

Her head went up. "I am not half-naked. And I did not take three hours. Only two. And a half. Stop looking at me that way. You'll make everyone stare."

"If you didn't want people to stare, you should have put on the rest of your gown."

"Oh, very well," she said. "Look if you must."

"Of course I must. There is that great diamond,

like a tavern sign, demanding my attention."

"Yes, Marcus," she said patiently. "I wore it on purpose to vex you."

He was vexed—not by the diamond but by the circumstances. Waltzing was very much like making love to music, but not enough like.

He wished her low voice didn't beckon so irresistibly. He wished he didn't find her combative retorts so adorable. Above all he wished that he hadn't found the woman of twenty-eight so very much more exciting and desirable than the girl of eighteen.

He drew her closer.

"I thought we were supposed to keep twelve inches apart," she said breathlessly.

"I'm too old and set in my ways to start following such stupid rules now," he said, also painfully short of breath. But then, waltzing wasn't the mildest of exercises.

She, too, was growing overheated. Her face was flushed, and there were traces of moisture at her temples. A strand of silky hair was coming loose near her left ear. It was making him desperate.

He drew her into another turn, steering her to a doorway, then through it, to the dimly lit hall that led to the backstairs.

"I think we'd better talk," he said. He let go of her waist and, taking her by the hand, led her into the shadows. He was aware of her body tensing in resistance, though she didn't try to break away.

"I suppose, because I asked you to dance, you've leapt to certain conclusions," she said, a shade of belligerence in her voice.

"Yes," he said.

"I suppose as well that you think my gown constitutes a deliberate provocation."

"Oh, yes."

"I don't see why I must dress like a dowd or obey every persnickety rule of behavior to please you," she said.

He bit back a smile. "But you aren't trying to please me," he said.

"Certainly not."

"You're trying to drive me distracted."

"I'm not trying to do anything."

"And you've succeeded." He brushed the wayward strand of hair back with his thumb. She trembled.

"I suppose you think I'm going to kiss you now," he said. "I suppose you think you're irresistible."

"I suppose you think *you* are," she said.

"I must be. You couldn't keep away."

"I did not drag you into a dark hallway."

"I didn't *drag* you."

"You said you wanted to *talk*."

"Must you always have the last word?" he asked impatiently. "Will you not give one inch?"

After a moment's consideration, she let out a sigh. "Very well," she said. "Kiss me if you must. You might as well get it out of your system."

"Very well," he said. "If you *insist*."

Still holding her hand, he bent toward her. Her head tilted back ever so slightly, ever so reluctantly. Her fingers tightened on his and that small pressure vibrated through him . . . a pulsing current, irresistible.

He bent closer. A breath away from her lips he paused, his heart hammering. He remembered vividly the aching loss, the grief and rage . . . weeks, months of it. But he also remembered the sweetness and tender yielding of the kisses he had stolen long ago.

His lips touched hers and there was a shock, sharp and sweet at once, and softness, too, so familiar . . . and the piercing ache of yearning. It was the yearning that made his arms slip round her to gather her close, and kiss her long and deeply . . . as he'd never dared to do all those years ago.

But it was different now. Christina was no longer a naive young girl, easily frightened by desire. Her mouth parted to his coaxing tongue and she melted against him, answering his erotic summons with a woman's tender passion.

She was as warm in his arms as homecoming, warm as love and belonging. Yet this was no safe hearth, either, he speedily discovered, for her warmth fueled his need, and the fire built swiftly.

Her firm breasts pressed against the wool of his coat, but it wasn't enough. His hands moved over her back, pressing her nearer, but still not close enough, for this was gloves on silk, and he wanted flesh on flesh. His hands moved to the base of her spine, to the sweet curve of her hips. She was near enough to be aware of his aching arousal. He wanted her closer still, wanted to crush her to him, but that would only make matters worse. He was already losing control.

He released her mouth. He meant to release her altogether, but the instant she began to pull away, his hands fastened on her waist.

"You can't go back now," he said thickly.

"You're all . . . mussed." Delectably mussed. Her neat coiffure was tumbling undone, her gown was tantalizingly rumpled, and her breath was coming in quick gasps. He thought about how much more tousled and heated he might make her, and his own breathing grew more labored. He tugged her closer. She stiffened, resisting.

"Don't tease, Christina," he said. "I only want another kiss."

"No," she said. "I gave you the inch you wanted, and you took ten *miles*. Then you have the audacity to tell me I'm mussed—as though I did it myself— on purpose to vex you, I suppose."

"I plead guilty to the charge of mussing," he said. "But you did cooperate."

"You seem to have a certain skill in eliciting cooperation," she said. "But then, you had it ten years ago. Evidently, my powers of resistance remain some years behind your powers of persuasion."

"You never even tried to resist, then or now," he said, bridling. "On the contrary, you deliberately sought me out, both times, and led me on."

"Very well, I led you on," she said. "You're a helpless victim of my irresistible wiles once again, though you're a successful, powerful man of four-and-thirty. And because I don't care to be seduced on your brother's back stairs—just as I didn't care to run off with you and be ruined—I'm a heartless tease." She glanced down at his hands. "Perhaps it's time I released you from my wicked clutches."

For one furious instant, he wanted to hurl her aside, out of his sight, out of his thoughts, out of existence.

He caught his breath and looked down at his rigid hands . . . then at her. As he searched her hurt, angry eyes, his own rage washed away, leaving him chilled.

"Dear God, is that what you thought?" he asked. "That I only wanted to seduce you?"

He took his hands away. She didn't move.

"I wanted to *marry* you, Christina," he said. "I told you so, again and again."

"You told me a great many things," she said tightly. "All lies."

He felt a surge of anger, instantly swamped by a flood of grief. Old grief. He drew a shaky breath. "You're wrong," he said softly. "I think we need to talk, but not here." He held out his hand.

He wouldn't have blamed her if she hadn't taken it, but she did—and that was a start, he thought, a proper beginning. He wasn't sure he could make a proper finish, but something, obviously, must be done. They must lay the ghosts to rest, regardless how painful the process might be. Otherwise, the past would taint everything he and she felt for and wanted from each other.

He led her down the back stairs, down another hall, and into a small, quiet parlor at the rear of the house.

He closed the door, firmly shutting out the rest of the world. She slid her hand from his and moved to the window.

"It's started to snow," she said.

He joined her, and looked out into the darkness at the fat snowflakes lazily drifting down. "I did love you," he said. "I did want to marry you. Did you believe *nothing* I told you?"

"I believed everything you told me," she said. "Every word you said to make me fall in love with you, then, every word you wrote later, showing me what a fool I'd been. You wrote that I needn't worry that you'd trouble me again. You thanked me for making an otherwise dull fortnight tolerably amusing." Bitterness edged her voice. "You said I mustn't mind my lack of sophistication, because I was pretty, and the world requires no more in a female. According to you, my future husband would be content merely to look at me. My heart untouched by any base human emotion, I should provide him the same tranquil pleasure a lovely painting or statue offers. There was more, all put very cleverly. You described everything that was wrong with me in words I might take for flattery— if I were the empty-headed miss you thought I was."

His face burned with shame. "It was a childish letter. I was . . . very angry."

"You had spent two whole weeks weakening my mind and morals. But in the end, I wouldn't run away with you and be ruined. Certainly you were angry. You had gone to so much trouble for nothing."

"You've got it all wrong," he said. "That may be what everyone else would believe, but not you. You understood me, trusted me, I thought."

"I loved you," she said. She spoke quietly, not trying to convince, merely stating a simple fact. He believed her.

"In other words," he said, "I had your love—then killed it with my letter."

She nodded.

He had been a fool. A proud, hotheaded fool.

"The letter was all lies," he said. "It was—" He searched his heart for the truth. "I was unacceptable," he said. "I knew that. All the world knew it. You saw how the chaperons watched me. You, like the rest of the young misses, must have been warned to keep away from me."

"Yes, I was warned," she said.

"I was warned as well. Before you came, Julius told me about your strict parents and about Arthur Travers and his spotless reputation and his forty thousand a year. Julius asked me not to flirt with you, because if your parents heard of it, they'd have you sent home, and Penny would be heartbroken. I promised both Julius and myself that I'd have nothing to do with you. Then I spent two weeks pretending, sneaking about, snatching stolen moments—and hating myself and all the world because I couldn't court you openly."

"My conscience wasn't easy, either," she said softly.

"And all the while, time was ticking away," he went on. "I knew your parents would arrive the day of the wedding—and that would be the end, because they'd take you away and I'd never be allowed within twenty miles of you. I knew—perhaps you did, too—that I hadn't a prayer of winning their approval. Ever."

"I . . . knew."

"I was terrified of losing you, Christina. That's why I plagued you to elope with me. That night before Julius's wedding was our last and only chance. I was so sure you'd meet me, as you promised, at the gatehouse. Everything was ready.

The carriage was packed, waiting. I waited, hours, and you didn't come. And when at last I gave up and returned to the house, I found your note in my room, and I . . . I just wrote out all my rage and hurt in a letter I should have burnt, not sent."

She turned to him. "I couldn't do it, Marcus. I couldn't break my parents' hearts. I couldn't subject Arthur to public humiliation."

"I know," he said. And he did, at last. He understood now what he'd been too heartsick to recognize then. "If you had, you would have been the flighty, unfeeling creature I claimed you were in that letter." He turned his gaze back to the night. "The whole situation was hopeless, wasn't it? I should have faced it and accepted it, like a man. Instead I lashed out at you, like a spiteful child. That was . . . unforgivable."

She shook her head. "I think now that it was better you wrote as you did. Otherwise, I might have grieved for what might have been for—well, a long time. Instead, I was able to pick up the pieces of my broken heart, telling myself I'd had a lucky escape, and go back to Arthur, and be a good wife to him."

Arthur's wife, when she should have been his, Marcus thought bleakly. Arthur's children, when they should have been his. She had gone back to Arthur, while Marcus had gone on, heartsick, for . . . oh, months only, though it had felt like years. But he'd picked up his broken bits of heart, too, and gone on to build his empire. He'd been too busy to be lonely. And there had been other women. He had fallen in and out of love half a dozen times at least.

But never so deeply. Never again had he loved, body and soul, as he had loved one eighteen-year-old girl. He had taken many risks since then, but never fully, with all his heart. Never had he been tempted to do so. Until now.

His gaze slid back to her. He hadn't even wanted to like her again, but he couldn't help it. She'd grown not only more beautiful and desirable but cleverer, bolder, infinitely more . . . exciting. If he let himself fall in love again, he had no doubt he'd fall harder. And then . . .

How would it end—if he let it begin—this time?

"It sounds as though we forgive each other," he said cautiously.

Smiling, she moved away from the window. "Yes. How mature we've managed to be, despite an unpromising beginning. Perhaps we might even manage to stop bickering."

"I don't mind bickering with you. It's—"

"Stimulating." She pushed a lock of hair away from her face. "However, I'd rather not return to the company looking quite so *stimulated*. I had better go to my room and put myself to rights." She headed toward the door. "If you're in a mood to be chivalrous, perhaps you'll explain to Julius and Penny that you accidentally stepped on the hem of my gown and tore it. That may, just barely, explain my overlong disappearance."

She hurried through the door before he could answer.

She would have to leave Greymarch, Christina told herself several hours later while she lay awake, staring at the ceiling. She had finally put her life together as she wanted it and was at last becoming the woman she wanted to be. She couldn't let Marcus Greyson turn everything upside down again. She'd spent only two days under the same roof with him, and already the world was tilting dangerously askew.

He had played havoc with her morals ten years ago. He said tonight that his intentions had been honorable, and she believed him. *Then*, however, wasn't *now*. This night, the instant he'd taken her into his arms, her morals had disintegrated completely.

He hadn't taken any outrageous liberties. His hands hadn't wandered where they shouldn't. He hadn't unfastened a single fastening. Nonetheless, in a few simmering minutes, without so much as taking off his gloves, Marcus Greyson had done to her what her adoring husband had never come close to doing in seven years of conjugal intimacy.

She was all too hotly aware of what Marcus might do to her if he took off his gloves.

She had thought the tension between them was because of the past, and even the physical attraction must somehow be part of it, because it was too feverishly intense. He was an attractive man, admittedly. All the same, he shouldn't make her feel so . . . desperate.

Yet even after they'd laid the past to rest and forgiven each other, the desperate feelings remained. She had fled the room to keep from hurling herself right back into his arms.

She closed her eyes. Heaven help her. Two days in his company and she had turned into a besotted schoolgirl . . . if not something worse.

*   *   *

Despite a restless night, Christina rose in time to go with Penny and the children to church. The men were still abed when they returned, and only Julius came down to luncheon. After that, Christina took the children outdoors. It had snowed throughout the night, leaving a thick blanket, the perfect consistency for sledding.

Aware that Kit could be trusted to take his brother down the small hill safely, Christina could give most of her attention to her own and her daughters' entertainment, which she did with gusto. She had two years' practice to give her confidence and two thrill-seeking seven-year-olds to encourage daring. They raced the boys, beat them twice, and were beaten twice.

It was during the fifth race that her skirt caught on a runner. The sled went out of control, veering toward a tree. She was aware of shouts above, then of flying through the air, Delia clasped in her arms, before she landed hard, a few feet from the tree.

Delia rolled free, shrieking with laughter, while Christina lay stunned and breathless, blinking at the vivid blue sky. In the next instant, she was staring into the very white, rigid countenance of Marcus Greyson.

Before she could utter a syllable, he caught her in his arms and pulled her tight against him. His chest heaved as though he'd been running for his life. She could have told him she was quite uninjured, and the only damage she was like to suffer was if he crushed her ribs. But she held her tongue. She wasn't in any hurry to be released.

"Me, too," Delia demanded.

Marcus's ferocious grip relaxed. He gave Delia a hug, then helped Christina to her feet. "That was well done," he said in a muffled voice. "I was . . . congratulating your mama on her fine handling of the sled."

He briskly brushed snow from the back of Christina's coat. "Why don't you go to the house and change into something dry?" he said. His voice was not altogether steady. "I'll look after the children."

"I'm all right," she said. "A little snow won't hurt me."

"You're soaked to the skin," he whispered fiercely. "You nearly broke your neck. In another moment, I shall shake you until your teeth rattle. *Go away*, Christina."

She turned away, her eyes widening in astonishment. He was very agitated, more than she'd guessed. Very likely he *would* shake her.

She straightened her bonnet and walked back to the house, her heart thrumming with hope.

Marcus was well aware that he'd just made a complete fool of himself. He had rushed down the slope in blind panic—doubtless alarming the children—and clutched Christina to him in a perfectly demented manner. He had all but wept with relief to find she was still breathing. Then, to cap the performance, he'd threatened to shake her.

After a half hour of brisk exercise with the children, he still hadn't recovered.

He had behaved like an idiot, but he wasn't one. He knew perfectly well what the trouble was. What he'd felt in that chilling moment when he'd thought he'd lost her told him all he needed to know. Somehow, in less than three days, he had stumbled out of his senses and fallen in love with her.

He looked down at the little girls trotting alongside him, confidently holding his hands. He loved them, too. That, too, in only three days. And in less than three weeks they'd be gone. Unless he could manage a miracle.

Christina didn't see Marcus again until shortly before dinner. She had just settled down to tell the twins a bedtime story when he appeared in the doorway.

"I just wanted to say good night to the young ladies," he said. He made a courtly bow. "Good night, Miss Delia, Miss Livy. Happy dreams."

Two childish countenances fell.

"What has happened to your manners?" Christina asked them. "Say good night to Mr. Greyson."

Delia's lower lip jutted out. "He's too far away. Livy can't kiss him."

Livy kicked her twin under the bedclothes. "You can't, either."

Christina looked at Marcus, her eyebrows raised.

He hesitated briefly, then entered and advanced to the bed. "I beg your pardon," he told the twins. "My mind was addled. I forgot the rules." He bent and politely accepted a kiss and a hug from each girl. The pouts vanished and he was bid smiling good nights.

Without another word, he left.

Christina turned back to her children.

"Mr. Greyson is very nice, isn't he, Mama?" Delia whispered.

"Yes. Very nice."

"He likes us, doesn't he?" Livy asked, gazing hopefully at her mother.

"I believe he does."

The girls glanced at each other.

"Do you like him, Mama?" Delia asked.

Christina bit back a smile. "Certainly. Didn't I just agree that he was very nice?"

"He has gold speckles in his eyes," Delia told her. "He said the fairies did it."

"Us, too," said Livy. "He told Delia she had silver fairy dust, and me, too, and you, too, Mama."

"And he said the angels dropped the stars and they turned into diamonds," Delia said.

Christina remembered nights long ago when the heavens were alight with shooting stars. "They're diamonds," he'd whispered as they watched. "We'll travel the world, and I'll find them for you. I'll shower you with diamonds. I can do it, love. Believe in me and I will. I'll give you the world."

"Is it true, Mama?" Livy asked.

Christina came back to the present. "It very well may be," she said.

That night, Marcus remained in the drawing room after the others went up to bed. He touched the book Christina had held and thought of her gloved hands curled about his neck when he'd kissed her. He thought about her low, foggy voice. He thought about her soft, welcoming mouth and her sweet curves melting against him. He thought about tumbled coiffures and rumpled sheets and silken skin.

He thought he had better stop thinking about it and do something.

At breakfast the next day, he tried to start an argument with her about the Corn Laws. She couldn't debate that topic, she said defensively, because she knew little about political economy. Immediately after breakfast, he drove to Bath and found a copy of Adam Smith's *The Wealth of Nations*, which he gave her that afternoon. Then he offered to show her a more challenging hill for sledding.

He took her and the children sledding that day and skating the next. The next day he took them on a tour of Bath, which he conducted in French, so that the girls could practice for their trip abroad. The following night they attended a ball. Though he danced with her only twice—for propriety's sake—he didn't keep entirely away the rest of the time. He had a campaign to conduct.

And so he wandered back to her side from time to time to share an amusing observation or a bit of gossip or a joke. He couldn't keep the other men away—not without committing violence—but he could make sure she didn't forget he was there. She would have to get used to having him about, after all, and learn that this wouldn't be a bad thing.

With this goal in mind, Marcus exerted himself in the following days to display all his good points. Rather like a horse offered at auction, he thought wryly.

At a concert in Bath, he made up his own ludicrous lyrics to the music, which he sang softly off-key in her ear during the interval until she was breathless with laughter. He taught the three Travers ladies Italian folk songs. He bribed his brother's cook, and spent an afternoon in the kitchen teaching Christina how to make Greek pastries while the fascinated twins looked on. He argued with her about education, religion, and art, and spent hours with her, poring over maps while they debated international politics.

Not once during this time did he make anything that might be construed as an improper advance. It wasn't easy. Nothing he'd done in the last ten years, in fact, had been so difficult. Never in that decade, however, had so very much been at stake. If he succeeded, Marcus reminded himself, he would have a lifetime for lovemaking. He could certainly endure another week or so. Besides, all the signs were promising. After ten days' steady campaigning, he felt sure he was making progress.

She was no longer uncomfortable with him. She shared her own observations and gossip and jokes, and her face lit up with glee when they launched into an argument. Twice when she'd been busy at some task and the twins had repeatedly interrupted with their squabbles, Christina had distractedly waved them away and told them to go bother Mr. Greyson.

Most encouraging of all was a minor episode the night before Christmas Eve, when they were preparing to leave for a musicale at the Nichol's. The clasp of her pearl necklace came undone as Marcus was helping her with her wrap. Though Penny stood only a few feet away, Christina turned to Marcus to refasten the pearls.

She was beginning to take him for granted, he reflected happily the next morning when he came down to breakfast. She wasn't simply getting used to his being there; she was beginning to count on it.

His pleased grin faded when he discovered only Julius at the breakfast table.

"Where is—where are the ladies?" Marcus asked.

"Where do you think? It's Christmas Eve day. They're locked in the sitting room amid a heap of silver tissue and ribbons. They're wrapping gifts this morning because there won't be time this afternoon," Julius elucidated. "We're taking the children to play with another thousand little beasts at Alistair House."

"No one mentioned Alistair House to me," said Marcus, moving to the sideboard.

"They'll probably spring it on you at the last minute. But you needn't come. It's meant mainly for the children, and very exciting it is, too: a fir tree in the hall, lit with candles, with a lot of gaudy trinkets and ribbons hanging in the boughs. I suppose we'll have to do it next year. The Duchess of York's German customs appear to have taken permanent hold. I wonder how many houses will burn down before we adopt a less hazardous foreign custom."

"I think it's an excellent custom," said Marcus. Next Christmas he would have a tree lit with candles, he decided. There would be a silver star at the top, and a lot of shiny geegaws hanging from the boughs. And angels. Three golden-haired angels in the tree. He had seen some in a shop in Paris. They had tiny golden halos and gossamer silk wings and gold threads in their snow white robes.

He brought his plate to the table and sat down. "I'll have to be excused from Alistair House," he said. "I've something to do in Bath."

"Something," Julius repeated expressionlessly. "You are too confiding, Marcus. You must try for more self-restraint. Though I am your brother, you really needn't tell me everything."

"I beg your pardon, Julius. I shall try to contain myself in future." Grinning, Marcus took up his knife and fork.

By eleven o'clock that night, they gave up waiting for Marcus and prepared to go to church.

The twins were beside themselves. They had been looking for him and asking for him since they'd returned from Alistair House. They had refused to nap because he hadn't come to wish them happy dreams—which meant, according to Delia, that they would have horrid ones. Because they hadn't napped, they were contrary and petulant.

After a lengthy struggle, Christina got them into their coats, mittens, and bonnets.

"But we can't go now, Mama," Delia wailed as Christina led them to the door.

Livy tugged at her mother's coat. "Can't we wait a little more? Can't I wait for him?"

"No, I'll wait," said Delia. "You go to church with Mama and I'll come later with Mr. Greyson."

"No one will wait," said Christina. "Mr. Greyson is perfectly capable of getting to midnight services by himself, if he wishes to. Come along. The others are already in the carriage, and Kit and Robin's papa is waiting in the cold."

"It isn't fair, Mama."

"Mr. Greyson will be all by himself. Maybe he won't know where we are."

"He'll be sad, Mama."

"He might be lost. Maybe we should look for him."

Christina knew it was no use trying to reason with them. If she was going to get them to midnight services, she must be an utterly heartless mama. She hustled them to the carriage and ordered them in. As they sulkily obeyed, she turned to apologize to Julius for keeping him waiting.

"I was happy to wait," he said gallantly. "It gave me an opportunity to gaze at the heavens and be properly awed."

Christina looked up. It had snowed off and on during the day, but the sky was rapidly clearing, the last wispy clouds chased by a brisk wind. It was an awe-inspiring sight, as Julius said. The heavens stretched out like a robe of blue-black velvet set with countless winking diamonds.

"The angels are putting the stars back," she murmured. "How busy they must be, and yet so careful. There is Orion, precisely as he always is, with three stars in his belt, and there—"

She caught her breath as a star shot past the astral hunter and down, to disappear behind the fir trees.

"A falling star," she said softly. "Isn't that—"

"There's another," Julius said.

There was another and another, a shower of falling stars, all dropping behind the fir trees that surrounded the old gatehouse. But of course they hadn't. It only looked that way.

All the same, her flesh prickled. She thought of angels dropping stars that turned into diamonds. She took a step away from the carriage, then another. She looked at Julius.

"I can't go to church," she said. "I have something to do."

"Something," he repeated. "Yes, of course. Some of us have something to do and some of us haven't. I beg you will not tell me what it is. I had much rather die of suspense." He made an elegant bow. "Good night, my dear. I shall see you . . . eventually, I trust."

"You're very understanding, Julius."

"I'm one of the two most understanding fellows in England." He smiled and climbed into the carriage.

Blushing, Christina hurried back to the house.

Marcus reached the house not long after the others had left. He had scoured Bath without finding the angels he wanted. As a result, he had spent a great deal of money and waited a great many hours while a dollmaker transformed a trio of tiny china dolls according to Marcus's specifications. He would have reached Greymarch in time for dinner if he hadn't come across a carriage accident and decided to be a good Samaritan.

Still, he did have the angels, and if he made a push, he could join the others before the midnight service ended. He gave the packages to the footman with orders to put them in his bedchamber.

Marcus was moving to the front door when his glance lit upon a side table. A hymnal lay upon it.

"Mrs. Travers forgot her hymnal," he said.

"Oh, Mrs. Travers didn't go to church, sir," the footman said. "She said she had a headache. She went out a few minutes ago to take a turn about the garden. She said a short walk in the cold air often helps."

Marcus changed direction and headed for the ballroom, whose French doors opened onto the terrace. From the terrace, he surveyed the formal gardens. There was no sign of her.

Out of the corner of his eyes he caught a flash of something, but when he looked that way it was gone. The wind rustled the leaves of the rhododendrons.

"Christina?"

Where in blazes was she? Where could she have gone in the dead of night, in the dead of winter?

Tonight, Christina. It must be tonight.

He shook his head, but the recollection wouldn't be shaken off. Then it began again: the past crowding into his mind and tangling with the present as it had done two weeks ago, before they laid the ghosts to rest.

Run away with me, Christina.

"No, I'm going to do it right this time," he muttered. "Courting and a church wedding and—"

Meet me at the gatehouse at midnight. Promise.

Yes, I'll be there. I promise.

His gaze moved to the fir forest where the old gatehouse lay hidden from view . . . where the flash had come from.

She couldn't be there. He was losing his mind—which was hardly surprising. These last ten days of keeping his hands to himself were taking their toll. He was probably going mad with frustration.

All the same, he couldn't keep himself from hurrying through the garden and down the path to the stream, then across the narrow bridge. He broke into a run when he reached the path leading to the gatehouse. It was nearly midnight. He couldn't be late, he thought wildly. He didn't know why. All he knew was that he mustn't, couldn't be late.

He reached the clearing just as the village church tolled the first stroke of midnight. A lantern stood on the stone ledge of the gatehouse window.

A figure stood in the shadow of the doorway.

He raced across the clearing and swept her into his arms.

If she had taken leave of her senses, Christina reflected a while later, at least she wasn't the only one.

They should have simply returned to the main house. But she had shown him the gatehouse key she'd stolen from Julius's desk, and Marcus had unlocked the door and taken her inside. Then, because she was shivering, he had built a fire. She wasn't at all surprised that the place was well stocked with coal, and not at all amazed to see the stack of blankets and cushions heaped near the hearth, just as though she and Marcus had been expected. This night, she could believe anything.

It also seemed the most natural thing in the world to be snuggled cozily with him in front of the fire. It was right that she should be in his arms, her head resting on his chest while she tried to explain how she had come to be there.

She didn't even try to make up a face-saving excuse. She couldn't think why she needed to save face.

"There were stars falling," she told him. "It was a shower of stars . . . and I just had to come . . . to find diamonds, perhaps . . . or maybe it was myself I came to find."

"Yourself?"

"From long ago. I did what was best then, I know, because it was hopeless for us. And my life hasn't been empty or miserable. I haven't been pining for you all this time. I was a good wife, and fond of Arthur, and content, and I had two children to love frantically. And yet tonight it seemed . . . it was as though I left some part of myself behind that night ten years ago. And I think it was the girl who loved you and wanted to follow you to the ends of the earth."

"And did you find her?" he asked softly.

"Yes."

"Will she follow me to the ends of the earth?"

"Yes."

He gave her a quick, fierce hug. "It may be enough if she marries me. Will she?"

"Oh, yes. She's been waiting for you to ask." She looked up at him. "I was beginning to think you'd *never* ask."

"It's only been—" He frowned. "Gad, Christina, it's been two weeks. Just like the last time."

"Yes. You work very quickly."

"I was trying to proceed slowly, to work my way into your affections by degrees, until you found it impossible to live without me. I wanted you to have no doubt that we're ideally suited, that I'm the perfect mate for you and shall make a superior papa for Delia and Livy."

"You did that very well." She smiled up at him. "You've made me fully aware of all your many assets."

"Not all of them." His eyes burned into hers. "But that can wait until after we're wed. I love you very much. I can wait."

"So can I," she said.

He nuzzled her head affectionately. She pressed a bit closer. His lips touched her forehead. Her hand slipped under his coat to his waistcoat. His hands slid down her back to the base of her spine. And tightened. She tipped her head back. His mouth brushed hers. Her fingers strayed under the waistcoat to the soft linen of his shirt. His mouth brushed hers again, then lingered. Warmth trickled through her, but it tingled, and she shivered. His arms tightened around her and the kiss deepened.

Then his hands were moving over her, stirring muscles and flesh to aching awareness. The world dissolved to haze, and the trickling warmth built to a torrent of heat. It raced through her veins and whirled in her head.

The haze darkened and fiery stars danced in it.

Things came undone ... buttons, hooks ... his, hers. His coat fell away, her gown. A neckcloth slid to the carpet, a shirt, a chemise ... shoes, trousers, stockings. Her hands moved restlessly over rock-hard muscle while her body strained and yearned under his simmering caresses, and her flesh sizzled under the hot touch of his lips and tongue.

She felt the worn carpet, soft as velvet against her back, as his powerful body bore her down. She heard his voice ragged with tenderness, coaxing, reassuring. She tried to answer.

"Marcus . . . oh, dear God . . ."

"I love you."

His hands moved insistently, willing her farther, on to the brink and beyond. Then, in the instant that rapture claimed her, the thrust came, and there was raw power surging inside her, driving her farther still. She cried his name and her love, and they blazed together at last, and became but one shooting star.

When Livy woke on Christmas morning, she found an angel on her pillow. It had golden hair and a tiny gold halo and silk wings and gold threads in its white silk robe. There was one just like it on Delia's pillow.

They gasped and exclaimed and laughed and hugged the angels. At last they noticed the two adults standing by the bed.

Then they noticed Mr. Greyson's hand, which was tightly clasping their mama's.

Twin blue gazes lifted questioningly to their mother. She quickly erased her smile.

"As you can see, I found him," she said.

"Oh, yes. Thank you, Mama," Delia said.

"Yes, thank you, Mama," Livy echoed.

Their voices were breathless.

"I thought I had better hold on, so he doesn't get lost again," Christina explained.

"Yes."

"Oh, yes."

"But I can't hold his hand forever," she went on. "And so I was thinking I might marry him."

Two eager nods.

"But then he would be your papa," she said dubiously, "and that might be rather a bother, you know. We should have to go live with him in his house, and give him kisses every single night—maybe sometimes even in the daytime. And sometimes I would have to let him tell the bedtime stories, and I am quite sure that now and then when we were naughty he would scold us."

Their gazes swung to Marcus.

"Well, I might," he said.

They looked at each other.

Christina heaved a sigh. "Perhaps we'd better not marry him," she said. "It will be a great deal of work."

They considered.

After a moment, Delia said, "I'll help you, Mama."

"Me, too," said Livy.

Marcus released Christina's hand to sit down upon the bed. "Are you quite sure?" he asked. "I would try my best not to be a terrible bother, but—"

"Oh, you won't be." Delia hastily crawled out from under the bedclothes to pat his arm reassuringly.

Livy quickly followed. "I'll help you be good," she said.

Marcus looked up at Christina. "Well, Mama?"

"He's very nice," Delia said, patting his head as though he were a puppy.

"He can teach us to cook," Livy pointed out. "And he sings funny songs."

"And he speaks French."

"And he can make the sled go very fast."

"And he has gold speckles in his eyes."

"And he came on the star."

Christina blinked. "He *what?*"

"On the star?" Marcus said, equally startled.

"You remember," Delia said as she crept onto his lap. "The clock chimed twelve times and the star fell. And you came."

"And I came," he said wonderingly.

Livy elbowed her sister onto one knee, and claimed the other. "The angels sent you on the star to be our papa," she explained.

His eyes met Christina's.

"I see," she said. "Angels. That explains everything. Well, he shall have to marry us, I suppose. I wouldn't dream of disappointing the angels."

At this the twins went into transports. They hugged him and kissed him and jumped up and down. Then they flung themselves off the bed to hug and kiss their mama and promise to help her take care of him. Then they grabbed their angels and rushed out to shriek the news to the household.

Christina called out a rebuke, which was completely ignored. She shrugged and turned back to him. "You came on a star," she said.

"The angels sent me."

"To be their papa."

He grinned. "And all this time I thought it was you playing tricks on my mind and luring me with provocative gowns and diamonds."

"Certainly it was me," she said, lifting her chin. "The instant I saw you in the hall I said to myself, 'Here's an eligible man. I think I shall catch him.' "

He laughed.

"But I didn't make you come to Greymarch," she said. "What made you come?"

What had it been? Boredom? Restlessness? No, worse.

"I believe I was lonely," he said rather sheepishly. "I wanted to be with my family, among those who loved me."

"And so you came and found an eligible family, and decided to trap us," she said. "You see how simple it is? It wasn't angel magic. The angels take care of the stars. The rest is up to us. If we want magic, we must make it ourselves. And so we did."

"And so we did," Marcus repeated, his gaze traveling possessively from her tidy slippers to the top of her slightly touseled head. A wash of pink tinged her cheekbones.

He rose from the bed. "I'd much rather believe it was our own doing. I'd rather not be dependent upon angels all the rest of my life." He gathered her into his arms. "I'd rather count on you," he said softly.

"I'll be there," she whispered as his mouth lowered to hers. "I promise."

MERRY CHRISTMAS
from . . .
LORETTA CHASE

I live in Worcester, Massachusetts, in a seventy-year-old house with my remarkably supportive husband and too many books. It's long been obvious to him that I am a fount of obscure and useless knowledge. (He wonders, for instance, why I can trace on a map six different mail coach routes from London to Brighton, but can't find fifth gear on my VW.) Nonetheless, he's twice taken me to England for the acquisition of additional impractical information. Wiltshire, the setting of "Falling Stars," is one of his favorite areas. The story itself was inspired by a photograph of an elaborately fanciful gate-house—all that remained of a centuries-old estate.

Gifts of
the Heart

Judith E. French

Who could know heaven save by heaven's gift ...
                                    —MARCUS MANILIUS

*New Hope Plantation, Maryland Colony
1670*

HE'S NOT COMING BACK. NOT EVER. JILLIAN'S throat constricted, and she blinked back the tears that clouded her vision. "No," she whispered fiercely. "I won't believe that. I can't ..."

She turned away from the frosted casement window and the gently falling snow that made her boxwood maze a sparkling fairyland in the fading twilight. She would not mourn her husband tonight. It was Christmas Eve, and for a few hours yet, she would keep Rory alive. She would remember his strong arms around her, the twinkle of his dark Irish eyes, and the provocative lilt of his deep, husky voice as he called her name.

Laughter drifted from the entrance hall, mingling with the clink of dishes from the kitchen wing. Her guests were arriving, and the servants were preparing for New Hope's traditional Christmas Eve supper and celebration. There would be music and dancing, games and riddles, and the warm fellowship of good friends.

It was not possible for Jillian to cancel Christmas. Doing that would be to admit that Rory MacDaniel was dead. It would mean giving up the last bright ribbons of hope and consigning her heart to the grave with the man she loved. This night had always been special to them, and she knew that if Rory was still alive, he'd cross hell's fiery pit and spit in the devil's face to be here with her.

For an instant, an image of Rory's coat with the silver buttons—the garment that lay carefully folded in the chest at the foot of her bed—flashed across her mind. The fine wool was pierced by a musket ball, the handsome gray color marred by ugly bloodstains . . . stains that would not come out, no matter how hard she tried to wash them away.

They had brought his coat to her, tied across his saddle, exactly four weeks and three days ago. It had been a little after one o'clock, and Jillian had been taking the dinner meal with Reverend Steele when she'd heard the whinny of a horse. It was a cold, overcast November day. She remembered it well. How could she not? Pain knifed through her as she recalled the shock of that bitter message.

A dark-haired man had been found murdered near Jackson's trading post five days' ride from the bay. The victim had been shot in the back and scalped. The white trappers who'd found him had buried the body and taken the horse and coat to Jackson's. There the victim had been identified by an English crown contract found on his person, a receipt for the delivery of white oak logs to be used as ships' masts. Eventually a surveyor had brought Rory's bay gelding and his personal effects home to New Hope.

Logic told Jillian that her husband of twenty-six years was dead, but her love for him would not concede defeat. Not yet. Not until she held his broken body in her arms or ran her fingers through his silver-tipped, crow-black hair. There were a hundred reasonable explanations why some other man could have been shot wearing Rory's coat and riding his horse; any one of them would do.

It was her willfulness that had sent him into danger . . . And if Rory had died on that lonely forest trail, she would be as much to blame as if she had pulled the trigger.

They had argued, and they never argued. She had shouted at him, and finally wept and pleaded with him to investigate this new rumor. Stubbornly, she'd begged him to follow just one more lead . . . one more, after so many had proved to be false. And he had given in, as he always did—given in and ridden away into a wilderness inflamed by tribal warfare and old blood feuds.

Rory had kissed her one last time and swung up into his saddle on the first day of October, a week after she had missed her woman's courses. She had not told him, of course. What need to raise his hopes after so many years of barrenness? But this was Christmas Eve, and her bleeding had never come. In its place was morning sickness, tender breasts, and a puffiness in a stomach normally as flat as any boy's.

She carried Rory's child; she was certain of it. In her forty-third year, God had answered her prayers and quickened her womb for the second time in their long marriage. At a time when her wheat-brown tresses were tinged with gray and most women were dandling grandchildren on their knee, she was pregnant. It was the gift she'd meant to give her husband for Christmas, this precious secret that heaven had blessed them with another chance.

And now, Rory wasn't here to receive her wonderful present.

"Miss Jillian! Miss Jillian!" Nell's excited voice broke through her reverie. "Miss Jillian!" the plain-faced bound girl cried. "Miss Sibyl and Master Walter are here. They've brought their little dog, and she's ever so cute. Her name is Taffy and she has a curly tail. Miss Sibyl is afraid that Bear will hurt him. May I take Miss Sibyl's dog into the kitchen? She'll be safe there, I promise. The Widow Smith had a little dog at home, and she let me feed it once. I know how to look after little dogs, I vow I do, Miss Jillian."

"Enough," Jillian said mildly. Nell's Cornwall accent was as heavy as clotted cream, and it was all Jillian could do to follow what the child was saying. In spite of all her instructions otherwise, Nell alternated between periods of painfully shy silence and long speeches delivered at breakneck speed.

She had come into service at New Hope only last summer, and although she'd shot up several inches since then, she was still as thin as a beanpole. Tonight, Nell's mouse-brown hair was slicked back into braids so tight that they pulled up the corners of her eyes, giving her a strangely Oriental look. Her starched mobcap and apron were a little too large, and her skirts a little too short, but her feet were decently covered with thick wool stockings and new leather shoes.

Still more child than woman, Nell was one of the reasons that Jillian couldn't slight the holiday season this year. The girl had come from a poor family of fifteen siblings. Before she'd crossed the ocean to become a bondservant, she'd never had a birthday pudding, a new dress, or even a shift that hadn't been worn thin by older sisters. This was her first Christmas at New Hope, and Jillian wanted to make it a memorable one for her.

"But, Miss Jillian," Nell insisted, "Cook says he won't have me—"

"Tell Cook that I said you can mind Miss Sibyl's dog and still help out in the kitchen." Jillian patted the child's cheek. "Bear wouldn't hurt a kitten. He's much too gentle. But I'll explain that to Sibyl. You run along now, and don't make yourself ill by eating too many sweets."

Nell gasped and her eyes widened in astonishment. "Oh, no, mistress. I'd never do that."

"Go now," Jillian repeated. "And tell Cook that as soon as supper is ready, I'll come down to the kitchen and pass out the Christmas shillings."

Nell bobbed a curtsy and hurried from the great hall, nearly running into Isaac. The gray-haired black man spoke sharply to the girl. She mumbled an apology and fled.

"That young'n is too flighty, Miss Jillian," Isaac said, lifting a flaming taper to light the candles along the wall. "She needs to learn manners afore she serves company."

Jillian smiled sympathetically. "She's in your charge, Isaac. It's up to you to see that she's instructed properly in her duties."

"Lord knows I try," the older man grumbled. "But these maids get younger and more foolish every year. They come off the boat with onions for brains. I don't know why you bother with them."

"You are the steward here, Isaac. If you feel that Nell is really—"

"I never said she was hopeless, Miss Jillian. I seen worse get sense with age and the right trainin'."

"I couldn't run New Hope without you, Isaac. I wouldn't know where to start." Jillian noticed that Isaac was dressed in his finest breeches, coat, and waistcoat. The pewter buckles on his black shoes shone like stars, and the stock at his throat was snowy white. Isaac's crippled arm was tucked neatly into his waistcoat as usual. "You do look fine tonight," she said. "I believe the cut of your coat is more stylish than that of Reverend Steele's."

"In his line of business, he don't need to look like a gentleman. If I don't dress proper, I show disrespect for New Hope and for you and Master Rory."

Jillian drew in a long, slow breath. "He will come home again, won't he, Isaac?"

The black man gazed back at her intently. "Certain, Miss Jillian. Certain he'll be here. It's Christmas, isn't it? I never knew Master Rory to miss a Christmas Eve frolic."

"Everyone else believes he's dead. They pretend in front of me, but I know what they're thinking."

"Don't matter what they thinks, does it? The master comes ridin' home, and every last one of them will swear they never had a doubt."

"Has the supper board been set in the west parlor?"

"Yes'm."

"With the great pie? It came out all right?" Cook had been preparing the fancy pastry late into last night, and he'd been frantic that the crust would crack or the meat gravy would leak through. Cook's great pie had never failed yet, but he put them all through agonies of suspense every Christmas.

"Set on the silver platter in the center of the table, Miss Jillian. Young Ben is standing guard over it. Cook said if Bear got into the parlor and touched that pie, he'd skin him for a rug."

"You're sure we'll have plenty for all our guests? The Goldsboroughs will be coming, and David Hazlett and his—"

"Not to worry. They's enough raw oysters, smoked rockfish, and crabmeat to feed all of Master Hazlett's boys. Cook told me he has oyster stew, chicken-corn soup, and clam chowder, as well as ham, cold duck, and roast beef for the first course. Not to mention peas and mushrooms, succotash, onions, greens, pumpkin bread, apple fritters—"

"Oh, stop!" Jillian interrupted, laughing. "I should have known better than to ask. Between you and Cook, I think you could feed the whole of the Maryland Colony."

"For the second course," Isaac began.

"Surprise me," she insisted, unable to hold back another smile.

"Eleven sweets for the dessert board. I doubt the Reverend Steele has tasted anything to beat Cook's dried strawberry pie with whipped cream."

"I'm sure you're right," Jillian answered, looking around the hall to make sure everything was in order. The furniture that usually stood here had been removed to another part of the house to make room for dancing. Only a few chairs and a settee lined the walls, and a low platform had been erected for the musicians in the west end of the chamber. The harpsichord stood between the east windows, far enough from the fireplace so that the heat wouldn't damage the delicate instrument. Jillian played—not so well as she had when she was younger, but well enough to entertain her guests.

Boughs of pine and holly had been woven into a garland by the serving girls and draped over the windows and fireplace mantel. A mistletoe ball, Isaac's specialty, hung over the doorway that led from the great hall to the entrance hall.

On the brick hearth, an apple log glowed red. The sweet smell of the applewood permeated the room. The traditional Yule log, always of oak, was too large this year for any fireplace but the one in the winter kitchen. It burned there now, a symbol of the fortunes of New Hope Plantation in the coming year. Jillian knew that Cook would sleep wrapped in his old cloak beside the kitchen fire to make certain the Yule log burned to the last before going out.

"Cook said the first syllabub punch wouldn't hold a froth, so he's held that back for the servants' table. He whipped up a second that came out perfectly. That's standing on the hunt table beside the stairs," Isaac informed her solemnly.

Jillian nodded. Both of them knew that Cook always made an extra bowl of sweet cider, lemon rind, milk, and egg whites, flavored with grated nutmeg, for his kitchen staff, and he never failed to insist that it was a concoction unsuited for Jillian's guests. But Cook was such a treasure that she gave him free rein in the kitchen, and closed her eyes to minor deceptions.

The first strains of violin music drifted from the kitchen wing. "Moses is practicin' up," Isaac said.

Moses was the young black slave Jillian had purchased in Chestertown two years before. He'd showed such a natural talent for the violin that she had provided lessons for him. But Moses had soon learned everything that his instructor could teach. She intended to send him to Boston in the spring to an even finer school. She supposed that she would have to write to friends in London about his future. Rory would free the boy when he was twenty-one, as he had freed all their slaves after four years of service.

Jillian winced. Would Rory be able to sign the papers that would manumit Moses Singer, or would that task and all the others fall to her? Oh, Rory! she cried inwardly. Where are you tonight?

"There you are!" a man's hearty voice called. "Thought we'd come to supper and found our hostess missing!"

"Henry, mind what you say," Henry Horsey's wife admonished. Sally Horsey, Jillian's nearest neighbor, came toward her with outstretched hands. Her husband gave Jillian a sound hug, then took his wife's cup of wassail so that she could do the same.

"Welcome to New Hope," Jillian said. Henry and Sally were good friends. Henry had helped to get in the harvest after Rory left, and Sally never failed to come over every few days and try to cheer her up.

"Any word from—" Sally began. Jillian shook her head. "Well, I'd not bury that rascal yet if he was mine," Sally said. "Rory MacDaniel would stand toe to toe with the devil and come home with a bucket full of coal."

Jillian met Henry's eyes for an instant and saw the sadness there. Henry believed that Rory was dead, but he was willing to keep up the charade for the sake of Christmas.

Sally caught Jillian's hand. "Come along. You've got to hear all the news. My oldest girl Jane's in the family way, and Beatty's boy has his first tooth."

Sally's my age, Jillian thought. This should be me, talking about my grandchildren.

"Sally." It was Henry's turn to try and change the subject to something less likely to offend their hostess. "The wassail is first-rate, Jillian," he bellowed. "First rate. Even the parson had two cups. Another, and we may get him into a jig with the Widow Lockhart again."

As they talked, they whisked her along into the entrance hall and on toward the blue room where a dozen guests had already gathered. Reverend Steele was posing a riddle, the same one he asked every year, but neither Sibyl Johnson nor the maid Nell— who was peeking around the doorway—seemed to have heard the puzzle before.

"What is it?" Reverend Steele asked between sips of wassail. "What is it that goes on four legs in the morning, two at noon, and three in the evening?"

"A dog!" Sibyl shouted excitedly. "It stands on its hind legs—that makes two. And three is—"

"Not a dog," the cleric replied smugly.

"A cat," Nell whispered. "It's a cat."

Jillian pretended not to see her, an easy trick since Rory's dog, Bear, bounded in through the front door with an arriving guest and jumped up on Jillian's green satin gown with muddy paws. "Down. Down, Bear," she ordered. Bear was the size of a four-month-old calf and as black as soot. He had the run of the house, but she'd given instructions that he was to be locked in her bedchamber until everyone was there to keep him from running in and out and doing to another woman's gown just what he was doing to hers. She caught his collar and turned to Henry. "Would you find one of the servants and have him taken upstairs?" she pleaded.

"Do it myself," Rory's friend agreed. "Easier than hunting down a girl in this madhouse."

"A horse!" Sibyl cried. "A horse—"

Reverend Steele chuckled and drained his cup. "Not a horse either."

" . . . disgraceful, I say," came a whisper from a woman at a card table in the corner of the room. "Not a sign of mourning and her man . . ."

Sally's loud voice drowned the gossip. "My Henry says that the same thing happened to Will Gest over on the Eastern Shore, and he turned up right as rain a month later. It seems that . . ."

"A man," Reverend Steele pronounced. "He crawls when he's a baby, walks in full manhood, and goes with a cane in old age."

"A man. That's wonderful," Sibyl said. She turned to Jillian. "Oh, thank you so much for having us," she gushed. "I've met Cat Bennett from Queen's Purchase. She's expecting her first baby too." Sibyl put her fingers over her lips and blushed. "I mean we're both . . ." she stammered, clearly embarrassed.

"Bound to become good friends," Jillian finished for her smoothly. "Mary Stewart and her husband are coming too. Mary's only two years older than you, and she just arrived from Bristol last spring." Sibyl was just seventeen and homesick for England and family. Jillian couldn't have told her that there'd be no celebration at New Hope this Christmas. Plantation life was often isolated, and gatherings like this were the only chance for young people to meet others their own age.

Cook carried in a huge frosted cake with crow foot around the plate, and a holly sprig on the top. "Look at this," Jillian announced. A single candle flickered on top of the grand confection. "Cook tells us that in the lower counties on the Delaware, it is the custom to bake a cake with a silver penny inside. Whoever finds the penny in his piece will have good luck all the next year."

"I'd say the good luck is not to swallow the penny," said Widow Lockhart. Everyone laughed, and Cook's beet-red cheeks grew even rosier.

"We'll cut the cake now," Jillian said. "It's not so sweet that it will ruin your supper. And the one who finds the penny will lead off tonight's dancing."

With much confusion and merriment, Jillian sliced the cake and portioned it out to her guests. And for a few minutes, in the midst of the teasing and laughter, she was able to forget Rory's absence.

Then Henry found the penny, winked at his wife, and dragged Jillian off to begin the first reel of the evening. Everyone followed, partners were found, and the musicians took their places. As Moses drew his bow across the violin strings, Jillian closed her eyes and imagined that it was her husband who held her hand. That it was Rory who would whirl, and clap, and stamp his feet, and that it was his merry brown eyes that would follow her as she moved to the lively country dance.

By holding his image in her mind, she was able to smile, and laugh, and keep up with the steps. Breathless at the end of the first set, she beckoned Sally to take her place and retreated to her bench at the harpsichord.

It was still snowing outside; big flakes were drifting lazily down. It was full dark now, and only a small section of the garden was illuminated by the glow of candles from the windows. Jillian felt herself drawn back into the memories of another snowy Christmas Eve long ago. She leaned close to and pressed her fingertips against the thick bull's-eye glass. "The first time I saw you . . ." she murmured softly. "The very first time, I was ten years old, and you were twelve . . ."

Mandeville House, England
Christmas Eve, 1637

"WHY ARE YOU SO DIRTY, BOY?" JILLIAN DEMANDED, drawing herself up to her full height and placing her small fists on her hips.

Fierce black eyes glared back at her from under a shaggy thatch of unruly dark hair. Slowly, almost defiantly, the ragged youth raised a grimy knuckle to his forehead. "M'lady," he said. His Irish brogue was so thick that Jillian could barely understand the words.

"Don't you speak English?" she asked.

"I be speakin' it," he muttered.

"You're Irish, aren't you?"

He grinned at her insolently. "Born and bred."

Jillian sniffed and stepped back, raising the hem of her cherry skirts to keep them from dragging on the flagstones. From the far end of the great hall came the strains of a lute as her grandfather's aging minstrel delivered a rasping encore of the "Cherry Tree Carol." In honor of the night, she'd been permitted to leave the nursery and join her older brother and the adults at the high table.

At first, the excitement of sitting beside her step-grandmother and being addressed as Lady Jillian by the servants had made up for the endless grown-up chatter and the stiffness of her new clothes. But after two hours, the starched lace collar had rubbed a sore on her neck, and her tight corset made it impossible for her to enjoy the rich food. She had toyed with the slices of stuffed swan, the jellied eels, and portion of roast suckling pig on her silver trencher despite Lady Mandeville's stern frowns of disapproval. Next, Jillian had wiggled on her stool and stared out the great Elizabethan window at the gently falling snow until her brother Charles had kicked her sharply with the toe of his elegant red boot.

Realizing that she could never win in a public battle against Charles, and that she was in imminent danger of being sent back to the nursery in disgrace, Jillian pleaded nature's call and slipped away from the high table to explore the crowded hall.

Tonight it seemed that the whole world had crowded into her grandfather's hall to share the bounty of his table and see the entertainment. There were visiting lords and ladies, a sheriff, two black-garbed clerics, three plump merchants, a span of country squires and their households, and more than a hundred lesser folk who counted themselves as quality.

Nor were the poor people forgotten on this night. Servants dashed back and forth carrying huge trays of bread and meat for those who labored on the Mandeville estate or worked their meager farms as tenants. Tankards of ale were downed by men, women, and children alike. Dogs whined and barked, and sparrows flew down from the smoky rafters to snatch up crumbs of food.

Jillian enjoyed the jugglers and the gypsy's monkey who did tricks. She even cheered the religious mummery put on by a group of roving players, and she clapped as loudly as anyone when the villagers dragged a huge Yule log into the great stone fireplace.

Charles complained that the old Christmas customs such as bringing mistletoe and holly into the house were pagan practices and should be banned, but her grandfather scoffed at his heir's criticism. A Yule log had burned on the hearth at Mandeville House for hundreds of years, he'd insisted. And as long as he was lord there, nothing would change.

"When I am earl, I will keep a decent Christian household," Charles whispered sullenly to Jillian. "You'll see."

Jillian hoped that her grandfather would live forever. She and Charles had never seen eye to eye on anything. He was fourteen to her ten, and he acted as though forty years stood between them, rather than four. In Jillian's opinion, Charles was a sour prig who cheated at games and had the brains of a cabbage.

This dirty Irish boy didn't seem to be much smarter than Charles. He wasn't as tall, but he was huskier than her brother, so she wasn't certain how old the urchin was. "This supper is only for Mandeville people," she said. "Beggars aren't allowed in the great hall. You must go to the kitchen door and ask for food there."

"I'm no beggar."

"I've not seen you before. What's your name?"

"Rory MacDaniel. My stepfather be second huntsman to Lord Mandeville."

"Hmph." Jillian sniffed again. "Do you know who I am?" He nodded, but she stated her full name and title just to put him in his place. "I am Lady Mary Jillian Elizabeth Stanley, oldest granddaughter to the earl."

Rory pushed back his shapeless knit hat and folded his arms over his chest. They were standing in the shadows of a forest of antlers and dusty boar tusks that lined one end of the three-storied hall. Rows of long wooden tables and dozens of men-at-arms and villagers blocked any view of the high table. "Your brother be the heir," the boy said.

"Yes." It seemed safe to admit that much. She brushed at a clump of dog hair on the folds of her silk gown. "Charles will be the next Lord Mandeville when my grandfather dies."

"Where's your da?"

"Dead." Her father had been killed in a hunting accident in Northumberland when she was still a babe in leading strings. She didn't remember him at all.

"My da too." He brought his left hand from behind his back cautiously. He was holding a cherry tart, somewhat the worse for wear. He glanced up at her through long, sooty lashes and grinned. "Want some?" he offered.

Jillian nodded. She'd left the high table before the sweet course was served. She watched as he broke the tart in half and gallantly gave her the larger piece. She nibbled at a corner of the pastry, then said, "My lady mother is dead too. She died in childbed right after my father was buried."

"Ye got no mam either?"

Jillian shook her head. "I have a nurse, and an Aunt Claudia."

"Not the same as a mam," he said.

"No." It wasn't, and there was no sense trying to lie about it. "I've got a little sister."

"Sure'n that's nothin' special," he replied. "I got four of them. Half sisters. And five half brothers."

"I've got my own pony," she declared, "and a dog."

He shrugged. "Seen the pony."

Jillian chewed at her bottom lip. Somehow, she felt that this rash upstart had gotten the best of her. Her eyes narrowed and she glared at him. Her gaze dropped from his stubborn chin down over his tattered vest and colorless homespun shirt. Below that, he wore baggy, coarse breeches with holes in the knees and soft, hide shoes that were little more than strips of leather wound around his feet. "You dress like a beggar," she said.

He straightened his shoulders. "And ye be naught but a babe wi' gooseberry on your chin."

Jillian felt her cheeks grow hot as she wiped her mouth with the back of her hand.

"Now ye ha' got it on your gown." She glanced down and saw to her dismay that she'd smeared purple jam onto her wide, white, starched collar.

"You're nothing but a horrid Irish bogtrotter," she said, trying to salvage her wounded pride. "And you're not supposed to talk to me. I'm a lady." She spun on her heel and stalked away from him.

"So tell on me," he dared. "Run back to yer nurse and cry like the spoiled babe ye be."

"I'm not crying," she flung back over her shoulder. "And I hate you, Rory MacDaniel. I hope I never see you again. Never!"

It was early summer before she saw him again, the day of the fox hunt . . . a glorious morning with the mist rising off the meadow and the sun shining brightly in a cloudless azure sky.

A horn sounded as a red fox burst from the hedgerow and fled across the open field with baying hounds strewn out behind him. Jillian urged her fat little pony, Ivory, toward the tangled hedge that the other riders in the hunt were taking by twos and threes. Lady Mandeville's bay hunter passed the dapple-gray pony and sailed over the jump, followed by two mounted grooms. Jillian's excitement grew as she neared the division between the two fields. This time Ivory would do it; she'd leap the barrier and allow Jillian to keep up with the hunt. She'd prove once and for all that she was old enough to ride to hounds with Charles. She'd started with the hunting party at the door of Mandeville House, and she'd be in on the finish.

But at the last possible minute, Ivory balked at the jump. She took the bit in her yellow teeth, shied left, and broke into a trot along the side of the hedge. Jillian kept her seat on the slippery leather sidesaddle and watched in dismay as the dogs and the other riders vanished at the far side of the meadow.

Unwilling to give up and go home in defeat, Jillian decided to follow the hedgeline to the far end of the field and cut through the chestnut woods. If the fox continued running in a straight line, she might be able to catch up with the hunt near the river crossing.

Once she reached the forest, Jillian followed an overgrown path for about a quarter of a mile, then turned off by a ruined hunting lodge. The way didn't look familiar, but she wasn't afraid, not even when the big trees blocked the sunlight above. This was all Mandeville land, and the chestnut woods covered no more than a few hundred acres.

The way was more difficult than she thought. Finally she was forced to dismount and lead Ivory around a fallen log, and then the stubborn animal refused to allow Jillian to get up onto the saddle again. Angry, knowing she'd be far too late to join up with the other riders, she trudged along, dragging the reluctant pony by the reins.

She'd gone a short distance when Ivory blew air through her lips in a sharp *purh-purrr* sound and stopped short. Jillian looked around, saw nothing but a squirrel scurrying up a tree trunk, and glanced back at the pony. Ivory's ears were back, her eyes wide and frightened. "What's the matter?" Jillian asked. "What's wrong?"

Then she noticed the dog. He was standing about thirty feet away from her, almost hidden by a brush pile. At first, she thought that this was one of the hounds from the hunt who'd become separated from the others, but something about the way he was watching her caused her to shiver.

This was a big dog, too tall at the shoulder for a pure hound, black with liver spots. His muzzle was grayish white, and his lips were drawn back to show long, sharp teeth.

"Go away!" Jillian cried. "Get out of here!" She'd never been afraid of animals, but this beast made the hair prickle on the back of her neck. She looked around for a stick, chose the likeliest she could reach, and shook it at the dog. "Shoo!" she said. "Go away." She glanced nervously at Ivory's back, wondering if she could get up into the sidesaddle without something to climb on. The pony nickered and danced sideways.

The dog growled.

Ivory pulled back hard on the reins. "Stop that!" Jillian ordered. She held on tighter to the leathers, and when the dog growled again and ran forward a few feet, the pony lunged backwards, pulling Jillian off balance. She went over in a tangle of riding habit, plumed hat, quirt, and leaves. As she scrambled up, the pony jerked the reins out of her hand and galloped off the way they had come.

Jillian thought of the foulest curse she'd ever heard Charles utter and threw it after her deserting pony. Ivory didn't stop. Jillian snatched up the stick, saw that it had cracked when she'd fallen on it, and backed up against a tree. Her mouth went dry and her heart was pounding with fright.

The dog lowered itself until its burr-tangled, matted belly dragged along the ground. It was close enough now that Jillian could see its emaciated ribs and lolling tongue. "Go away!" she yelled, throwing the remainder of the stick at it.

The dog advanced, ears back against its head, eyes wide and staring. The low growls had become a menacing snarl. Jillian wanted to run, but she knew that a mean dog always attacked anything that ran away. There wasn't a tree with limbs low enough for her to climb in her cumbersome riding habit, and there wasn't anything she could use as a weapon but her quirt.

"Go away," she said again, trying to keep the fear from her voice. Great gobs of white slobber drooled from the creature's gaping mouth. "Please . . ." she whispered, "Go . . . go away."

"Don't move!" A boy's voice came from behind her. Before she could answer, an arrow flew past her and struck the dog in the chest. The animal let out a howl of pain, then a muffled yelp as a second shaft drove into its chest.

A figure in green dashed between Jillian and the dog. She heard the twang of a bowstring, and the dog dropped, kicked twice, and lay still.

Jillian stared at the dead animal, and then at the hooded youth as he knelt beside the dog. There was something familiar about the sturdy set of those young shoulders, and the lock of black hair that peeked along the side of the leather hood. She also realized, with a start, that two hares were dangling from a string on his waist.

"He's dead," the boy said and turned to look at her. "Are ye all right? He didn't bite ye, did he?"

"You!"

"Aye. Who did ye expect? A wood's leprechaun?"

"You've been poaching." She pointed at the hares. Last summer her grandfather had ordered a poacher's hand cut off for snaring a pheasant in these woods. The sentence had been carried out in the village square, and she and Charles had had to watch. As long as she lived, she'd remember that man's scream, and the awful gush of blood before a soldier had plunged the bleeding stump into hot tar. When she'd wept, her grandfather had scolded her and told her the poacher was lucky. A second offense, he said sternly, meant hanging.

Jillian began to tremble. There were other arrows in the boy's quiver. Would he shoot her to keep her from telling? It was all she could do to hold back the tears.

"Ye might start by thankin' me," he reminded her. "I did save your neck, ye know. What are ye doin' here, all by yourself? A wee colleen, alone in the forest?"

He was calling her a baby again. The insult made her forget her fear. "I was with the hunt, *boy*," she flung back.

He grinned at her insolently. "I have a name. Ye know it. Rory MacDaniel. Say *Thank ye for savin' my life, Rory MacDaniel*."

She glanced back at the dog and felt a sudden rush of shame. She was behaving like a child. He hadn't threatened her; he'd only come to her rescue like some knight in an old story. "Thank you for saving my life, Rory MacDaniel," she said in her most grown-up voice. She raised her eyes to meet his and couldn't resist a final shot. "But you were poaching hares in my grandfather's forest."

He shrugged. "Lord Mandeville doesn't pay his gamekeepers enough to feed eleven children."

She smiled back at him. "I thought you said there were ten of you."

He shrugged again. "That was Christmas. Mam has another babe, born just two weeks ago. She needed red meat to strengthen her blood." He deliberately struck a cocky pose, feet apart, hands on his hips. "I'd have shot her a deer, but all I saw were does. I hate to kill them this time of year. They're carryin' their fawns now."

"A deer?" Her eyes widened in shock. "You'd shoot a deer?" If Grandfather would cut off a man's hand for taking a bird, what would he do for a deer? Rory

MacDaniel would be lucky if he survived with his male parts intact. "Lord Mandeville hangs poachers," she ventured.

"Hang or starve. It doesn't much matter, does it?"

"Is your family really hungry?" she asked. She'd seen poor people in the village, of course, but it had never occurred to her that they might go without food. "If you come to the kitchen door, I can ask Cook to—"

"MacDaniels aren't beggars," he snapped.

"But poaching is the same as stealing," she protested. "It's a sin."

"An English sin, maybe." He scowled at her. "What right does Lord Mandeville—or any rich man—have to claim the fish in the streams and the birds that fly in the air? God made the deer and the hare. I say they belong to the man who catches them."

She shook her head sadly. "You have strange ideas for a gamekeeper's son."

" 'Tis my stepfather what's the gamekeeper. My da owned his own piece o' land. He was beholdin' to no one but his Savior. I'll do the same some day."

"Land is expensive," Jillian replied. "Most yeomen inherit their farms. I've never heard of a poor boy who—"

"I'll not be stayin' here in England, I can tell ye that," he declared. "I'll go across the sea to the American Colonies, where a man can have land for the takin'. I'll make my own place and damn devil or lord who tries to snatch it from me."

"Such talk is dangerous," she said. "If my grandfather hears of it, he'll turn your family out."

"Do I look a fool, Lady Mary Jillian Elizabeth Stanley?"

She giggled. "No. You don't, Rory MacDaniel." She glanced at the ground shyly. "You remembered all of my name."

"And why wouldn't I? It's a silly grand name for such a wee snip of a colleen."

This time she smiled.

He turned away and retrieved his arrows from the fallen dog. "Likely he weren't mad," Rory said. "Just old and hungry. But dangerous, just the same. An empty belly makes for desperation."

"You talk good for a—" she'd started to say *gamekeeper's son.*

"I've had book learnin'. Hedge school, they call it. Priests teach us behind the English backs. 'Tis against the law to educate the Irish, ye know." He fixed her with a steady gaze. "I may be poor, but I'm not stupid, Mary Jillian Elizabeth."

She sighed. "No. I see you are not." For a moment, they stood facing each other, neither speaking. "I . . . I have to go," she said. "I won't tell on you."

"I know ye won't." He shouldered the bow. "I can put ye back on your pony, if ye want—and show ye the way back to the big house."

"Ivory ran away," she answered. She nibbled at her lower lip again. Once Grandfather found out that she'd lost control of the pony, he wouldn't let her ride with the hounds again.

"Not far. I tied her to a tree back that away." Rory looked scornfully at her. "If I had a pony, I'd be able to get on it without help."

She took hold of her wide skirts. "Not a sidesaddle, you wouldn't. Not in these."

He laughed. "More foolishness."

"Would you have me ride astride like a boy?"

" 'Twould make a great deal more sense, don't ye think?"

"If you help me mount, maybe I can get home ahead of the others. Then Grandfather won't be mad."

Rory motioned to the dog. "Would he whip ye if he found out what happened?"

She shook her head. "No. But I'd spend a few weeks in the parlor, working my sampler. And he might take Ivory away. Charles says a pony is a needless expense. I only got her because Lady Mandeville likes to ride, and she asked Grandfather to buy Ivory for me."

"Then, if ye do not tell, you're home free."

"I couldn't lie," she said fervently.

"Oh-ho, wee babe," he replied, "you've a lot to learn about the world. For there's a great space between out-and-out lying and just not sayin' what will bring ye grief."

"You're not a grown-up, you know. You're only twelve."

"Aye," he said. "I am that, but I'm thinkin' that twelve years as the gamekeeper's Irish stepson add up to a lot more than ten as Lady Mary—"

"Jillian," she corrected. "If we are going to be friends, you must call me Jillian."

"Only if ye promise never to call me *boy* again."

She smiled at him. "I promise." She took a few steps, raised on tiptoe, and kissed his cheek.

"Arahhh!" he cried, jumping back and wiping a grimy hand across his face. "What did ye go and do that for?"

She giggled. "It was a kiss of peace," she said, "a bond between us."

"Well, I need none of your English bonds or kisses," he said, rubbing at his cheek again. "For you're nothin' but trouble. If I hadn't had to stop and help you out, I could have had another hare."

A warm, happy feeling rose in the pit of Jillian's stomach. It didn't matter what Rory said. She knew he liked her. What if he was a papist and a poacher? He'd come to her rescue, hadn't he? She smiled and extended her hand. "Friends?" she asked.

Hesitantly, he took her small hand in his dirty, bloodstained one. "Friends," he muttered. "But best for us if we never lay eyes on each other again."

Mandeville House, England
Christmas Eve, 1640

THE CHRISTMAS THREE YEARS LATER WAS NOTHING LIKE Jillian's early ones. Mandeville House was deserted except for herself, her lady companion, and a dozen servants. Her grandfather had gone to London with Lady Mandeville, her brother, and the bulk of the household. Due to the trouble between Parliament and the king, the country was in turmoil. Her grandfather's localities were divided. He was a nobleman and an Anglican, not a Puritan, but he had grievances against King Charles and sympathy for the Parliamentary cause. It was rumoured that there might be war between the opposing factions.

Jillian, at thirteen, had been left at Mandeville as a token representative. Since the family was still in mourning for her younger sister who'd died the summer before, the usual holiday celebrations had been canceled. No guests crowded the smoky great hall; no performers sang, no Yule log burned on the hearth, and no Christmas feast was prepared by the kitchen staff. Even the villagers and yeomen were absent. Lord Mandeville had left orders that bread and meat were to be distributed from the church door, so much to each family.

The only people at the high table for Christmas supper were Jillian, the aging Lady Martin—a poor Knight's widow who'd come to Mandeville House to instruct Jillian in the duties of her class—the dour Reverend Winthrop, and a senile gentleman, Lord Dacre. Since Lord and Lady Mandeville had taken the head cook and his first assistant to the London house, the meal was plain and simply prepared.

Jillian's only Christmas gift had been a prayer book and a letter from her grandfather reminding her of her many failings in deportment. She had sat through the supper with cold feet and a lump in her throat. She was thirteen years old and no longer a child, they said. But she didn't feel grown-up, and her future looked as bleak as the dark, echoing hall.

Later that night, when Lady Martin had fallen asleep, Jillian threw a cloak over her shoulders and went out to the stables to take Ivory a carrot.

Her lantern made a pool of light in the shadowy darkness of the nearly deserted barn. Under her feet, the bricks were cold and damp. From above in the hayloft came the squeaks of rodents and furtive rustling. Only a few horses remained; most had gone to London with Lord Mandeville's party. Long before she could see Ivory's stall, Jillian heard her lonely nickering. She ran the last few yards to throw her arms around the furry gray neck and bury her face in the pony's warm hair.

"What are ye doin' here at this time of night?" a male voice demanded.

Jillian spun around, nearly dropping the light. It was Rory MacDaniel, taller and broader than she had remembered him, but the black scowl was the same.

"Do ye mean to burn down the stable?" He stepped forward to take the lantern from her hand. "And you've no business being here alone," he scolded.

"What are you doing here?" she countered. "My grandfather—"

"Lord Mandeville would not want ye wanderin' the stable yards, and well ye know it." He stared at her for a long moment. "What place is this for a lord's daughter on Christmas night?"

"I have a right to be here," she insisted, refusing to be bullied by a gamekeeper's brat. She had not seen Rory for many months, and then only at a distance. When had he lost the look of a boy?

"Nay, ye have the wrong of it, Lady Jillian," he said. "Since most have gone to London, the steward hired me as groom here. Tonight I was ordered to the house to carry wood for the hall. If you'd but once looked down from your high table, you'd have seen me."

"But why aren't you with your family? Even grooms are given time off for the holy night." Her fear melted away. Rory wouldn't hurt her. She remembered the kind heart that hid behind his tough exterior.

"I followed ye." His dark eyes narrowed. "Have ye no one to be with on Christmas Eve but this dumb pony?"

A sharp reply rose to her tongue, but her own emotions betrayed her. A single tear rolled down her cheek. "My lord grandfather says I am too old for a pony. Ivory has been sold to a squire's household. They come to fetch her tomorrow morning. I thought to say goodbye."

" 'Tis true, you've grown. I imagine you're to have a fine blooded horse now."

Jillian shook her head. "Grandfather says that I will be married soon enough. He says it would be a waste to buy a horse for me when there are plenty of horses in the stable. He says it is for my husband to do that."

"You're young for marriage. Still a babe."

"I am not," she protested, stiffening. "I am thirteen. I have been . . ." She felt her cheeks go hot. She could not tell him that she'd begun the monthly cycle that made her a woman. "Not yet. Not yet will I wed," she stammered. "But by sixteen at the latest. My grandfather has had several offers for my hand."

Rory scoffed. "I hope he's getting more for you than for the pony."

"You don't understand," she protested. "My grandfather loves me. It is only natural that he choose a husband—"

"I understand well enough. You have no loving mother to look after you, my lady. Poor my family may be, but God willing, my sisters shall choose their own husbands. My mother has vowed that and sworn on her father's soul. Common folk have some blessings ye will never know."

"Catholic. You are Catholics." Jillian exhaled softly. For a papist, he did not seem so odd. To hear her brother, Charles, tell it, all Catholics had the horns and tail of the devil.

"We are." Rory's gaze hardened. "Does it matter to you?"

"No," she answered. A bubble of rebellion rose within her. Her hateful brother thought all Catholics should be driven from England. Her grandfather ranted that they were little better than pagans. "No," she repeated with daring. "I don't care."

"Then ye wouldn't mind comin' to my mother's cottage to share a cup of cider and a carol or two."

"Me?" She blinked. "To your house?"

"Yes, to my house. Are ye deaf?"

"I couldn't."

"Have ye somewhere else to celebrate the Lord's birthday? There will be games and dancing. Mam will not notice another head in the crowd."

"I shouldn't."

"Has your grandfather ever forbidden ye to cross my mother's threshold?"

"No, but—"

"Does not Lady Mandeville visit the village when a child is born or someone dies?"

"Yes," she admitted. Her step-grandmother did go into the commoners' homes on occasion.

"Then come with me or admit that ye are a babe in apron strings, too scared to have a cup of apple cider on Christmas Eve."

So she went to Rory's house, a tiny cottage nestled at the edge of the woods. And she sat wedged between babies and toddlers and nibbled hot Irish soda bread and joined in with the old carols.

Rory's plump, rosy-cheeked mother was as nervous as Jillian was when she first entered the cramped dwelling. But Morna gamely refused her husband Duncan's efforts to turn Jillian from the door, and after a few uncomfortable moments, she seemed to forget that the lord's granddaughter was there at all.

"Mam's had her share of hard cider tonight," Rory whispered in explanation.

There was a Yule log burning gaily on the hearth, and the crude mantel was nearly hidden by ropes of greenery. In the center stood the tiny, hand-carved wooden figures of Mary, Joseph, and the baby Jesus, images that fascinated Jillian.

"Mam is as Irish as the mossy walls of Tara, and my stepfather is half-English and half-Scot," Rory whispered. "Between the two of them, they do know how to bring in an old-time Christmas."

Late as it now was, every child in the household, eleven in all, was still awake. They took turns dancing an Irish jig, reciting silly poems, telling riddles and stories. Rory even read a passage from the Bible about the first Christmas and the birth of the infant Jesus.

Rory's stepfather handed out gifts of handsewn rag dolls and leather balls to the smallest children, and stockings to the older ones. And when the little ones had fallen asleep, the adults roasted chestnuts on the open hearth and sipped mugs of cider heated with a hot poker.

It was after midnight when Rory rose to walk Jillian back to the big house. His mother insisted that two of his sisters walk with them. "To be fittin'," she said. "So none can accuse my boy of wrongdoin', do they catch ye."

Rory's half sisters hung back and giggled as he escorted Jillian to the unlocked garden door that she'd used to slip out of the manor. " 'Tis sorry I am that I had no gift for ye," he whispered to her in farewell.

"Oh," Jillian replied, "oh, but you did give me a gift. You gave me Christmas."

His only reply was to lean down and kiss her lightly on the lips. Jillian felt a sudden rush of excitement that made her toes tingle and her head go all awhirl. She stepped back in surprise and touched her fingers to her tingling mouth.

" 'Tis only a Christmas kiss, little one," he said. "A kiss of peace between friends."

But Jillian knew that it had been more than that. And as she hurried up the cold stone steps to her bedchamber, she never felt the chill.

Winter faded into an uneasy spring in England. In summer, Jillian's family returned to Mandeville House. But as the drums of civil war grew louder, it seemed to Jillian as though her grandfather forgot that she existed. She saw only glimpses of Rory around the estate, and if he did see her, he seemed to have forgotten that they had ever shared a kiss on an enchanted Christmas Eve.

In September, when Lord Mandeville prepared to go to London again, he sent both Jillian and her stepgrandmother to stay with friends at a forbidding castle on the Welsh border. It was to be four long years before Jillian saw Mandeville House or Rory again.

And when she did return in the autumn of 1644, the world had turned upside down. Cromwell's Roundhead armies were marching across England in a whirlwind of blood and smoke. In July, the king's

Royalist followers had suffered a terrible defeat at Marston Moor, and her grandfather had become a fiery supporter of the Parliamentary faction. Her brother—Lord Mandeville's heir—was fighting as an officer under Cromwell's command, and Mandeville House was more an armed camp than a country home.

Jillian didn't have long to wait to find out why she had been summoned from Wales. Lord Mandeville called her into his chamber and informed her that she was to be wed at Christmas to Sir Vernon Pyle.

"I made the betrothal after his wife's death last winter," her grandfather said. "Pyle is a wealthy man and a Puritan. He and Cromwell are the best of friends."

"Do I know him?" she'd asked, too stunned to think of anything more sensible to say. A Puritan! Her heart sank at the thought. She had known she would have no say in whom she took as a husband, but she had expected to be wed to an Anglican. The only Puritans she'd ever met dressed in somber clothing and had long, sour faces.

An alliance had been formed for her with a baron when she was fifteen, but that suitor had chosen the wrong side in the civil war and her grandfather had broken off the arrangement. Since then, no one had mentioned marriage to her. Life on the Welsh border had been dull with no young people of her rank to talk to and few freedoms. She had spent most of her days sewing or walking in an enclosed garden. Still, that seemed vastly superior to the thought of becoming the bride of a faceless man in black.

"You'll meet a few days before the ceremony. He's a sensible sort, but I warn you, he'll have none of your flighty ways. He keeps a strict household."

"How old is he?" she'd dared, trying frantically to remember anything she might have heard about Pyle. "Will I be a stepmother?"

"Pyle's oldest son is your brother's superior officer. There are other children—girls, I believe. One is married, two are still at home." Lord Mandeville leaned forward and glared at her. "What possible business is his age to you? You will wed where and when I tell you, and you'll be an obedient wife—a credit to your breeding. God knows you need a strong hand. You've always been a flighty chit. I've been far too lenient with you, and that's the truth. You are long past the age of marrying. Were it not for the war, you'd be bouncing a babe on your knee by now."

Having delivered the news, Lord Mandeville promptly forgot her again and returned to the paperwork on his desk. Jillian stumbled from the room, numbly deciding to enjoy her two and a half months of freedom before leaving Mandeville House forever.

Before Jillian had been called to her grandfather's office, Lady Mandeville had given her permission to go riding. A saddled horse was already waiting for her at the entrance stairs, and Jillian's maid, Gwen, was at the door. Not wanting to listen to Gwen's maddening chatter, Jillian waved her away. "I'll not need you until the supper hour," she said.

"You can't ride alone, m'lady," Gwen replied.

"I'll have the groom," she argued, trying not to let Gwen see how upset she was. "And there are enough soldiers here to make Mandeville House the safest spot in England." She was trembling as she took her riding gloves and quirt from the maid and swept through the double doors. Pulling on her gloves, she tried to maintain her composure as she descended the outer marble steps and offered her hand to the groom. Then he snatched the hat off his dark head, turned, and looked full into her eyes . . . changing her life forever.

"Rory MacDaniel." The words came out a whisper.

"Lady Jillian." Simple words. Proper. But her name on Rory's lips sounded as sweet as rainfall in a desert.

Somehow, she was seated on the sidesaddle with the leather reins in her hands, but she couldn't remember mounting. Her chest felt tight, and her breath came in short, strangled gasps. Her fingers and toes felt numb, and her stomach was full of fluttering birds' wings.

There wasn't a cloud in the sky, but lightning had struck her as surely as if it were the heart of a violent summer thunderstorm. Her skin burned where he'd touched her, and she couldn't keep her gaze off him.

"Rory MacDaniel," she murmured again. Her mare began to walk, and his horse fell in beside her. Rory's eyes were focused straight ahead, but she could not keep from staring at him.

He was different. He was the same.

The prickly boy had become a man—a man so unlike the gentlemen she was used to seeing that he might be a hunting hawk in the midst of a flock of pigeons.

He was not big, as men went. The grizzled sergeant standing beside the gate yonder was taller and broader than Rory MacDaniel. Rory was muscular, but not so thewy that he resembled a blacksmith. The tight, doeskin breeches above his worn riding boots gave evidence of sleek, fluid sinew rather than bulky mass.

Rory's face was not even handsome in the classical sense. His browline was too sharp, his eyes too fierce, and his nose too definite. His chin was square and dimpled, but his mouth . . . his mouth beckoned like forbidden fruit. A faint scar trailed down one side of his face from cheekbone to chin, but it only added to his rugged appeal.

He sat the bay hunter as if they were not horse and rider, but a single entity—some pagan centaur. What stable groom had ever had such pride? He was a gamekeeper's son with the arrogance of a prince.

They turned the animals onto the orchard lane. Rory glanced over at her and smiled. And in that instant Jillian gave him her heart.

They laughed and talked as though three years had not passed since they'd last met. She knew it was wrong to allow him such liberties, but she would have given Rory anything he'd asked for.

Days drifted into weeks. Hands touched. Lips met, and lonely hearts reached out to each other. The difference in their stations meant nothing. All that mattered was the time they were together.

And, as Jillian reminded herself, she had done nothing wrong. What were a few embraces . . . a crown of autumn leaves that he tucked into her hair . . . a stolen hare roasted over a forest campfire and shared between friends? What were whispered hopes and dreams, as long as she kept herself innocent for her Puritan husband?

What mattered a few snatched hours of happiness when a lifetime of duty awaited her?

4

Mandeville House, England
December 1644

"I'LL PUT AN ARROW THROUGH HIS BLACK HEART BEFORE I let him lay a hand on ye, Jillian!" Rory exclaimed as he crushed her fiercely against him. "Oh, darlin'," he said with a groan. " 'Tis as black a sin as any devil ever committed—to wed a girl like you to such a monster."

"Don't. Don't say that," Jillian sobbed. "I couldn't bear it to have you commit murder for my sake. They'd hang you."

"Like your bloody betrothed hung that child for carrying Royalist messages?" He gripped her arms tightly and pushed her far enough away so that he could look down into her tearstained face. "Jesus and Mary! The boy was ten years old. He went to the gallows clutchin' a rag doll and cryin' for his mama."

Jillian was speechless. There was nothing she could say to mitigate the horror of what Vernon Pyle had done. By his orders, a child in the next village had been tortured with hot irons, and by his command the boy had been publicly hanged by his neck until he was dead. Rory had seen the execution with his own eyes, and he had seen Sir Vernon Pyle.

"He's a cruel, hard man," Rory said. "I stood not thirty feet from him as he watched that boy die. When the child's aunt begged for his life, Pyle said that God would know if the traitor was truly penitent or not, and gave the signal for the hangman to drop the trap."

"I will go to my grandfather and plead with him," she said. "Perhaps if I tell him that I cannot wed—"

"When has he ever listened to you, Jillian? When has anyone in your family cared for what you thought or wanted? Did they care when they left ye alone the Christmas ye turned thirteen? When they sold your pony? They care for your brother Charles, not you."

"Yes . . . you're right."

"I want ye for my wife, darlin'. I love ye more than I love my own soul. You've got to trust me."

Jillian closed her eyes and leaned against him, drawing strength from the clean, woody scent of his leather jerkin. She did love Rory MacDaniel. She loved him with all her heart and soul. And if she made a Christian marriage with Vernon Pyle, it would be a travesty.

"I know that I am penniless—" Rory began.

"I don't care about that." She drew in a deep, ragged breath. The thought of running away with Rory was overwhelming. The days and weeks that they'd spent together were the best times of her life, but she had never dared to hope that such happiness could continue. "My grandfather will have you killed," she said. "I'd rather spend the rest of my life with a man like Pyle than see you hurt."

"Nay. I'll not die if we are wed by book and marriage lines. Lord Mandeville might disinherit you, but—"

"Money means nothing to me."

Rory's face hardened. "Because you've always had it, ye can say it means naught. 'Tis another thing entirely to live on stolen hares and turnip soup when there is no coin to buy wheat flour for bread."

"I would do anything to be with you, but the risk is too great. I couldn't—"

"Jillian." He stopped her protests with a kiss.

His mouth covered hers gently at first, then when she yielded to him, he intensified the pressure against her lips until she lost her balance and swayed against him. Instinctively, she parted her lips and the tip of his tongue brushed hers. To her surprise, a bolt of white-hot desire rocked her. Her knees went weak, and her breath caught in her throat.

"No, darlin'," he murmured. "We must flee. We must marry. The risk is too great if we don't. For Pyle shall never have ye—not if I have to take on your family and Cromwell's army single-handed."

"But when? How?" She was so full of pent-up excitement and confused thoughts that she couldn't hold still. She didn't know whether to laugh or cry. She was as light-headed as if she had been drinking strong brandy wine. "Could we?"

"If we go," he said firmly, "we go now. I lied to my mother. I told her that I was going to join the army. I did not go home last night. She will think I'm on my way to enlist."

"And my grandfather believes that I am with Lady Mandeville." Her step-grandmother had ridden out very early that morning with her attendants to pay a visit to her ailing sister in the next shire. Jillian had been invited to go along, but a kitchen maid had brought a note from Rory just before bedtime last night. In the brief message, he had begged her to meet him on a matter of life and death at the place where he'd shot the wild dog so long ago.

She had told Lady Mandeville's servant that she was suffering from monthly cramps and wanted to stay at home. Lady Martin, Jillian's companion, never rose before noon, and she believed that Jillian had gone with her step-grandmother to Blackwell Castle.

Jillian had dressed in her plainest clothing, thrown her maid's cloak over her head, and slipped out the garden door without anyone seeing her. She had not even gone to the stables for a horse, but had run through the orchards and into the wooded parkland on foot.

"Lady Mandeville will not return for two days. Until then, no one will look for you," Rory continued. "By the time they do, we will be man and wife, and your family will have to accept it."

"What if they have our marriage annulled?" she asked.

"We will stay away until there is the chance you are with child. Better an Irish son-in-law than a bastard child." He looked at her with love in his eyes. "Once, the MacDaniels were a family to be reckoned with in Ireland. Were it not for the English, we would be wealthy still. I promise ye, Jillian, ye willna be poor forever. If ye do me the honor of becomin' my wife, I swear, I'll give ye everything—"

"You are all that matters to me," she whispered.

"Then ye will marry me?"

"I will."

"I will not." The dour cleric scowled at them from the entrance of St. Stephen's Church. "Go to your own village priest. I'll have no part of this."

As the black-robed man slammed the door in their faces, Jillian stepped back and looked at Rory in despair. "Four days," she murmured. "Four days and three men of god. And all of them have turned us away."

Rory took her arm and led her quickly through the cemetery. "There has to be a way," he said. "There has to be."

"If they catch us before we're married, they'll hang you." She tried to keep the desperation from her voice.

"They won't catch us."

"But they will," she insisted. "You don't know my grandfather."

"If ye think I'll give ye up, Jillian, ye don't know me."

They trudged on through the churchyard gate and into the woods. Jillian was tired and hungry, and she had a blister on her left heel. The hem of her gown was torn and dirty, and she looked as if she'd slept in her clothes.

She had. They'd spent the night in a farmer's haystack, and the night before that they'd slept in a mill. It was unseasonably warm for December. Otherwise . . . Jillian shivered. She didn't want to think what it would be like if there was frost on the ground.

The first minister had turned them away because Jillian looked too young and Rory sounded Irish. The priest had refused to marry them until Jillian showed proof that she was Catholic. The second minister had demanded to know their real names and threatened to call the sheriff. And here, on December 24th, at St. Stephen's in the Wood, they had received no explanation, only rejection.

"I'm ruined if we go back," Jillian said. "Everyone

will think we—" She broke off, unable to finish. But they hadn't done anything wrong. Rory had treated her with tender care. He'd found her food and kept her warm at night, and he'd not done anything that would touch on her honor.

"I promised ye that I'd care for ye," he soothed, "and I will." They crossed a meadow and entered an older woods, following a game path until it faded, and then continuing on through the thick forest for nearly an hour.

Jillian followed, too heartsick to ask where they were going, until suddenly Rory stopped short and pointed.

"Look!" Just ahead, in a clearing, stood the crumbling remains of an ancient stone chapel. "Look at this," he said, taking her hand.

As they entered a break in the walls, a rabbit hopped away. Jillian started, then laughed at her own foolishness. "It's beautiful," she said. She didn't speak too loudly, because there was a sense of holiness about the ruins. She stopped and looked around her, sighing at the empty windows and stone arches covered with wild grape vines and mistletoe. "It's a ghost church."

Moss grew thick beneath their feet, and in one corner of what had once been the choir, a trickle of clear water ran down to form a fern-edged pool. Sparrows sang overhead, and one flew down almost at Jillian's feet to drink from the stream.

"Not a ghost church," Rory said. "A fairy church." Jillian smiled at him, and he squeezed her hand.

"We could pledge our vows here," she suggested shyly. "A handfast promise."

"Before God," Rory agreed, taking her other hand.

"Do you, Jillian, take me as your wedded husband? To have and to hold, in sickness and in health, for richer for poorer, until death do us part?"

She smiled at him. "I do."

"Now ye must ask the same of me," he urged.

"And do you, Rory MacDaniel, take me, Jillian, to be your wedded wife, to love and to cherish, until death us do part?"

"I do," he said solemnly. "And in the name of our love and this blessed spot, I pronounce us husband and wife."

She went into his arms and raised her face to be kissed. "I will always love you, Rory. And I will never, never wed another," she murmured. "On my immortal soul, I swear it."

And the sweetness of that kiss was such that Jillian could remember it as clearly on this Christmas Eve, in Maryland twenty-six years later, as if it had been only this afternoon.

Oh, yes, she thought. I remember Rory's kiss, and I remember the night that followed . . . our wedding night.

"This be it," the innkeeper's jovial wife said, throwing open the door. "Private and clean. Just what I promised ye." She held the Betty lamp high. "Wood and tinder's on the hearth. My girl will light it for ye, and bring along bread and meat." She chuckled. "The mister says take only coin, but I've a young'n that will fancy your bow and arrows for a Christmas gift. Good luck to ye both." She laughed again. "And I'll send up a little wine as well. I remember my own wedding night. A little wine helps to calm the nerves. For both of ye."

Jillian looked around the tiny attic room. The floor-boards were swept bare. There were no furnishings but a crude washstand with a cracked pitcher and bowl, and a pallet on the floor. The straw-tick mattress took up most of the available floor space, and the roof was so low that Rory could only stand upright near the doorway. But dried herbs and flowers hung from the open rafters and ivy covered the single window. The garret chamber smelled of summertime.

"This isn't—" Rory began.

"It will do nicely," Jillian said to the woman. "Thank you."

When they were alone, Rory pulled her into his arms. "I love ye, Mistress MacDaniel."

"And I love you, but you didn't have to trade away your bow for this room. I could have slept in a hay-stack again."

"Not tonight," he said huskily.

A shyness overcame her then, a fumbling, hot-cheeked awkwardness that lasted through their shared supper of beef and biscuits and homemade gooseberry wine. She was starving, but she could hardly force herself to eat.

"You've nothin' to fear from me," Rory said as he fed sticks to the small fire.

"Have you . . . have you ever . . ." she stammered. "I mean, have you . . ."

"Made love to a woman?" He turned and looked at her with those sloe-black Irish eyes. "No, darlin', ye are the first."

"For me too," she said.

He laughed. "I hoped as much."

And she laughed with him. She'd supposed that Rory had done it before—that all men knew of such things. But the thought that this was as new to him as it was to her was comforting.

"Will we get it right, do you suppose?" she dared.

"I think we will."

He came to lie beside her then, on the clean quilt. She was still fully dressed, except for her shoes. Those stood neatly by the door. Her one stocking had a hole in the heel, and she hid it from him. He slid an arm around her and she tensed.

"There now," he murmured. "None of that, Mistress MacDaniel. We'll do nothin' that ye do not wish to do. God willin', we shall be married for fifty years, and there's no hurry. All I want of ye is a kiss." She flattened herself against the mattress and he leaned over her.

She closed her eyes, held her breath, and their lips touched. She sighed. It was only Rory, after all, and only a kiss like so many they'd shared. Still, she could not help the trembling in the pit of her stomach.

"Sweet Jillian," he whispered. His lips were warm against hers.

She sighed again as he kissed a path of gentle caresses from her mouth to the ticklish spot under her chin. Delicious shivers washed through her. Boldly, she stroked his cheek and felt the texture of his dark hair. "My husband," she murmured. His hair was thick and clean. It slid through her fingers like raw silk.

The tip of his warm tongue touched the hollow of her throat, and she gasped. He whispered her name again as his strong fingers played along the neckline of her gown. Jillian found each breath harder to draw in as he held her tighter against him.

This is right and good, she thought. This is my

God-given husband, and this is how it was meant to be between us. She closed her eyes and gave herself over to the wonder of his next kiss. Somehow, without her consciously deciding to do it, her lips parted, and she felt the velvet thrust of his tongue.

She went all giddy and her stomach churned. No man had ever kissed her like this. And no whispered servants' gossip had told the glory of this daring act. Rory's tongue was in her mouth and she was tasting him as she had never done before. The sensations were sweet and wild. They made her breasts swell and tingle against the confines of her stays.

Rory's hand cupped her breast, and she opened her eyes wide and gave a little cry of delight. She wanted him to touch her, wanted him to pull away her gown and chemise and fondle her bare skin. As she wanted to feel his . . .

She clutched his shoulders, pulling him ever closer, while the flame of their growing passion flickered in her most secret places. And when he asked her to let him undo her gown, she obediently rolled onto her side and lay breathless as he fumbled with the back laces.

"You are so beautiful, Jillian," he said as he slid the gown off her shoulders and kissed each one in turn. "So very beautiful."

Trembling with anticipation, she helped him to remove her gown, linen petticoats, barrel pad, and stays, leaving her garbed only in a simple calf-length cambric chemise and her silk stockings.

"Now you," she said. She swallowed the rising knot in her throat and watched as he took off his shirt.

Years of drawing a long bow had built muscle and sinew on his sturdy frame. His chest was covered with a fine sprinkling of dark, curling hair. She could not keep her bold gaze from dropping lower, over his flat belly to the second line of curling hair and above the waistband of his low-slung leather breeches. His lean, hard body was so beautiful that it brought a sudden rush of anticipation through her and she felt no shame. Instead, she smiled at him and held out her arms in wanton invitation.

"I might have known it," he teased. "Sooner or later, every Englishman has the shirt off an Irishman's back."

"An even trade—my shirt for yours."

"Aye, sweet, that it is." He took her in his strong arms again, and they kissed until she lost all track of time or place. She couldn't get enough of his touch, of the exquisite feel of his tongue against her . . . or of his heavy weight pressing on her. She wanted to taste and touch every inch of him as he was doing to her.

His mouth was on her breast. His warm, wet tongue caressed and teased her nipple until it ached. And then, when she could stand it no more, he gently drew her nipple into his velvet mouth and suckled until she writhed with passion.

And when he caught her hand in his and drew it down to the growing proof of his desire, she gloried in the wonder of his silken power, taking joy from his ragged breathing.

"Jillian." He groaned. "Jillian, my sweet." His seeking fingers found the dampness between her thighs and slipped between the sensitive folds. "I want ye," he gasped.

Jillian's eyes were closed tightly. His words seemed to come from far away. She had forgotten where she was and why. Her heart was pounding as though she had run half a mile with hounds on her heels. All her concentration—all her senses—were centered on the wonderful sensations that Rory was creating with his slow, sensual touches.

His fingers moved deeper within her, and she gasped. Something was happening . . . something she had never dreamed of . . . Waves of intense pleasure rocked her. She clung to him as stars burst through her consciousness, bringing small sounds of rapture from her throat. "Rory, Rory, Rory," she cried.

Before her mind had stopped spinning, she became aware of his weight on her . . . his weight and a hard fullness. Her eyes flew open as he entered her, deeper than she could ever have imagined. There was a brief, sharp pain, an uncomfortable stretching, and then the stirring of renewed excitement as he began to move against her.

When Rory withdrew, Jillian gave a low cry of protest and arched her hips. He sighed and joined with her again. His mouth was on her breast, and the sweet joy spiraled through her body with growing intensity. A few attempts and she caught the rhythm, receiving him within her and holding him, taking and giving until he stiffened his entire body, shuddered, and plunged deep to fill her with his need. Her own climax followed his within seconds, and she drifted into a sparkling nothingness of bright light and utter peace, followed by an exhaustion as complete as anything she had ever known.

With another sigh, he cradled her against him and whispered her name into her hair. For a while they slept, and when she did awake, Rory's breath was warm on her face in the darkness.

"I love ye," he whispered. "More than my immortal soul."

"And I love you."

"Forever and a day?"

"Forever and a day," she answered sleepily. He kissed her bruised lips, and she smiled, then fell asleep again.

Sometime before dawn Jillian awoke. A blanket was tucked around her, but the pallet beside her was empty. "Rory?" she whispered. "Rory, where are you?" Frightened, she sat up. "Rory?"

"Shhh." The door opened and she heard his footsteps. He knelt beside her and she threw herself into his arms.

"You were gone," she said. "I woke up and—"

"I will never leave ye, Jillian." His arms tightened around her. "Now, ye must be very brave. No. Shhh," he soothed as she gave a little cry. "Shhh, listen to me." He closed the door and leaned close to her ear. "The innkeeper's wife said that soldiers came to the inn just after midnight."

"No!"

"Aye. Now, listen. Vernon Pyle has offered a reward for us—twenty pounds silver to any who gives information leading to our arrest."

"Arrest? For what?"

"Murder. Your companion Lady Martin was found dead in her bed."

"Lady Martin? Murdered? But she was old and sick. Who would do such a thing?"

"I know not. They did not say what she died of, only that she was dead. She may have passed away in her sleep. But I'd not like to try and prove that to a judge in Pyle's pay, would ye?"

"Surely my grandfather can't believe that I would ever—"

"The reward is twenty pounds for us alive, Jillian, but fifty pounds dead. If they catch us, we'll not survive to plead innocence."

Jillian began to shiver. "What will we do? The innkeeper's wife must suspect—"

"Aye, she knows who we be, right enough, but she has no love for Pyle and Cromwell's soldiers. She lost a boy at Marston Moor, fighting for the king. She'll not turn us in, but she cannot say as much for the maid who brought our supper last night. We must get far away from here, Jillian, and we must do it now."

"But where? How?"

"America."

"Yes, we could go there. But passage money . . . It would take more than we have. No one would take us aboard a ship without—"

"There is a way, but it will be hard. More for you than me, darlin'. The innkeeper's wife says her cousin's son has signed on with the captain of the *Golden Hart* anchored in Bristol harbor to go to the Maryland Colony as an indentured servant. Four years he must serve in return for his passage. She says that her cousin told her that there is such a demand for bond-servants that the captain asks no questions. So long as you be young and healthy, they care not what laws ye have broken. Could you do it, Jillian? Go with me across the sea to this Maryland?"

She did not hesitate, so great was the relief, so bright the hope. "I would follow you to the ends of the earth, Rory MacDaniel," she replied. "Follow you to hell and scrub the devil's pitchfork, so long as you were there beside me."

"They say that wild Indians roam the forests. And that there are poison snakes, and bears, and all manner of fierce creatures."

"Can any be as cruel as Vernon Pyle?"

5

New Hope Plantation, Maryland Colony
Christmas, 1667

"AND NONE WAS AS CRUEL AS VERNON PYLE," JILLIAN murmured to herself as she stared out her window at the drifting snow. Here, in the new colony, they had found only welcome arms and a bright future. She smiled at the sounds of her guests' laughter, not really conscious of them, letting her mind drift back to a happier Christmas Eve. How well she remembered that special Christmas of 1667, over two decades after they left England, the year their precious little son was five. Jillian closed her eyes and in her mind she could see Rory and Jamie here by this very window . . .

"On Christmas, twenty-three years ago, your mother offered to go to hell with me," Rory said to his son. "Fortunately for you, my fine lad, the ship to hell had just sailed and we had to get on another ship that brought us here to Maryland."

Jamie giggled and looked up at Rory with huge

dark eyes full of mischief. "Mama says don't say *hell*. That's a bad word, Da."

"She's right, o' course," he agreed, pinching the boy's freckled nose playfully. "But what could ye expect from a rascal like me?"

Jamie giggled again and bounced hard on Rory's knee. "Tell me about the whales," he said. "I want to hear about the whales in the big ocean."

"Rory MacDaniel, what blasphemy are you filling that child's head with?" Jillian demanded, coming into the great hall. "You told me you were putting him into bed a half hour ago." She smiled at them both, taking the sting from her scolding. Watching the two of them together always made her feel so light and happy inside that she was surprised she didn't float up to the ceiling.

In all their years of marriage, the good Lord had seen fit to send them only this one child. Just one blessed babe—but he was the best and most beautiful that heaven could fashion. Jillian swallowed the knot of emotion in her throat. Father and son—she loved them more than anything in the world.

"Blasphemy? Not me," Rory defended with a wink. He sat the boy down and ruffled his dark curls. "We were just after tellin' a few stories."

Jillian came to stand beside Rory, and he rose and put an arm around her shoulders. "Are you sure it was so long ago that we came to Maryland?" she asked. He tilted her chin up and kissed her full on the mouth, and the sweet music flowed over her as bright and magical as ever it had.

"Aye, darlin', it has been. Twenty-three years since I stole away the finest prize any poacher ever took." He smiled down at her and caught a curling lock of her hair between his fingers. "And fair as ever ye were at seventeen, I'm thinkin'."

"Go on with you, Rory," she said, straightening her lace cap. Her cheeks grew hot. He could still make her blush like a bride, even if she was almost two times twenty and her wheat-brown tresses were streaked with gray.

"Are ye glad, colleen? Have ye never wished for the grand house and fortune ye left behind when ye came away with me?"

"No," she replied. "For what other husband could I have chosen who would still flirt so outrageously with me after so many years of marriage?"

"And why shouldn't I admire such a vision in a rose brocade gown? What do ye say, son? Isn't your mother beautiful?"

"Yes," Jamie agreed. "The prettiest mama in the world."

"A little rounder than when we first wed," Rory teased, "but your smile warms my heart like no other on earth."

"Stop it, both of you," she insisted. "Give me too many compliments, and I'll think you're up to something you shouldn't be."

Rory's features became serious. "Truth now, darlin', do ye ever miss your old life in England?"

"Never," she answered softly.

"No regrets?"

"None. Except . . ."

Rory kissed her on the forehead.

There was no need for her to explain. He knew her too well. Deep in her heart, Jillian still worried because there had been no priest or minister to read their marriage lines. They had pledged their troth alone.

And once they had signed on to come to America and settled here in the colony, they'd not wanted to bring shame on themselves by saying that they were not technically wed.

"Ye are my wife, darlin'," he murmured, breaking into her reverie. "In your heart, ye know it to be true."

She sighed and nodded. "I know, but—"

"But it's time Master MacDaniel here was into his bed. Our neighbors will be here to help us celebrate the night, will they not?"

Jillian laughed. "What was I just saying? It's time Jamie was in bed."

"A present," Jamie said. "I want a present."

"Tomorrow, my dumplin'," Rory said. "Tomorrow mornin' if ye are as good as good can be." He grabbed Jamie and swung him up onto his shoulders.

"Git-up horse," Jamie cried, grabbing hold of Rory's hair.

"Easy, easy," Jillian warned. "You'll pull your father's hair out, and at his age there's none to spare."

"What?" Rory cried. "What are ye sayin', woman? With me possessin' as fine a head of hair as any lad in—" The sound of sleigh bells came from outside and Rory went to the window. "There's the Bennetts. I guess it's bedtime for ye, my boy."

"I'll call Isaac to tuck him in," Jillian said. She went to the door and pulled the bell cord.

"I want to sleep in your bed," Jamie insisted.

"Till we come up," Rory said, "but then—" He winked at Jillian. "Then it's into your own bedchamber where ye belong."

The early hours of Christmas morning had always

belonged to Rory and her alone, she thought. Tonight would be no different. They would laugh and sing with friends, and later they would share old memories and try and make a few new ones.

"I want a light. I don't like dark. I want to sleep with you and Mama, Da."

Jillian bent and kissed his cheek. "Tessie May sleeps in your room, and there is light from your fireplace. We're just across the hall. You're a big boy, Jamie. Big boys sleep in their own beds. Go along now, and I'll ask Isaac to tell you one story. And don't forget your prayers."

"Two stories," the child bargained.

Rory laughed. "Ye heard your mother, Jamie. One story or none? What will it be?"

Jamie's lips puckered. For an instant it looked to Jillian as though he might cry, but then he shrugged and flashed a smile that was an exact copy of Rory's. "One story, Da—but a long, long one."

Jillian shook her head as Isaac came to lead the boy to bed. "He's a handful, that one. Do we spoil him, do you think, Rory? I don't want him to turn out like my brother."

"Not a chance," Rory answered. "Jamie doesn't have a mean bone in his body. He's a child, and all children want their own way. Keep doin' what ye've been doin', and he'll end up a fine man."

"Like his father," she replied.

Rory shook his head. "What did I ever do to deserve a woman like you, Jillian? You can take credit for our son."

"And who delivered him with his own hands? Who walked with him at night when he was sick with measles? Who sewed up his finger when he cut it with

Cook's knife? You are a rare father, Rory MacDaniel, and Jamie's a lucky boy to have you."

"I missed havin' my own da. My stepfather was a good man, but he favored his own blood more than me. 'Tis only natural I'd take an interest in my own lad."

"Neither of us had a father's guidance. I pray our child never has to face that loss."

Rory grimaced. "I'll try and remember not to trip over a pig and break my neck."

"I'm serious. I don't know what we'd do without you."

"Fair enough. For I'd be helpless as a milk cow on ice without the two of you, darlin'."

Jillian glanced at the table. "Does everything look all right?"

Rory gazed around the great hall. "Aye, sweet,'tis all in order, though this room would hold three of the house I was raised in."

A log blazed on the hearth and greens decorated the mantel and windows. The long walnut table groaned beneath the weight of silver platters of cold meats, pies, and cakes, raw oysters, jellies, jams, apples, nuts, and all manner of delicious-looking food. The chairs and hunt board along the far wall had been especially crafted in Dublin for New Hope Plantation and shipped there at terrible expense the year before Jamie's birth. Jillian felt a surge of sinful pride as she admired her chairs. She was certain there were none in the colony to match them. "You're sure I haven't forgotten anything?" she asked.

"No, wife," he said. "It looks mortal fine." He grinned. "I'd say I've come a far piece in my lifetime from a penniless lad without a second shirt for his back or sound shoes for his feet to a man of substance."

"You did it all," she said. "Whatever we have, you made for us." The land of New Hope Plantation had been bought with Rory's sweat and backbreaking work, and the emerald necklace her step-grandmother had sent her ten years back when the old earl had finally died. In twenty-three years, the two of them had crossed the chasm from bondservants to gentility.

Their original land had been a tract of one hundred acres, all virgin forest, a gift from John Parker's widow when they'd finished their four-year term of service. She and Rory had been fortunate enough to have their indentures sold to good people, and when John Parker drowned crossing from the Eastern Shore, Judith Parker had treated them more like family than servants.

Both of them had worked hard in the fields, in the woodlots, and in the stables. Jillian had peeled potatoes, fed chickens, and planted seeds, while Rory hoed tobacco in rain and broiling sun and cut down trees, hardening his hands to iron and adding lines to his face.

They had been so lucky. Lucky to have escaped Vernon Pyle's soldiers in England, lucky to be given fertile land of their own, and lucky to raise cattle in a year when there was a shortage of beef. Their first crop of tobacco had thrived and sold for more money than Jillian had dreamed it could. Yes, they had prospered in America. She couldn't imagine what their life would have been if they hadn't come to this New World.

"Not my work alone," Rory said, as though reading her thoughts. "*Our work* bought this land and all we have."

"We've been blessed."

"Aye, but of all my blessings, I count two as the greatest," he said. "Ye are as brave and loving a wife as any man ever wed. Granddaughter to an earl ye be, Jillian, yet ye never whined or shirked your duties, and never once did ye fault me for my common birth." He smiled at her. "Ye shared my dreams, woman. Ye argued with me when ye thought I was wrong, and stood shoulder to shoulder with me in times of trouble." His grin widened. "And ye've welcomed me to your bed, givin' me a gift that few men get— a passion that equals my own."

"It was no trouble," she teased. "Your bed is not something a woman would flee from."

"I hope not," he replied.

"And what do you count as your second blessing?" she asked, knowing the answer before he replied. It had to be Jamie, born to them when she'd reached her mid-thirties and they had all but given up hope of being parents. Jamie had a warm and loving nature, a genuine fondness for animals, and a quick mind. Jamie had been born here in the Colonies, and he had a pride and independence beyond any Rory had known in the old country. He was a match for this wilderness, and when he grew to be a man, she was certain Jamie would leave his mark on it.

"You and my son, they are my real riches," he said. "The house, the fertile land, the good neighbors, they're all sauce for my goose."

"Master Rory," Nell called. "Mr. Bennett—"

Jillian tugged at her husband's hand. "We can't keep our guests waiting."

"Lead on, woman." Dutifully, he followed her to the entrance hall and their Christmas Eve celebration.

* * *

Jillian reined in her mare and shaded her eyes against the setting April sun. At the far side of the corn field, beside the woods, she could just make out Rory's black gelding and her son Jamie on the dapple-gray pony they'd given him for Christmas.

Rory had dismounted, left his horse, and had a bag of seed corn hung over one shoulder. He was walking down the row dropping kernels into the freshly turned soil. Ahead of him, Giles, their new indentured bondman, guided the horse and wooden plow that cut a shallow furrow in the newly turned soil.

It was early for planting corn, even in this high, sheltered field, but last summer had been a dry one, and Rory had been determined to get this one field of Indian corn seeded. That way, if there wasn't a late freeze, the abundant showers of May and June would give the crop a good start.

Elsewhere in the field, Jillian saw two other teams of servants engaged in the same tasks. There was no need for Rory to do field labor anymore; God knew they had both done their share in the early, hard years in Maryland. But Rory wanted his son to learn each step of farming. When he was older, Jillian knew that Rory would put the boy in the fields.

"Ye can't teach a servant to do a thing unless ye be master of that skill," Rory always liked to say. He believed in working with his people, teaching them, and continuing to learn as the seasons passed. "Lord willin', our Jamie will have a fine education, but he needs to know where his roots are. A planter can't be too high in the stomach to get his hands dirty in his own soil."

Jillian touched her mare's rump lightly with her

quirt and rode around the end of the field. As she drew nearer to Jamie, she couldn't resist a smile at the serious expression on the boy's face, or the proud manner in which he sat in his small saddle.

Jamie had been riding since he was three, but always on a lead line, or riding double with his father or one of the servants. They'd had no pony or horse gentle enough to trust with the object of her heart. Jamie promised to be a good rider with a real feel for handling horses, but the child was still very young. Rory wasn't about to let him ride head-over-heels across the countryside alone. There would be time enough for that once they were certain he was an accomplished horseman.

The boy looked up and saw Jillian coming. He smiled and waved. She waved back, trying not to think how fast her baby was growing up. God grant that I live long enough to see his children, she thought.

For many years she had prayed for children. She'd wanted to give Rory a handful, laughing daughters and solid sons. But that was not to be. They had Jamie, and a mother with a boy like him would be greedy to ask for more.

As she watched, Rory straightened, rubbing his back. She called a greeting to him and he answered her with a grin and a wave. "It's time to call it a day," she shouted.

"We just want to finish these last four rows."

"It will be dark," she argued. "You can finish in the morning."

Rory said something to Giles that she couldn't make out, then he turned back to her. "All right, Mistress MacDaniel. We'll stop at the end of the row. Giles says his backbone is banging against his belly. He's afraid he'll starve if he doesn't get supper soon."

"Giles looks like he's starving," she called back. Giles stood six feet in his stocking feet and weighed fifteen stone. His size and appetite were an ongoing joke between them. "Pork pie for supper," she said.

Then a movement in the trees caught her attention and Jillian stared at the bronze stranger who moved from the shadows. "Rory—" she began uneasily.

The figure turned his head and Jillian saw streaks of black and yellow paint across his face and realized he was an Indian. Before she could shout a warning, he raised what looked like a stick. Instantly, there was a puff of smoke and the echoing crack of a musket.

Rory raised his arms and took a step toward the woods as other Indians appeared behind the first brave. Rory looked almost puzzled as he dropped to one knee and toppled over, clutching his midsection.

"Rory!" Jillian screamed.

More painted savages were pouring out of the trees. One ran toward Jamie.

"Da! Da!" he cried.

"Run, Jamie!" Jillian shouted. "Run!" She brought the quirt down sharply on her mare's rump and tried to go to his aid, but the Indians' howling war cries terrified the mare and it reared. Jillian fought to keep her seat on the sidesaddle. "Jamie!"

More shots were fired. Jillian saw Giles fall with an arrow in his back. An Indian leaped on him and metal flashed in the sun. Triumphantly, the brave held up a bloody scalp. A second warrior ran toward Rory's fallen body. Jillian screamed again.

Rory raised up, pointed his pistol at the Indian, and fired point-blank. The brave went down, kicked once, and lay still.

A huge Indian with a shaved head and copper hoops in his ears rushed toward Jillian. The mare reared again, catching him in the head with an iron-clad hoof. He sank back, his face covered in blood.

"Mama! Mama!" An Indian had Jamie's pony by the bridle. The pony lashed out at another man with both hind feet, then spun around in a circle. The Indian let go of the bridle and the pony reared up. Jamie slid off over the animal's rump and ran toward Jillian. A slim warrior wearing a blue military coat with wide cuffs and silver buttons reached out to grab her son, but Jamie dodged him and ran like a rabbit.

Three Indians moved in on Jillian. "Run! Run!" she screamed to Jamie. She slashed at the nearest man with her leather quirt, cutting a slice across his face.

"Get away from my mama!" Jamie shouted. He flew into the closest Indian brave, his small fists flying. "Get away from my mama!"

A savage seized Jillian's arm and dragged her from the saddle. She bounced off the ground, kicked him hard in the shin. When he still didn't loosen his grip, she lowered her head and butted him hard in the stomach. He gasped and grabbed his belly. She twisted away and ran around the kicking, squealing mare toward Jamie.

An Indian grabbed him around the waist. "Mama!" Jamie shouted. For an instant their eyes met, and she read the absolute trust in her son's eyes.

"I'm coming!" Then something struck her head and everything went black.

Jillian didn't open her eyes again for a long time. When she did, she found a neighbor standing over her. Her first word was her son's name. "Jamie?"

Tears rolled down Mary Bennett's plump cheeks. "Stolen away by the savages. He's alive, but taken."

"What? What are you saying?" Jillian demanded.

Mary shook her head. "Three of your people dead, four more are being cared for at the next plantation. They took four of your horses too."

"Jamie?" She knew the answer. Her head hurt, but she knew what Mary had said. She didn't want to believe it. She kept asking, hoping the next answer would be different.

"Likely you'd be dead and scalped like poor Giles," Mary said, "if it wasn't for the smoke from the Ironses' tobacco barn. They burned it and the Ironses' summer kitchen. Joseph Irons rode to our place to get help to keep the fire from spreading to the main house. Jered and the other men took a shortcut through your cornfield to get to the Ironses' plantation and came face to face with the war party. The Indians fired off a few shots, snatched your boy and the horses, and vanished into the woods."

"Jamie's gone?" Jillian repeated. The attack seemed like a bad dream. It couldn't be real. Here she was in her own bed with Mary Bennett offering chicken soup to her. Her only child couldn't be kidnapped by Indians. Not her Jamie . . .

"You lay back on those pillows now. You took an awful knock on your head."

"Rory?" Jillian murmured. An image of Rory's fallen body flashed across her mind. She couldn't ask about him yet. She couldn't. If she did . . .

Three dead, Mary had said. Giles. Giles and who else? Not Rory, she bargained with fate. She couldn't bear to lose both of them. "Is Rory . . ," She wouldn't cry. There weren't any tears. She felt dead and empty inside. "Is Rory dead? Did they scalp him too?"

She closed her eyes, ignoring the pain in her head, visualizing the awful moment when she'd seen the puff of smoke ... the moment when Rory had fallen.

"No, indeed. Don't think it for an instant," Mary said, taking her hand and sitting on the edge of the bed. "He took a musket ball along the ribs. He lost a lot of blood, but it didn't stop him. They brought him back here and sewed him up, and he rode off with the search party. Irishmen are tough as leather."

"He rode out hurt?"

"They couldn't stop him. He was bound to go. They'll find your boy, Jillian. Never doubt it. They'll find your boy."

"They have to, don't they?" she whispered. "They have to find him. It will be getting dark soon. He's afraid of the dark. He has to be home by dark."

A look of real pain crossed Mary's face. "It was yesterday, Jillian. This is another day. The search party hasn't come back yet. But I'm sure they'll have Jamie when they do. You can be certain of it."

Two weeks later, Rory returned, white-faced and bone-tired. His eyes were red and swollen, and his features seemed years older than when Jillian had last seen him.

She ran to him with open arms. "Are you all right?" she demanded. "Where's my baby?"

"Out there somewhere," Rory answered hoarsely. He pointed west toward the wilderness, a great wild forest that stretched for God knew how far without a road, or house, or hint of civilization. " 'Twas Susquehannas that raided us. Some fool English soldiers burned a Susquehanna village and killed twenty Indians. They took out their revenge on us."

"But Jamie? What of Jamie? Didn't you find any trace of him? How do we know if he's dead or alive?"

Rory pulled her against him, and she felt the weariness of his battered body. "We ran into some friendly Delawares. They hadn't seen the raiding party, but they said that our boy won't be harmed. The warrior that took him likely lost a son when the Indian village was burned. It's their way to take a captive in return."

"They can't have my son!"

"And they won't. I've told the Delaware that we'll give a big reward for his return. I had to come home. The men with me gave up weeks of spring planting to hunt for Jamie. I'll see our crops in the ground, and then I'll gather another party and go out again. I'll bring him back to ye, Jillian. I swear I will."

She wept then, great sobbing bursts of tears that would not stop. "He's just a baby," she said over and over. "He's just a baby."

"I'll bring him home to ye. As God is my witness," Rory swore, "I'll bring him home."

But that had been over two years ago, and despite all the times Rory had ridden out, he'd never returned with Jamie.

6

New Hope Plantation, Maryland Colony
Christmas Eve, 1670

HER GUESTS' LAUGHTER DREW JILLIAN BACK FROM HER
memories of the years gone by, and she suddenly
realized that Sibyl was standing in front of the
harpsichord speaking to her. From the expression
on the young woman's face, she had been trying to
get Jillian's attention.

"Oh, play for us," Sibyl begged. "Please play." Sibyl's cheeks were rosy beneath dancing blue eyes. She
looked lovely in the low-cut gown of flowered silk
that showed off her pretty freckled shoulders.

Jillian released her breath softly, smiled at the young
bride, and looked down at her instrument. Softly, she
began to play an old English carol, one she had first
heard in her grandfather's hall, as her friends gathered
around Sibyl and began to sing.

Go back to your dancing, Jillian wanted to say to
them. She didn't want to let go of her memories of
Rory and Jamie just yet. As long as she could picture
them in her mind, they were very close to her and
the new life she carried. But there was no way she
could hurt the feelings of those who had come to

celebrate Christmas at New Hope, so she joined her voice with theirs, laughed in all the right places, and smiled though her heart felt like stone.

If only she and Rory hadn't argued before he rode away the last time, Jillian thought. Pangs of guilt swept over her . . .

In the two and a half years since Jamie had been stolen, their hopes had been raised and dashed so many times that Rory had wanted to give up the search.

"He's dead to us," he'd insisted. "Accept that, Jillian. I love Jamie as much as ye do. I'd give my eyes to have him back, but it's not going to happen."

Rumors drifted back from the frontier wilderness time and time again. A white child had been seen living with a peaceful tribe of Shawnee. An English boy named James had appeared in Philadelphia. A light-skinned child had been living alone in the forest west of St. Mary's City. And each time they'd heard one of these tales, Rory had ridden off to track down the report. But always, these expeditions ended in heartbreak.

Sometimes there was no child at all; sometimes a girl was found instead. Once, a supposed captive turned out to be an albino native boy living with his own parents.

Rory had placed reward notices in newspapers. He had gone into the interior and met with friendly tribes to ask for information about his son. He had taken eleven trips in two and a half years, all without finding Jamie. Somehow, their son and the war party who had taken him had vanished without a trace.

"I will not believe that he's dead," Jillian had said stubbornly. "You promised me that you'd bring him home. Benjamin Bennett said that his brother Harry told him that a Delaware brave talked about seeing a dark-haired white boy last spring with Copper Knife's band of Susquehannas. Harry insisted that the Delaware had spoken with the boy. It's got to be our Jamie."

"Copper Knife's people have always been hostile to the English," Rory had said. "And Ben says his brother lies like a gypsy and drinks like a fish."

"It's Jamie, I know it is."

"It's not our son. Our son is dead, Jillian. He's dead, or at least dead to us, and the sooner you accept that, the sooner we can get on with our lives."

But she had not let up, and Rory had ridden off again. He'd gone because he loved her, even though he hadn't wanted to continue the search.

But this time was different. This time it was Rory who was missing and presumed dead. And if her husband never returned, she would have to live with the guilt and regret forever.

Jillian finished the tune just as Isaac threw open the double doors to the parlor where the food had been spread. Jillian stood up and gestured toward the dining area. "I believe Isaac would like us to come and—" A loud barking from upstairs caught Jillian's attention. "Please," she said to her guests. "Go in. Walter? Would you and Sibyl lead the way? I'll join you in a moment. If I don't see to that fool dog of Rory's, he may have the house down around us."

Jillian crossed the room and opened the door to the entrance hall just as Bear came thundering down the steps with Nell running behind him.

"Sorry. He ran over me!" Nell cried. "Bear! Bear! Come back here."

The dog whined, barked twice—a deep rumbling bellow loud enough to rattle the crystal candle sconces—and began to scratch with huge, hairy, black paws on the outer door.

"Sorry, miss," Nell repeated. "I heard him barkin' and I—"

"Never mind. I'll let him out. Then you can shut him in the cellar."

"Oh, miss, you'll catch yer death," Nell fussed. "That's me place to—"

"Give me your shawl then," Jillian said, taking Nell's worn homespun wrap and throwing it over her gown.

"Nell!" Cook's urgent shout came from the kitchen wing.

"Go on, girl," Jillian said, taking Bear's collar. "I'm capable of seeing to the dog. Go along to your duties."

Nell bobbed a quick curtsy and hurried down the hall. Jillian opened the wide paneled front door a crack, and Bear forced his way through, nearly knocking her over in the process. "Bear! What's gotten into you?"

The dog bounded off into the darkness, and Jillian pulled the worn wool shawl around her and stepped out into the still night, closing the heavy door behind her.

Candlelight from the downstairs windows pooled on the snow, and she could hear the faint murmurs of laughter muffled by the brick walls. Large, lacy snowflakes fell on her hair and stung her cheeks, but Jillian didn't mind the cold. The stillness of the night was comforting. It warmed her heart and made her think again of the happiness she had known since she'd come to Maryland so many years ago.

"No one would have expected our love to last," she whispered into the night. The early years here in America had been so very hard. She had worked in a dairy on a plantation across the bay, scrubbing brick floors, milking cows, and churning butter. She smiled, thinking how disbelieving little Nell would be if she tried to tell her that her mistress had once served as a bound girl. The hours had been so long that it had been hard for her and Rory to find time to be together.

For months, they had not even been able to share sleeping quarters. She had slept on a mattress in the kitchen, and Rory had spent his nights in the bachelor men's cabin beyond the stables. Sundays had been their only free days, and it was nearly impossible to find a place where they could be alone. "But we showed them all, didn't we, Rory?"

A tear slipped down her face. Their first Christmas in Maryland, they had been so poor that her gift to her husband had been a mincemeat pie with a broken crust that the cook had given her. "A crushed pie," she murmured, "too damaged to serve at the high table."

Rory had given her a single apple. She had cherished it so that she hadn't been willing to eat it. She'd kept her apple wrapped in her sleeping quilt until it withered and shriveled up. She'd cried and showed it to Rory, crying harder when he laughed at her.

But he'd taken her apple and grown a seedling from it for her. Today, that apple tree grew by the kitchen door and provided baskets of apples for the household.

"You always could make something from nothing," she said. "I ran away with a gamekeeper's brat and married a prince." A prince whose happiness had been complete when she'd quickened with her babe . . .

She closed her eyes and she could hear again the sound of Jamie's baby cooing and Rory's strong voice. She could see the pride in Rory's eyes when she'd handed him their infant son for the first time.

She blinked, straightening her shoulders. There was no use dwelling on what was past. She must look to the future, to the child she would bear in summer, and to making a good life for that babe.

In springtime, two of Rory's sisters and their families would be coming to New Hope Plantation. Rory had searched for them for years, sending letters to England and Ireland and waiting patiently for answers. He had learned finally that his mother was dead. One of his brothers had entered the priesthood, another had joined the army. But two sisters had replied, saying they would be pleased to come to the colony if he could send passage money.

It would be tragic for Rory's relatives to come all this way and find him gone, she thought. Tragic for them all. But for Rory's sake, she would make his family welcome and try to help them become established in Maryland.

"I have been blessed beyond what most women ever know," Jillian murmured. "No matter what comes, I have been loved by a good man." She touched her midsection and smiled as she imagined another child with Rory's dark, laughing eyes. "I'll tell you of him," she promised. "I'll have you, and I'll never let you forget your father or the love we—"

Bear barked once, then twice, before his bellowing rose to an ear-splitting volume, a sound that Jillian had heard him make in greeting only one person.

Doubting her own ears, she ran a few steps down the brick walk and peered through the falling snow. "Bear!" she called anxiously.

Hope rose in her breast, and she quickened her pace, leaving the walk and starting across the snowy lawn toward the single glowing lantern that hung from a post. Hurrying on, she paid no heed to the crunchy cold snow that came over the tops of her thin kid slippers. "Bear!"

The dog's booming voice echoed off the trees. "What is it, Bear? What do you see?" All she could make out of the huge dog was a churning mass of whirling snow as he circled a shadowy figure that could only be a horse and rider.

The man in the saddle—for Jillian could see now that the rider was too large and bulky to be a woman—was wrapped in a shaggy bearskin that covered him from the crown of his head to the bottom of his feet. She couldn't see his face, but she began to run toward him. "Rory?" Her heart thudded wildly in her chest. "Rory, is that you?"

"Jillian!" There was no mistaking the Irish music in that resounding shout.

"Rory!" she screamed. "Oh, Rory!"

He urged the horse into a trot, and as the distance closed between them, he rode into a yellow circle of lantern light and she could make out his dear, familiar features. "I'm home," he called amid the dog's excited clamor. "I'm home for Christmas, darlin'." And then he pulled aside his wrap, and there, nestled against his chest, lay the sleeping form of an eight-year-old boy. "I'm home," Rory repeated, and his voice cracked with emotion. "We're both home."

Jillian stumbled to a halt, unable to believe her eyes. Was this a dream? God knew she had conjured up this picture often enough! Rory and Jamie—both safe. She began to tremble, and her cries of joy lodged in her throat. It was too much, and she could not move or make a sound for fear their images would melt away like morning frost on her bedchamber window.

Rory dropped the reins and dismounted, holding his precious bundle carefully in his arms. "It's himself, darlin'. Our lad, sound as silver and right as rain." Rory's face creased in a grin as he walked toward her. "It's our Jamie, woman. Have ye been struck deaf and dumb?"

Then the boy stirred in Rory's arms and opened his eyes. He was so close that Jillian could have reached out her hands and touched his cheek. He blinked. His long, curling, dark lashes held sprinkles of snowflakes that sparkled like diamonds in the lantern light. He rubbed his eyes with the back of dirty hands and looked directly at her. "Ma-ma?"

Jamie's voice. Raspy, sleepy, aged since she had last heard that word fall from his lips, but she would have known him in the blackest night in the midst of the fiercest hurricane. "Jamie!" she cried. And then she was holding his warm little body against hers and covering both his face and Rory's with tears and kisses. And when Rory encircled her with his strong arms, she thought her heart would break with joy.

Somehow, the three of them reached the house with Bear leaping and licking their faces and threatening to trip them flat in the snow. And once in the entrance hall, Rory began to put all to order, sending one servant to tend his horse, another to fetch blankets for the boy, and yet another to take word of the miracle to his guests at Christmas supper.

Jillian was useless. She could not put the boy down, and she was torn between embracing him and squeezing Rory so hard that she would crush his bones.

Rory ushered them up the back servant stairs. There would be time enough to share the reunion with their friends. For a few minutes, he insisted, he wanted only to be alone with his wife and son.

"The boy be weary, wife. We have ridden one day in and another out without stopping to rest. Give him something hot to drink and let him sleep. You can bathe him—"

But the sight of Jamie's strange Indian leggings and loincloth, fringed vest, and moccasins were enough to wake Jillian from her trance. "Hot water," she demanded. "And soap." Later she would ask where he'd been for so long. Now she could fulfill a mother's duty and see her child bathed and tucked into bed. "Are you hungry?" she asked him.

Jamie smiled shyly and nodded. "Yes, Mama." His voice was strained and hesitant, as though the English words had to come from deep within, but there was no mistaking the love that shone from his dark Irish eyes.

"We looked for you," Jillian whispered. "We never stopped." She fingered his long hair, braided untidily into one thick plait down his back. "Bring me my scissors," she called to Nell. "I'll have this decently cut or know the reason why not."

"I waited and waited for Papa to come and get me," the boy confided. "Sometimes I cried . . . but . . ." His lips firmed as Jillian had seen Rory's do a thousand times before. "But I only cried at night, Mama. I didn't let them know. I . . . I didn't want them to think I was a milksop."

Rory put a hand on Jamie's shoulder. "Ye can be proud of him, darlin'. He escaped on his own from those who took him. He ran away. The Delaware braves that found him said he must have been alone in the woods for weeks."

"I ate berries and bird eggs," Jamie said, wrinkling his freckled nose. "I caught a fish too, but I couldn't make a fire, so I threw it back. Raw eggs taste ucky enough." He snuggled against Jillian. "I was little then," he bragged. "I can make a fire now and shoot a bow. I killed a rabbit. Honneekuis was going to take me deer hunting. He's a Delaware. I lived in his wigwam part of the summer and all fall. Honneekuis is a great hunter. He said that I shoot good enough to kill a deer. Will you take me deer hunting, Papa? I didn't bring my bow. I wish I had. I . . ."

All the while Jamie was chattering on, Jillian was busy unbraiding his hair, brushing the worst of the tangles out, and cutting his dark locks to fall just below his shoulders. She could not keep her hands off him. She wanted to inspect every inch of his body, count every hair on his head to make certain he was sound and healthy.

"He's fine," Rory assured her. "Strong and healthy. Not many boys his age could ride so far in this weather without complaining."

"Honneekuis was nicer than Copper Knife," Jamie confided. "I lived with Copper Knife for a long time, but I didn't like him. He tried to make me eat roast dog, and once he threw a stick at me. He hated me because my skin was white. It's not so white, do you think?" He pushed aside his vest and looked at his belly. "Whiter than the Indian boys, though. Of course, Copper Knife was a liar. He said you and Papa were dead. First he said that you didn't want me anymore. Then he said that you were dead. I thought maybe he was right, because I saw Papa get shot, but you weren't dead, Mama. I knew if you weren't dead, you'd want me to come home. And I was right, wasn't I?"

Jillian nodded, too full of emotion to speak.

"Copper Knife wanted to make me his son. He had a son, but he died of something. So he stole me. But he didn't like me much. And I didn't like him neither. He had two wives. One was Many Bowls. The other one was Sees Her Vision. Many Bowls made good corn bread, but Sees Her Vision's corn cakes were so bad we threw them to the dogs."

Just then Isaac entered the room with two male servants carrying a tin bathing tub which they set in front of the fireplace. Then Cook arrived with a bowl full of hot soup and a tray of meat and sweet rolls.

"What shall it be, son?" Rory asked, taking a slice of beef between his fingers. "Food or bath first?"

"Eat!"

"That's my lad," Rory said with a grin.

"He's not the only one who needs a bath," Jillian said, holding her nose in mock disgust. "You smell like the dead man we all thought you were."

"Ah? So ye thought to be rid of me, did ye, woman?" Rory teased. "Just because I had the bad luck to be ambushed and robbed by a man I thought to help was no reason to count me among the dear departed."

Jillian waved all the servants but Isaac out of the room and began to tell Rory about the dead man who had been found with Rory's horse and clothing. "They thought it was you," she said. "I have your coat with a hole from a musket ball through it."

"I met a man, Lucas Crane, who said he knew the woods. He was down on his luck, didn't even have a horse," Rory said. "I paid for food and lodging for him, and he was takin' me to the Delaware village. He was ridin' behind me when he struck me over the head with my own pistol."

"Were you hurt?" Jillian cried in alarm.

"Knocked cold as a tombstone. When I woke, it was dark and I was miles from nowhere. If a friendly Shawnee hunter hadn't found me, I might still be wanderin' in the woods. He took me to his camp, patched up my head, and finally when my head healed, he took me on to the Delaware village. They'd heard about Jamie living at another village five days' travel away."

Jillian bit her lower lip as she traced the red scar along the back of Rory's skull. "You could have been killed," she said.

"I believe that was the idea," Rory replied wryly. "Anyway, we were delayed by bad weather. Then we found that the camp we were lookin' for had been moved. It took us almost a week to catch up with them. When we walked into the Delaware village, the first boy I caught sight of was mine."

"But I thought he was with the Susquehannas," Jillian said.

"He was for two years. Last summer he escaped. He knew me right off and came runnin'."

"And meanwhile, this Lucas must have been ambushed and murdered by hostile Indians," she said.

"One dead white man looks much like another after a few days," Rory agreed.

"I saw Papa coming," Jamie put in. "He had a beard, but I knew him anyway."

While they sorted out the explanations, she got first one of her men bathed and garbed in clean clothing, then the other.

In less than an hour, Jamie was tucked into his own bed and fast asleep. Isaac sat in a high-backed chair beside the flickering fire and watched the boy's every breath.

"I don't want to leave him," Jillian said, leaning over to kiss Jamie's forehead. "I'm afraid if I leave him, he'll vanish again."

"No chance of that, Miss Jillian," the black man said. "I'm here, and neither devil nor Indian will come near that boy tonight."

"Aye, I'm certain of that," Rory agreed. "If Isaac had been with us in the cornfield, he'd have made short shrift of that war party."

"No need to poke fun at me, Master Rory," Isaac said. "You go on now to your guests. The reverend is there, and it don't look good for New Hope people to slight the reverend. They're hangin' on tenterhooks, every one of them, waitin' to see how you and Master Jamie came back from the dead. I'll watch over this boy for you. My, hasn't he growed, though. He was lost to us a tadpole, and he comes back lookin' like a young gentleman."

"Come along, wife," Rory said. "Isaac's right. Our guests will be feeling neglected if we don't share our good fortune with them. And a few prayers won't hurt any of us, considering that it could be me in that forest grave instead of that common thief. I have no use for any like him, but I'd not wish any man a death like he met, so I have no bitterness against him."

They left Jamie's room, and Rory closed the door tightly, then took her in his arms. "I missed ye, darlin'. I missed ye somethin' fierce."

"And I you, Rory." His lips brushed hers and a thrill ran through her. "You'll never know. I felt so awful, knowing I'd sent you out against your will."

"If ye hadn't, we'd not have our son back, would we?" He kissed the crown of her head. "I'm a lucky man, Jillian. Lucky to have you and Jamie."

She smiled, wanting to stay where she was, safe in his arms . . . wanting this moment to go on forever.

"And I was thinkin'," he said.

"Yes?" She looked up into his sparkling eyes. "What were you *thinkin*, husband?"

"Ye know what night this is?"

"Christmas night."

"More than that," he teased. " 'Tis our weddin' night. We took our vows on this night."

"Twenty-six years ago," she finished for him.

"Then . . ." He grinned down at her. "Then what could be more fittin' than that we ask the good reverend to renew our marriage with another ceremony tonight?"

"Renew our vows?" She looked at him. "But . . . Wouldn't that be dishonest? After all—"

"Woman." His voice took on a thread of steel. "Am I your husband before God?"

"Yes." Oh, yes, she thought. Forever and ever. There had never been and never could be any husband for her but Rory.

"And ye be my wife. 'Tis certain I am of that." He kissed her forehead lightly. "So what can be wrong with the good man readin' the lines for us in front of our friends?"

"Oh, Rory!" She threw her arms around his neck and hugged him as tightly as she could. "I do love you."

"And I ye, darlin'." He took her by the hand. "So let us go down and share this blessed Christmas with those we love. For I think that this is one night that neither of us shall forget so long as we live."

"Yes, Rory," she agreed. And then a bubble of happiness rose in her chest. "But there's one thing more."

"Aye?" He waited expectantly.

"I have a Christmas present for you," she murmured.

"Well, woman?" He grinned. "I'll not be turnin' down gifts on this night."

And laughing, she stood on tiptoe and whispered her secret in his ear.

"Truly?" he asked huskily.

"Truly," she replied. "Merry Christmas, darling."

And the glow in his eyes was enough to drive away the chill of all her lonely nights.

SEASON'S GREETINGS
from ...
JUDITH E. FRENCH

The Yuletide Season is a magical time of wonder and endless possibilities. What better time for a celebration of love, and the mystery that draws a man to his special woman?

When I was asked to contribute to *Avon Books Presents: Under The Mistletoe*, I was delighted. I have shared in the joy of reading Avon's earlier Christmas historical romances and I was excited to be a part of this year's collection.

Like small mysterious packages, wrapped in gold and silver foil, and tied with silken ribbons, each story is a treat to be savored and remembered.

So to each and every one of you, may I wish a holiday season filled with love and laughter and warm memories.

Judith is the author of fifteen Avon historical romances, including *The Fortune Trilogy*. Her latest release is *This Fierce Loving* (October, 1994). She and her husband Gary have been married for 35 years.

Surrender

Lisa Kleypas

To Patsy Kluck with love

Prologue
✳ ✳ ✳

December 1875
Boston

"COME ON IN," HALE SAID, THROWING OPEN THE front door with a flourish. He gestured for Jason to precede him into the house.

Jason followed him into the entrance hall, appreciating the house's splendidly dark interior and quietly luxurious atmosphere. He raised his eyebrows and whistled silently.

"I'm glad to see you're properly impressed," Hale remarked with a grin. A dour-faced butler approached them, and Hale greeted him casually. "Hello, Higgins. I've brought a friend from college to stay for the holidays. Jason Moran, a fine fellow. Higgins, take our coats and tell me where my sister Laura—no, don't bother, I hear her singing in the parlor. C'mon, Moran." Hale strode past the staircase toward a room off the hallway. Jason followed obligingly, hearing a thin, girlish voice crooning "Deck the Halls."

A tall Christmas tree laden with ornaments and tiny wax tapers trembled in the center of the room. A slim adolescent girl in a blue velvet dress stood on a chair that was close to toppling over. She clutched an angel with glass wings in her small hand, rising on her toes in an effort to place it atop the tree. Jason started forward, but Hale was already there, snatching the girl by the waist and whirling her off the chair. "Here's my girl!"

"Hale!" she cried, throwing her arms around his neck and peppering his cheek with enthusiastic kisses. "Hale, you're home at last!"

"What were you doing up on that chair?"

"Putting the angel on the tree."

Hale held Laura's fragile body aloft as if she were a rag doll and inspected her thoroughly. "You're prettier than she is. I think we'll put *you* up there instead."

She laughed and handed him the angel. "Here, you do it. And don't break her wings."

Instead of lowering Laura to the floor. Hale transferred her to Jason, who took her in a startled but automatic reaction. Afraid she might be dropped, she gasped with surprise and threw her arms around his neck. For a moment they stared at each other while Hale bounded onto the chair.

Jason found himself looking into a pair of soft green eyes fringed with dark lashes. He could have drowned in those eyes. Regretfully he saw that he was too old for her. He had just turned twenty, while she couldn't have been more than fourteen or fifteen. Her body was as light as a bird's, her breasts and hips not yet developed. But she was an exquisitely feminine creature with long chestnut hair that fell in curls down her back, and skin that looked as soft as rose petals.

"Who are you?" she asked, and Jason set her down with great care. He was strangely reluctant to let go of her.

"Ah, yes," Hale called down, in the midst of fastening the angel to the prickly sprice branch, "introductions are in order. Miss Laura Prescott, may I present Mr. Jason Moran.''

Jason took her hand, holding it as if he were afraid it might break. ''I am pleased to make your acquaintance, Miss Prescott.''

Laura smiled up at the tall, handsome man. He was making an obvious effort to speak carefully, but he couldn't hide the touch of a lilting brogue in his voice, the kind that housemaids and street peddlers and chimney sweeps had. His clothes were nice, and his black hair was thick and windswept. He was big and lean and healthy-looking, and his black eyes snapped with liveliness. ''Are you from Harvard?'' she asked.

''Yes, I'm in your brother's class.'' Realizing he was still holding her hand, Jason dropped it immediately.

''Moran is an Irish name, isn't it?'' As Laura waited for an answer, she sensed his sudden wariness.

''Yes,'' Hale answered for him in a loud whisper. ''He's Irish through and through.''

Laura's smiled at her brother. ''Does Mother know?'' she whispered back.

''No, I thought we would let her discover it for herself.''

Anticipating her narrow-minded mother's expression when she saw their Irish guest, Laura giggled softly and glanced at Jason. She saw that his black eyes had turned cool and unfathomable. Disconcerted, for she had not meant to give offense, she hastened to soothe him. ''Mr. Moran,'' she said, ''do forgive our teasing.'' She smiled, timidly placing her hand on his arm. ''We always tease our friends.''

For her it was a bold gesture, touching a man even in so impersonal a way. Jason could not know just how untoward it was. All he knew was that she was the most beautiful creature he had ever seen. Even in his ambitious dreams of being wealthy and having a fine home and a well-bred wife, he had not been able to imagine anything like her.

She was an aristocrat by birth, while he would never amount to more than a peasant in the Prescotts' estimation. For someone like him it was the highest honor just to be allowed to sit at their table. No matter how rich or important he became, he would never have a chance of marrying a Boston Brahmin. But he had beaten impossible odds many times before. Silently he vowed that he would do it again. When it came time to marry, Laura Prescott was exactly what he wanted.

It would take time and careful planning. Jason never counted on luck, which had always been in short supply in the Moran family. To hell with luck—all he had ever needed were his own resources. He did not return Laura's smile. In no way would he betray the thought that seared across his brain . . . that someday she was going to be his.

1

November 1880
Boston

THE LAST THING JASON MORAN EXPECTED WHEN HE opened the door of his library was the sight of his wife being kissed by another man. Perhaps someone else's wife would resort to clandestine meetings, but not his. There were no secrets to Laura . . . or so he had thought. His black eyes narrowed while the unfamiliar sensation of jealousy froze the pit of his stomach.

The pair sprang apart as soon as the door opened. The light Strauss music from the party drifted in, dispelling any illusion of privacy the two might have had. Laura raised her hands to her cheeks in surprise, but that did not conceal the fact that she had been crying.

Jason broke the silence in a mocking voice. "You're not being an attentive hostess, darling. Some of the guests have been asking for you."

Laura smoothed her chestnut-brown hair and composed herself with miraculous speed, assuming her usual emotionless mask. "Don't look so anxious, Perry," she said to the other man, who had flushed scarlet. "Jason understands a kiss between friends." Her green eyes flickered in her husband's direction. "Don't you, Jason?"

"Oh, I understand all about . . . friends," Jason replied, leaning his shoulder against the doorway. He had never looked as dangerous as he did in that moment, his black eyes as hard and bright as diamonds. "Perhaps your friend will be kind enough to allow us some privacy, Laura."

That was all the prompting Perry Whitton needed to make his escape. Mumbling something apologetic, he skittered through the doorway, pulling at his high starched collar as if to relieve the rush of blood to his face.

"Whitton," Jason mused, closing the door behind the retreating figure. "Not the most obvious choice for a romantic liaison, is he?"

Perry Whitton was a shy, middle-aged bachelor, a friend of some of the most influential women in Boston society. He had innumerable female acquaintances, but never showed a romantic interest in any of them. Whitton's looks were pleasant but unthreatening, his manner engaging but not flirtatious. Any husband would feel completely secure in leaving his wife in Whitton's company.

"You know it was not like that," Laura said in a low voice.

Perry had been an acquaintance of the Prescotts for years—the kiss had been a gesture of sympathy not passion. As Laura had welcomed him to the party, Perry had seen the strain on her face and the unhappiness beneath her social pleasantries.

"You are as lovely as always," Perry had said kindly, "but I would presume to say that something is troubling you."

It was indeed. Laura had no intention of confiding in

him about her problems with Jason, but to her horror she realized she was about to cry. She would rather have died than make an emotional scene. Understanding her dilemma, Perry had taken her to a private place. And before she could say a word, he had kissed her.

"Jason, surely you can't think there are romantic feelings between Perry and me," she said in guarded tones.

She quivered with unease as her husband approached her and seized her upper arms. "I own you," he said hoarsely. "Every inch of you." His eyes raked over the satin evening gown she wore. "Your face, your body, your every thought. The fact that I don't choose to partake of your favors does *not* mean I'll allow you to bestow them on any other man. You are mine, and mine alone."

Laura's astonished green eyes met his. "You are hurting me. Jason, you know the kiss meant nothing."

"No, I don't know that." He glanced down at her body in that insulting way again, his cruel gaze seeming to strip off her garments. "You're a beautiful woman, beautiful enough to make even Perry Whitton want you. He may have made the mistake of thinking he could find some warmth in that slender little body. Perhaps he isn't aware that you're as lovely and cold as a marble statue."

Laura flinched and turned her face away. Jason could see a moist patch on her cheek where her tears had not yet dried. He had never seen her cry, not in all the time they had known each other. "What were you crying about?" he demanded, his voice as rough as the blade of a saw.

Laura was silent, staring at him uncomprehendingly. In her family there had never been displays of anger or violence. Hale's boyish antics had provided the only excitement in the Prescotts' placid world. During the last years when her brother had been away at school, her life had been as quiet as a nun's. As Jason glared at her, demanding that she explain herself, she was too over-whelmed to speak.

Cursing savagely, Jason yanked her against him. Her racing heartbeat pounded against his, and her skirts flowed around his feet. His dark head bent, and his mouth crushed hers. She whimpered and tried to pull her head back, but he caught her jaw in his fingers and held her still. His lips were hard and bruising, his kiss infused with raw anger. She gasped and went rigid, enduring the brutal onslaught. .

Jason let go of her so swiftly that she stumbled back a few steps. "I can feel how my touch disgusts you," he jeered. "It must be humiliating for the daughter of Cyril Prescott to be fondled by a grocer's son. You were meant to marry a Boston Brahmin, but instead you became the wife of a workingman, a shanty mick. I bought you, paid for you with money so new the ink was barely dry. I know how your friends pity you. God knows you have reason to pity yourself."

Laura's face turned white, the marks of his fingers showing on her jaw. They stared at each other in the brittle silence. When it became clear he was going to say no more, she turned and fled the room as if the devil were at her heels.

Jason dropped his black head and rubbed the back of his neck wearily. He was filled with self-hatred. He had promised himself he would never hurt her, and once again he had broken that vow. He had spent his entire life trying to overcome his heritage and hide his rough edges. Most of all he had devoted himself to making money, for he had realized in his youth that being rich was the only way to compensate for the lack of a proper name and bloodlines.

In the past two months of marriage, Laura had orga-nized his life and provided for his comforts with an ef-ficiency he would never take for granted. Managing the household, entertaining their friends and guests, and accompanying him to social events were things she did with ease. Her taste was flawless, and he didn't question her opinions even when it came to his own clothes. Subtly she influenced him in matters of style and discrimination, and he valued her advice.

Jason knew how other men envied him for his wife, and he took pride in her accomplishments. Laura co-sponsored charitable functions for the benefit of the poor and was a member of the Ladies' Christian Association. Her leisure pursuits were all proper and respectable: attending lectures, going to the theater, and encouraging the arts in Boston. Everyone agreed she was a quiet but charming woman, a model of self-restraint. Not for a minute did Jason regret marrying her. But that did not make her contempt for him any easier to bear.

He remembered the day he had approached Cyril Prescott for Laura's hand in marriage. In spite of their distinguished name, the Prescotts' fortune was dwindling. Such "first families" sometimes found it necessary to sacrifice one of their daughters to the vulgar newly monied class. Marrying Laura had not been as difficult as Jason had expected. It had boiled down to a matter of money, and he had been easily able to meet Cyril Prescott's asking price. "I would not consent to this," Cyril had said, looking both indignant and shamefaced, "if I thought you would prove to be an unworthy husband to my daughter. But you appear to hold her in high regard. And there is obviously no question that you will provide well for her."

"She'll have everything she wants," Jason replied smoothly, concealing his triumph at finally obtaining the woman he had wanted for so many years. Afterward he had proposed to Laura in a businesslike manner, informing her of the decision that had already been made between him and her father. They never had a courtship—

Jason had felt it would be unwise to give her an opportunity to spurn him, which she most certainly would have done. Instead he had maneuvered the situation so that she had no choice but to accept him as her husband. He knew there was no other way he could have had her. She was desired by every eligible man in Boston. Had it not been for him, she would have become the wife of a gentleman with blood as blue as her own

In time, Jason had thought, she would learn to accept him . . . and then perhaps he could begin to reveal his feelings for her. Unfortunately he had not anticipated how repelled she would be by his touch. She had such obvious disgust for her socially inferior husband that, God help him, he—who had always been so self-contained—couldn't seem to stop himself from losing his temper around her.

Keeping her head down, Laura strode rapidly along the hallway, her only thought being to escape. A short distance away was the large music room, which also doubled as a ballroom. The crowd of guests indulged in light conversation and danced to the buoyant waltz being played by the orchestra. Oblivious to the music and laughter, Laura made her way through the entrance hall to the front door and slipped outside. The November air was damp as it bit through her brocaded satin gown. She shuddered in misery and wrapped her arms around her middle, staring out at the dimly lit street where lacquered broughams and liveried drivers waited for the guests to depart.

Drawing herself into the porch shadows of the fashionable six-story Beacon Street home, Laura wondered what she was going to do. It was obvious that Jason hated her. She could not face him anymore. She was a failure as a wife, as a woman. Tears welled up in her eyes, and she willed herself not to cry. Good Lord, what if someone saw her out here, weeping on the steps of her own home?

Suddenly she heard a cheerful whistle on the street. Anxiously she stared into the darkness. "H-hale?" she cried. "Hale, is that you?"

Her brother's gentle laugh drifted to her. "Hmmm ... why, yes, I believe it is. Have I crossed the line between fashionably late and too, too late?"

Laura gave a watery chuckle. "As always."

"Ah, you'll forgive me," Hale said, and leaped up the stairs with his customary vigor. "Have you been waiting for me? Damn, you're out here in that thin dress! How long—" He broke off as he took her face in his gloved hands and tilted it up.

Tears spilled from Laura's eyes, and she gripped his wrists tightly. "I'm glad you're here, Hale," she choked out.

"Laura, sweetheart." Alarmed, Hale pulled her head against the front of his wool coat. "My God, what's the matter?"

"I can't tell you."

"Oh, you can and you will. But not here." He ruffled her hair, carelessly disarranging her coiled chignon. "We'll go inside and have a talk."

Laura shook her head. "People ... people will see—"

"We'll walk around the house and come in through the kitchen." Hale shrugged out of his coat and draped it over her narrow shoulders. "It has something to do with Jason, doesn't it?"

Her throat closed painfully, and she nodded. Without another word Hale put his arm around her waist and guided her down the steps, shielding her from the view of the drivers and passersby. By the time they reached the kitchen, which opened onto the backyard, Laura was shivering violently. The heat and light of the kitchen engulfed her, but they did not take away her numbness.

"Why, Mrs. Moran," she heard the housekeeper's voice exclaim.

Hale favored the older woman with an appealing smile. He had matured into a handsome and solidly built man with green eyes, rich brown hair, and a thick slash of a mustache. His openhearted manner charmed all women. "Mrs. Ramsey, I'm afraid my sister has the vapors," he said. "Could you find a way to inform Mr. Moran— discreetly, mind you—that she has retired for the evening?"

"Certainly, Mr. Prescott."

The vapors, Laura thought wryly. Well, it would work. The excuse was always accepted with quiet understanding. Because of the spoonbill corsets and heavy haircloth bustles worn under their gowns, women often experienced dizziness and fainting spells. In fact, such episodes were considered proof of a lady's refinement.

"Oh," Hale added as he guided Laura out of the kitchen toward the stairs, "and would you have two toddies brought to the upstairs sitting room, Mrs. Ramsey?"

"Yes, Mr. Prescott."

Laura handed the coat back to Hale, and they began to climb the three flights of stairs to the sitting room. "You probably don't even know what the vapors are," she said with a sniffle.

He laughed. "No, and I really have no desire to find out."

They reached the sitting room. It was Laura's private place. No one intruded, not even Jason, unless she invited them. Like the other rooms in the house, it was comfortable and elegant, with a flowered Persian rug, velvet drapes, plush chairs, tiny polished tables covered with lace and ornaments, and a marble fireplace. Laura had chosen the carefully blended styles of furnishings for the entire house, all matters of taste being left to her discretion. Jason preferred it that way.

"Now," Hale said, sinking to his haunches in front of the fireplace, "tell me everything while I stir up the fire."

Laura gathered up the fringed train of her evening dress and sat in a nearby chair. Morosely she kicked off her damp satin slippers with their two-inch heels and tiny diamond buckles. It pleased Jason for his wife to be dressed in the finest of garments. "I don't know what to tell you," she said. "Jason would be furious if he knew—"

"Tell me everything," Hale repeated patiently, glancing at her over his shoulder. "Remember, I was Jason's closest friend until you married."

"Yes, I remember." Laura's mind turned back to all the holidays Jason had spent with her family. Although he and Hale had been in the same class at Harvard, Jason was two years older. He had never made pretensions about his background. His father had been a grocer, and his mother had peddled a fish cart.

It was highly unusual for someone of Jason's humble beginnings to have climbed as high as he already had. But Jason was intelligent, hardworking, and ruthlessly charming when he wished to be. Something in his voice and the way he moved proclaimed he was a man who knew exactly what he wanted—and what he wanted, he would get. And when he smiled, he was the most handsome man on earth.

"Laura, what's wrong?" Hale asked.

"Everything. It's been wrong since the beginning." She peeled her gloves off and wiped her stinging eyes. "Jason has no idea how overwhelming he is. I don't know how to please him, and when I try I fail miserably. I—I think something is wrong with me. Whenever we try to . . . be intimate, I don't do whatever it is he expects me to do, and—"

"Laura, wait." Hale cleared his throat uncomfortably, his cheekbones tinged with red. "If you're referring to the sort of thing that goes on in the bedroom, I think you had better discuss it with a woman."

Laura thought of her prudish mother and her straight-laced sisters. "Who do you suggest?" she asked.

Hale groaned and clutched his head in his hands, looking down at the flowered carpet. "All right," he said in a muffled voice. "Tell me. But keep in mind that a fellow doesn't like to hear about his sister and . . . that."

She shook her head. "There is nothing to tell you." After a brief pause, she repeated meaningfully, "Nothing."

Hale's astonished green eyes met hers. "Are you trying to tell me . . . my God . . . that you and Jason have never . . . *never*?"

"No," Laura said, embarrassed but strangely relieved to be telling someone.

Hale opened and closed his mouth several times before he could form another word. "Why not?" he finally managed to ask.

She held her head in her hands much as he had a moment before, while her words burst out in a swift torrent. "Jason has approached me a few times, but I— I make him so angry. The last time we argued he accused me of being cold, a-and I suppose I must be, but I can't seem to help myself! I thought that as time passed we might come to some kind of understanding, but things only worsened. He spends his days at his business offices, and he dines at his club, and whenever he is in the house we avoid meeting in the same room! There's not the least bit of trust or friendliness between us. The best we've been able to manage is politeness, but now even that seems to be beyond us."

"I see," Hale said, sounding strange. He stroked his mustache and shook his head.

"And tonight," Laura continued, "I was in the library with Perry Whitton, who kissed me—"

"He *what*?" Hale gave her a disapproving glance.

"Perry and I are friends, nothing more."

"All the same, Laura, you shouldn't have allowed it."

"It happened too quickly for me to say or do anything! And of course Jason walked in and misinterpreted the situation, and said that I must be ashamed of being the wife of a shanty mick . . . and I don't even know what that is!"

"That's what they call an Irishman, one from a peasant family so poor that even the women have to work." Hale sighed heavily. "A mick, a blackleg, a greenhorn. A few of the fellows at Harvard didn't give a damn about his being Irish, but most of them did. Jason was excluded and subtly insulted at almost every turn. After all, his background was the same as that of their servants. You know how they can be." He made a face. "Frankly, I can't blame Jason for being upset if he saw you with Perry Whitton. He is the epitome of all Jason could never be, a gentleman with the right name, the right family, the right upbringing."

Laura nodded in understanding. Boston society was fastidious about every entry in a family's genealogy. Change was regarded with suspicion, and everything depended upon who one's grandfather had happened to be. It was considered vulgar to work hard or make much money. The ideal Bostonian man was genteel, dignified, and intellectual. Someone like Jason, ambitious and driven, a self-made man, was a shock to the more refined Bostonians such as the Whittons.

"Hale," she said fervently, "if I had wanted a man of Perry's ilk, I wouldn't have married Jason. How can

I make him understand that?''

"I don't know.'' Her brother looked guilty. "It won't be easy to convince him. Your entire family disapproves of his heritage. We all know that Father only consented to the betrothal because of the extraordinary amount of money Jason's made in real estate. And I . . . well, I told Jason at the beginning that I was against the marriage because he's Irish.''

"Y-you couldn't have!'' Laura exclaimed, horrified. "Hale, you don't really feel that way!''

"Oh, yes.'' He nodded stubbornly. "I explained to Jason that I valued him as a friend, but I couldn't approve of him marrying one of my sisters. Especially not you. I knew how difficult it would be for you, never quite belonging in one world or the other. I had known for a long time that Jason wanted to marry someone with a name, someone who could gain him entry into our circles. And—hell, I'll be frank—he comes from crude beginnings, Laura.''

"That doesn't matter to me,'' Laura said, and cleared her throat awkwardly. "It has never mattered to me that Jason is Irish.''

The maid knocked at the door and brought in their toddies on a small silver tray. Laura took the tray from her and dismissed her with a wan smile of thanks. She gave Hale his drink and sipped slowly on hers, welcoming its bracing effects.

"Well,'' Hale said, "let's address this business about this 'coldness' of yours. I'll wager some of this is Mother's influence.''

"Hale, I can't blame her for—''

"Don't defend her, sweetheart. She raised all three of her daughters to believe that it is natural for a husband and wife to live as strangers. For years I knew about the ridiculous things she told you and Anne and Sophia, but it wasn't my place to contradict her.'' He sighed and regarded her sympathetically. "These matters are not complicated, Laura. It's very simple. All you have to do is show Jason that you're willing to accept his attentions, and he will take care of the rest of it. He is an experienced man. Just allow him to . . ." He stopped and began fiddling uneasily with the silk fringe of the brocaded chair. "He wouldn't be cruel to you, Laura, not in that way."

She clasped her hands together tightly. "I wish I could believe that. But I don't know what to think about him anymore. I find myself wondering why I married him."

"Well, why did you?" Hale demanded.

"Father wanted me to, and it was a help to the family."

"Father and the family be damned! You know he wouldn't have forced you to marry Jason. The wedding would never have taken place had you uttered one word of objection."

Laura bit her lip and nodded, ashamed. "Yes, you're right. I . . . the truth is, I was more than willing. I wanted to be a wife to Jason." She drew her legs up and tucked them beneath her. "Jason thinks he doesn't need anything from anyone. But I knew the first moment I met him that he needed someone like me, to help and comfort him, to bring some warmth into his life. I was so certain I could soften him, and bring out another side of him." She laughed shakily. "And instead he seems to be changing me into something I never wanted to be."

It was three hours later when Hale made his way downstairs and discovered that the last of the guests had departed. Sliding his hands in his pockets, he ambled through the ballroom, where the musicians were packing their instruments.

"Was it a success?" Hale inquired of the young lank-haired violinist.

"Quite lively for your kind of crowd," came the cheerful reply.

Hale grinned and wandered past a pair of Irish maids carrying trays of empty glasses. "Pardon, miss," he inquired of one of them, "where might Mr. Moran be? Retired for the evening? No? Ah, drinking in the library. I'm not surprised. Mr. Moran does have a taste for whiskey, doesn't he?"

Jason was sitting in a chair before the fire, holding a bottle of liquor loosely in his hand. His legs were stretched out, his head resting against the brocaded upholstery. His black evening coat had been discarded, while the sleeves of his starched white shirt were rolled up to the elbows. His eyes were half-slitted as he stared into the flames, while the firelight played over his raven hair. He did not move as Hale walked into the room and closed the door.

"*Usquebaugh,*" Hale said, using a Gaelic word Jason had once taught him. He gestured casually toward the whisky. "You micks call it the water of life, don't you?"

"Go to hell."

"Very likely." Hale dragged up a heavy chair with his foot and collapsed into it. "First, however, I'm going to have a talk with you."

"If you're half-witted enough to think I'm going to listen—"

"I believe I'll begin with a few observations." Green eyes met black, and they exchanged a long glance, the glance of adversaries who knew each other's secrets. "So far everything has gone according to your plan, hasn't it?" Hale said. "Remember telling me about the plan years ago? Remember what you said?"

Jason arched a black eyebrow. "I said that by the time I was twenty-five I would have graduated from Harvard with honors."

"And established yourself in the Boston business community."

"Yes."

"And married a girl whose name would allow you into the most elite social circles."

"Yes."

Hale smiled ironically. "At the time, although I admired your ambition, I didn't believe you could do it. But you've accomplished all that. You married my own sister. You're being referred to in Boston as 'that damned Irish tycoon,' and by the time you reach thirty, you'll have multiplied your fortune several times over." He leaned forward, losing some of his flippancy as he demanded, "What, then, is the cause for bitterness? Why are you behaving like such a bastard to Laura, when you have everything you ever wanted out of life?"

Jason swished the whisky in the bottle and stared into its swirling contents. He was tempted to confide in Hale, but he could not let go of the grudge between them.

"Don't answer, then," Hale said. "I already know why."

Jason's eyes gleamed dangerously. "You've always known all the answers, haven't you? A Prescott's prerogative."

Hale shrugged.

Jason extended the whisky bottle with a scowl, and Hale took a drink without hesitation. "You've been talking with Laura," Jason said.

"Yes, and she's owned up to a few things I've been suspecting for some time."

"It's a dangerous game, prying into matters that have nothing to do with you."

"Nothing to do with me?" Hale exclaimed, his temper sparking. "Laura is my sister, my *favorite* sister, and you're making her miserable! Of all the girls in Boston you could have married and made miserable, why did it have to be her?''

Jason rested his forearms on his knees, a shock of black hair falling over his forehead. He answered slowly, watching the fire with a brooding gaze. "There weren't all that many girls to choose from. It had to be someone with a name, and someone with the qualities I wanted in a wife. And most of all it had to be someone whose family was in financial straits and had need of a rich son-in-law.''

"So when it came time to marry, you cast your eyes around and there was my youngest sister—"

"I decided to marry Laura the first Christmas I spent with your family.''

Hale frowned, the ends of his mustache curving downward. "That long ago?"

"Yes. Laura was only fifteen. When the family sat down to dinner I nearly made some excuse and left. I would rather have faced a firing line than confront that endless row of spoons and forks at each plate. I didn't know which one to pick up first, or how to eat the damned asparagus. And there was your mother, watching every move I made like a hawk. But Laura was slower and more painstaking than everyone else, and I was able to imitate everything she did. Halfway through the meal I realized she knew I was aping her. She was being slow and precise in order to make it easier for me.''

"Hell, *I* never bothered with Mother's blasted rows of forks.''

"You didn't have to," Jason said flatly. "You had nothing to prove.''

"And so you decided to marry Laura because she helped you get through a meal?"

"Because I knew she would be the kind of wife I needed.''

Laura had said much the same thing. Hale set down

the bottle of whisky and stood up, glaring at his former friend. "Ah. A housekeeper. A social companion. A teacher of etiquette. A pretty ornament to impress the hoi polloi. There were other girls you could have married if that was all you wanted. Laura has more to give than that, and she deserves more than to spend the rest of her life trying to make you into a gentleman."

Jason smiled nastily. "You think she's too good for an Irishman?"

"Not at all. I think she's too good for *you*."

Retrieving the whisky bottle, Jason gestured toward the door. "Understood. Now get the hell out of here."

Hale paced around the room in frustration. "I've never seen Laura as high-strung and nervous as she was tonight. You're crushing all the fire and spirit out of her."

Jason stood up to face him. "*Fire* and *spirit*," he repeated sarcastically, thinking of his pale, poised wife, "are not words I would apply to your sister, Hale."

"Oh? Now I'm beginning to understand how little you really know her. She's the most adventurous, free-spirited girl I've ever . . . why, once on a dare she sneaked into Father's room and cut off half his mustache while he was sleeping. She loves swimming and skating and riding. She's a crack shot, a first-rate pianist, an excellent dancer. She's always dreamed of going to Egypt and seeing the pyramids, and traveling up the Nile in a *dahabeah*—"

"A what?"

"*Dahabeah*. One of those long boats."

Jason stared at him with narrowed eyes. "Hale, I don't know who the hell you're talking about, but it isn't my wife."

"It damn well is! And there's something else you should hear—"

"I've heard enough."

"Falling-out or not, I should have talked to you before

the wedding about Laura. This notion you both seem to have—this supposed coldness of hers—''

"Out," Jason said tersely, herding him toward the door.

Hale talked rapidly. "Dammit, Jason, you obviously haven't realized how sheltered she's been. My other two sisters had a devil of a time adjusting to marriage after the way they'd been reared. If Mother were a Catholic, she'd consider the *convent* too permissive for her daughters. Most girls have opportunities to flirt and hold hands with men, enjoy a stolen kiss or two. My sisters had none of that. As you know, Jason, I have a great deal of respect for my mother—but there's no denying that she's a bitter woman. My father has been unfaithful to her, not once but many times. My parents' marriage went sour long before Laura was even born. Laura's been brought up with some mistaken ideas about men and women, and by God, you've probably confirmed every last one of them! All because you seem to expect her to hop into your arms like some barmaid!''

"The lecture is over," Jason snapped, kicking the door open with the side of his foot.

"*Listen*, damn you! Before she married you, Laura had never been alone with a man before, not for a minute. She's not cold, she's an innocent, a complete innocent who doesn't even know how to kiss. She's always been shy around men, especially those with a tendency to be overbearing. And all you do, all you've *ever* done, is frighten and accuse her! How is she supposed to be responsive to you?''

Jason's hands dropped to his sides, and his black eyes fastened onto Hale's agitated face.

"If you treat her with just a little patience or kindness you might be able to make her happy," Hale said in a cutting voice. "I've seen you with women. I've seen you seduce the most hard-hearted of them inside of a quarter hour. But for some reason all your renowned charm seems to vanish when it comes to Laura.'' He tugged his own sleeves down and straightened his coat lapels. ''You've been married for two months, and so far all you've done is build a mountain of misunderstandings. You and I may no longer be friends, Jason, but for Laura's sake and your own, I hope you give some thought to what I've said.'' Turning away, Hale walked to the front hall, snatched up his greatcoat, and left without a backward glance.

Jason stared after him, his brows drawn together in a frown. Slowly he went to the stairs and sat down, raking his hands through his disheveled hair. He thought of his wife in bed, clad in one of her demure white gowns, her long hair braided loosely, her skin flushed with sleep. He had gone in there countless nights to watch her while she slept, being careful never to awaken her. The sight of her never failed to arouse him unbearably.

When Laura was awake, however, her green eyes seemed to say what everyone else did, that Jason was unworthy of her, that Cyril Prescott's daughter should never have married so far beneath her. But . . . what if that expression in her eyes was not disdain? What if it was something else entirely? Was it possible that he had made his own wife afraid of him?

Cursing, Jason thought over the past weeks and counted the scant number of times he had been gentle with Laura—God, no, he had been too busy dwelling on her resentment of him. As much as Jason hated to admit it, Hale had been right about something. There were misunderstandings that had to be cleared away, for both their sakes.

Laura's cup rattled in its saucer as Jason's broad shoulders filled the doorway of the breakfast room. Hastily she set the saucer down and lowered her gaze to the linen

tablecloth. The silence was agonizing. Should she say
something? Something accusing, something appeasing.
Words of forgiveness? . . . reproach? Perhaps—

"Laura."

His voice was quiet and serious. Blankly she looked
up at him, her eyes shadowed from a sleepless night.

Jason was struck by how young she looked, silhouetted
against the white lace curtains at the window. Her chestnut hair was pulled into a coiled braid at the nape of her
neck and tied with velvet ribbons. The pointed basque
of her chocolate-brown dress was buttoned high up to
her throat, the sleeves long and puffed at the tops. In
spite of the strain evident on her delicate features, she
was as lovely as always.

Jason could not stop his gaze from flickering to the
curve of her breasts molded beneath the tight-fitting bodice, and the flash of white throat above the tiny lace
collar. Quickly he looked away before she could read
his overwhelming desire. He wanted her desperately. It
would have been a simple matter to find release with
another woman, but Laura was the only one he wanted.
Perhaps, he thought cynically, it was a just punishment
for his past sins, being married to a woman who was
revolted by his touch.

"Jason," Laura said, gathering up her courage. "After
last night, I—"

"No," he interrupted. "Let me speak first."

She fell silent in confusion. There was an expression
on Jason's face she had never seen before, earnest and
uncomfortable. The way his eyes searched hers caused
a wave of heat to rise from her neck to her face.

"I'm sorry for what I said—and did—last night,"
Jason said in a low voice. "I was angry. I wanted to
hurt you."

Unconsciously she raised her fingers to her throat.
"You did," she replied softly.

"It will not happen again."

Laura had never been so surprised, not even the day he had proposed to her. She heard herself murmuring something, but the voice did not seem to belong to her. "This is the f-first time you've ever apologized to me."

Jason smiled at that, his eyes alight with self-mockery. "It may be the first time I've ever apologized to anyone. I've always thought of it as a sign of weakness I couldn't afford."

Laura did not know if she was more relieved or astonished by his oddly agreeable manner. "Will you have some breakfast?" she asked, trying to hide her nervousness.

"No." Jason ventured further into the room, lean and handsome in his tailored black coat, gray trousers, and quietly patterned vest. As he came close to her, she rose from her chair and backed away a step or two. He appeared not to notice her involuntary movement. "I have a great deal of business to attend to this morning," he said. "And I'll be home late tonight." A brief hesitation followed before he added, "I thought that tomorrow morning we would leave to spend the rest of the week at your sister's home in Brookline."

"Brookline? But your work—"

"The world won't come to an end if I stop working for a few days."

Laura was astounded. For as long as she had known him, Jason had been obsessed with his work. "We have never accepted Sophia's invitations before," she said. "Why would you want to spend time with my family when you've made it clear—"

"Yes, I know what I've made clear—and what I haven't." He took another step toward her, and she skittered back once more. "Laura," he said gently, capturing her wrist with ease. He held her hand so lightly that she could have pulled away with little effort. "If you would rather not go to Brookline . . ."

"Oh, no, I—I think it would be a fine idea."

His thumb slipped into her palm and lingered in the soft hollow, and she felt the sensation of his caress all the way down to her knees.

"Good," he murmured.

They were standing close enough for her to detect the scent of his cologne. She felt him looking down at her, and in vain she waited for him to release her hand. But he waited patiently as well, making no move to let go. After long seconds dragged by she raised her head.

"You haven't said you'll forgive me," he remarked.

"I—I do."

His thumb still played idly in her palm, and she knew that he could not help but be aware of her agitation. Slowly, easily, his free arm slid around her. Laura endured the closeness for a few seconds before a natural reflex caused her to break free of him with a sound of protest. Horrified, she retreated to the side of the room, certain he would jeer at her. She waited for a rebuke that never came. Instead there was silence.

Jason approached her with the smoothness of a panther, not stopping until she was flattened against the wall and he was just inches away. He rested one forearm over her head, his body looming over hers. For an instant she recalled how it had felt to be crushed against that hard body.

"Laura . . ." His voice was husky. His hand slid to the back of her neck and tilted her face toward him. "In the past two months you've guided me in many things. And in spite of my display last night, you've even managed to teach me a few manners. But now . . ." Before she could move, he brushed his lips across her forehead. "Now there are some things I'd like to teach you."

Nervous chills ran down Laura's spine. She could not deny him. It was a wife's duty to submit to her husband's embrace, no matter how much she dreaded the prospect. "Whatever you wish," she said emotionlessly, her nerves writhing in turmoil.

A smile pulled the corner of his lips at her dutiful answer. "What I wish for is a kiss from my wife."

Laura searched his midnight eyes for mockery, and found an oddly challenging gleam. He expected her to refuse, she thought. She would show him that she was not afraid of him. Only a kiss . . . it was not such a dreadful request.

She held her breath and summoned all her courage, standing on her toes to accomodate the difference in their heights. Gingerly she pressed her lips to his, her palms falling to his shoulders for balance. To her surprise, the closeness was not unpleasant. His mouth was warm against hers, his shoulders hard and steady underneath her hands. He did not crush her in his arms or frighten her as he had so many times before.

Red-faced and trembling, she ended the kiss and sank to her heels, beginning to breathe again. But it appeared Jason was not through with her. His dark head bent, and his lips drifted over her temple, the curve of her cheek, the tiny hollow behind her earlobe. Laura's hands clenched into fists against his shoulders.

He slid his hands over her silky hair, pushing her head back. He took his time with her, noting that although she was not responding to him, she was not rejecting him either. Gently he brushed her lips with his own. She kissed like a child, her mouth innocently closed. Jason realized that the sexual urges so familiar to him were only just awakening in her.

The tip of his tongue traced her lower lip, lingering at the center. Laura jerked away from him in surprise, touching her fingers to the damp surface. Why had he done that? Was it wrong for her to allow it?

Jason's eyes held her in a dark, velvet prison. Carefully

he pulled her back against his body. "It's all right," he murmured, his breath mingling with hers. "It's all right, Laura . . . did I frighten you?"

"No," she said faintly.

He smoothed her hair and kissed her temple, careful to keep every movement slow and gentle. "Would you put your arms around my neck?"

She hesitated and then obeyed, her breasts resting against his chest. The warmth of his hands cupped her jaws, holding her head still, and his lips teased hers with fleeting touches. "Kiss me back," he whispered.

Laura felt light-headed, her fear dissolving in a wave of slow, sensual curiosity. She relaxed in his arms, her lips no longer closed so firmly, accepting the gently playful mouth that moved over hers. The tip of his tongue ventured further and further, probing until she opened her mouth with a gasp. She felt his tongue begin a languid search for hers, stroking deep in a way she had never dreamed of.

Eventually he lifted his mouth, and she realized dazedly that she did not want the kiss to end. She rested her head on his shoulder, soothed by the long, repeated strokes of his hand along her spine. His palms pressed her buttocks and hips forward until there was not an inch of space between their bodies. They were separated by the thick layers of her skirts and petticoats, but even so she could feel the hard ridge of his loins.

Jason held her close between his thighs, allowing her to become accustomed to the feel of a man's body. His lips wandered over her moist forehead, while the uneven gusts of her breath against his neck caused his manhood to swell even more blatantly. He felt her trembling as he fondled the downy nape of her neck. "Afraid?" he asked.

"I . . . I don't know."

"There's nothing to be afraid of." He rubbed his lips

over hers in a roughly teasing caress. When she did not respond, he raised his head and looked at her questioningly.

Her eyes were luminous and turquoise-green, while her kiss-reddened lips were softer and fuller than usual. Wonderingly she lifted her hand to smooth back the hair that had fallen over his forehead.

Suddenly they were interrupted by the opening of the door to the kitchen. It was Phoebe, a housemaid who had been in the Prescott's employ for nearly ten years. Phoebe's round face turned the color of raspberries, and her mouth fell open at the sight of husband and wife clasped together in the breakfast room. "Oh, my. Excuse me," she exclaimed in horror, and disappeared behind the door.

Laura tried to smooth her hair and dress, while her skin burned with embarrassment.

"We are married," Jason reminded her dryly, tightening his arms around her back.

"You should let me go—"

"Not yet. Is it so unpleasant to be held by me?"

"I would not like anyone else t-to break in upon us again." She closed her eyes as she felt him nuzzling her ear.

"If you would prefer some privacy," he said in a soft voice that raised every hair on the back of her neck, "we could go upstairs."

She tried to pull away from him. "I—I have many things to do today if we are to leave for Brookline so soon. I do think you should let me go—"

"Then go, if you're so damned eager to fly out of my arms." He released her with a slight scowl. But his tone was far more gentle than usual, and she felt his gaze caressing her as she turned away. "Laura."

She stopped without looking at him. "Yes?"

"I am not going to force you to do anything," he said

quietly. ''I have wanted you for a long time, and I haven't yet forced you.''

He was more overwhelming in his gentleness than he had ever been in anger. Laura was astonished by the feelings that swept over her: the desire to walk back to him and press herself against his body, to slide her fingers through his coal-black hair, to feel his mouth on hers again. She left the room quickly, her heart pounding with the knowledge that in less than a few minutes her husband had turned her entire world upside down.

2

A FRESH SNOW HAD COVERED THE GROUND, GIVING THE rebuilt farmhouse a picturesque appearance. As the driver opened the door of the double brougham, a burst of icy air swept away Laura's pleasant lethargy. The drive from Boston with Jason had been surprisingly enjoyable. In response to her questions, he had talked to her about his construction enterprise in the Back Bay, an apartment building of twenty-five flats complete with elevators and steam heating.

''I would like to see it,'' Laura had remarked, and he regarded her with a skeptical smile.

''I'll take you there when we return.''

Laura nodded in assent, while her insides quivered in

delight. Jason had never been so nice to her. She began to think that the next few days might not be as harrowing as she had feared. Since their marriage, they had never spent longer than an afternoon with her family. When any of the Prescotts were near, Jason was quiet and abrupt, his manner challenging. The Prescotts, in turn, were stiff and polite. Laura always felt caught between two opposing forces, and she was miserable when they were all together. But if everyone made an effort to be pleasant, it might pave the way for future gatherings.

Jason stepped out of the carriage and reached up for her, catching her around the waist. Laura pulled her hands from her tiny fur muff and grasped his shoulders. He swung her down without letting her feet touch the portable steps.

"Thank you," she said with a breathless laugh.

His dark eyes studied hers, and he smiled ruefully. "A house full of Prescotts," he said, keeping his hands on her waist. "I feel as if I'm about to brave a lion's den."

"You got on well enough with them before we were married," Laura pointed out.

Suddenly he grinned. "Yes, until I made you a Moran." Still holding her, he looked over her head at the large house, surrounding fields, and wooded copses. Well in the distance was the outline of the Boston State House dome, and the tall buildings near it.

The Prescotts often gathered at Sophia's Brookline home during the winter. The firstborn of Cyril Prescott's children, Sophia was a plain but sociable woman. She had a talent for entertaining, and it was universally agreed that Sophia was one of the most accomplished hostesses in Boston. Her husband, Judge T. Horace Marsh, was a rather stiff-necked blue blood, but Sophia's influence had caused him to soften during the past few years.

Sophia was one of the rare breed of Bostonian women

who liked to dispense with unnecessary formality. In her home the younger people were allowed the free use of first names, a custom which irked the older generations. No one was allowed to remain a stranger in the Marshes' gatherings. They were all cajoled into joining the constant rounds of whist and backgammon, sleigh rides and dancing parties.

Sophia appeared on the landing of the outside steps, her lips curved in a welcoming smile. She was clad in a stylish winter dress of gray cashmere and garnet velvet. "My dears, how wonderful to have you here at last," she said, pressing Jason's hand between hers, then embracing Laura. "Come inside at once. We have a splendid fire, and hot tea for the ladies, and something stronger for the gentlemen. Anne and Howard are here, and so are the Warrens—oh, and Jason, you'll be pleased to learn that Hale arrived not an hour ago." Sophia inclined her head toward them confidentially. "I believe Hale is seriously thinking of courting the Warrens' daughter Prudence. I told him that the two of you might not be averse to chaperoning them on the sleigh ride this afternoon."

Laura and Jason exchanged a questioning glance, and Jason replied while holding his wife's gaze. "Of course I'll chaperon Hale," he said, a little too nicely. Laura suppressed a laugh, pitying her brother.

Jason guided her into the house with his arm at her back, pulling her to the side as the servants moved past them to carry their trunks upstairs. Slowly Jason untied the laces of Laura's velvet-trimmed mantle. She was unable to look at him as she felt his fingers at her throat.

Jason handed the garment to the waiting arms of a maid, and glanced over Laura's head to his sister-in-law. "I wouldn't mind a glass of the 'something stronger' you mentioned, Sophia."

"I suggest you join Hale and the other men in the parlor," Sophia replied. "They are congregated around a bowl of hot punch, discussing whatever it is men discuss amongst themselves." She slipped an arm around Laura's shoulders and smiled. "We sisters must confer with Cook about the dinner preparations."

Jason's black eyes glinted with amusement. "Certainly," he said, and although his voice was bland, it was obvious he knew they were planning to gossip.

Together Sophia and Laura watched his broad-shouldered form as he left, then they wandered toward the kitchen. "Now, out with it," Sophia said. "How did you manage to drag Jason here?"

"It was his decision," Laura replied. "No one is more surprised than I."

"Hale confided to me that he had a talk with Jason, but he would not reveal what was said between them."

Laura frowned darkly. "I will not have Hale interfering in my marriage, no matter how well-intentioned he is. I will speak to him about it."

"Oh, don't be cross with him! You know how Hale adores you. He cannot bear to see you unhappy." Sophia peered at her younger sister. "*Are* you unhappy? Jason is not being unkind to you, is he?"

"Not at all." Laura folded her arms in a stubborn gesture.

"Hmmm. The two of you look well enough. And Jason is as wickedly handsome as ever. If it were not for his regrettable background, he would have been the prize catch of Boston." With studied casualness, Sophia added, "But of course there will always be those who say you must be pitied for marrying a shanty-born Irishman. No one would blame you for feeling ashamed."

"Why should I be ashamed of a man who has lifted himself from poverty to prosperity? Jason has had to fight for everything he's ever had. Nothing has been given to him. Nothing has been easy for him. He is a man of intelligence and strength. I'm *not* ashamed of him, yet for some reason Jason finds that as difficult to believe as everyone else!''

There was a gleam of satisfaction in Sophia's eyes. ''Then you must persist until you do convince him. It is a woman's duty to make the best of her lot, Laura. And there are *certain things* a wife owes to her husband.''

Laura turned red up to her hairline at Sophia's delicate emphasis on 'certain things.' ''Hale told you everything, didn't he?'' she asked, feeling betrayed.

''I won't deny it.''

''I should have known I couldn't trust him to keep my confidence.''

''Hale felt you would benefit from the advice of an older sister,'' Sophia said implacably. ''You and Anne and I were not given an adequate education in how to be good wives. We learned all of the practical things and none of the truly necessary things. We never learned about trust and affection, and most of all loyalty. Father's philandering embittered Mother years ago. She never wished for her daughters to risk the danger of loving a man and perhaps being hurt by him.''

Laura regarded her speculatively. ''I wouldn't have expected such frankness from you, Sophia.''

''I have discovered many things in the past few years. I have learned to love my Horace, and not to withhold myself from him.'' She raised her eyebrows slightly. ''I suspect that Jason has not been the shining example of a devoted husband. But a good wife could make him into a good husband. *If* he's as intelligent as you claim. And the best revenge, my dear, against those who would mock or pity you for your common red-blooded husband, is simply to be happy.''

What seemed to be at least a dozen children ran and cavorted around the four sleighs lined up in front of the house. Some of them were Sophia's offspring, others belonged to the Warrens, and the remainder were distant Prescott cousins. Laura stopped at the top of the circular steps with Prudence Warren, a vivacious and friendly girl she had met once or twice before.

"How lovely the sleighs are," Prudence exclaimed, and Laura agreed. Each vehicle with its shiny black runners was pulled by two horses with festive tassels and bells affixed to their harnesses. A driver in a top hat sat at the front of each sleigh. Laughing young men and women were piling into the sleighs and covering themselves with wool and fur blankets, while others were helping the children clamber aboard.

"Now I can believe Christmas is only three weeks away," Prudence said.

Laura looked at her with a faint smile. "Are you and my brother planning to exchange gifts?" she could not resist asking.

"That depends on Hale," Prudence said airily. "If he gives me something proper and acceptable—candy or a book are all Mama will allow—then I shall give him something in return."

The two of them watched as Hale stomped toward the last sleigh with two giggling children under his arms, loudly demanding that someone relieve him of his burden. Jason walked around to him, reached for the children one at a time, and settled them into the vehicle. The little boy reached for the ends of Hale's mustache and refused to let go, causing Jason to laugh. The scene reminded Laura of the days when her husband and brother had been close friends, and she smiled wistfully. It was good to see them being civil to each other. She could not help but hope that they might someday regain their closeness.

"Your husband is quite charming," Prudence said, following her gaze. "And good with the children."

He was, Laura saw with a touch of surprise. Expertly Jason separated a pair of quarreling siblings, rescued a tot who was wandering close to the horses' hooves, and carried a little boy on his back from one sleigh to another. While Jason organized the group and conferred with the drivers, Hale bounded up the circular steps to Laura and Prudence.

"Laura, sweetheart," he said cheerfully, grasping her small gloved hands.

Remembering the way he had confided her private affairs to her sister, Laura pulled her hands from his and gave him a frosty glare. "I've had a revealing talk with Sophia," she said.

He looked sheepish, but didn't bother to pretend he didn't understand. "I'm sorry."

"I didn't give you permission to tell anyone about Jason and me."

"Sophia hit upon it with some damned clever guesses, and hang it, I couldn't lie to her."

"You could have said nothing," Laura said coolly.

"But with Sophia that's the same as admitting everything! Sweetheart, don't get all ruffled, there's a—"

"I have a right to be ruffled, you traitor." Laura folded her arms over her chest and turned away.

Swearing under his breath, Hale regarded her guiltily and then offered his arm to Prudence.

"Hale, whatever is—" Prudence began, but he interrupted her with a scowl.

"Don't ask, Pru. With three sisters, a fellow's always in one stew or another." He walked Prudence down the steps, while Jason passed by them on the way up.

Jason raised an eyebrow as he looked from Hale's face to Laura's. He smiled at the sight of his wife dressed in a smart sleighing costume of black satin and brocade, and a lynx-trimmed mantle. A tiny black bonnet trimmed with red ribbons and ostrich plumes was perched on her head. Every hair was in place, every ribbon and pleat perfectly arranged. Jason wanted to scoop her up and kiss her right there on the steps.

Laura's glare faded immediately as she saw him. He was especially handsome today, his black hair smoothly brushed, his wool overcoat tailored to his broad-shouldered form. "I was coming to find you," he said, sliding his hands over her ribs, his thumbs resting just underneath her breasts.

She held onto his arms, her green eyes shyly meeting his. "It is quite a large sleighing party," she said.

"Yes, and we're the only married couple of the group. I hope we can keep all of them in order."

"I have no doubt of it." She used her mittened hand to whisk away the snow that clung to his shoulder. "A horde of Prescotts should provide no difficulty for you."

Jason tilted his head and regarded her with a slow, quizzical smile that made her heart turn over. "We'll see if your faith is justified." He kept his arm around her as he helped her down the steps. "We're riding in the last sleigh to keep all the others in sight."

He lifted her into the sleigh and strode to the front of the line of vehicles, where the first driver awaited the signal to go. Slowly the sleighs began to move. Laura sat opposite Hale and Prudence, while Sophia's four children were bundled between them. The youngest, a seven-year-old girl named Millicent, crept into Laura's lap and huddled under the woolen robe.

Jason came to join them, climbing into the empty space beside Laura. Together they arranged the blankets, the child, and their tangled legs, until Laura began to laugh. Finally she was tucked securely against Jason's side, her leg wedged against his muscled thigh, her head near his shoulder. Disregarding Hale and Prudence's interested gazes, she leaned against him.

Millicent sat up in Laura's lap, asking questions about the horses, the trees, and anything else that struck her fancy. Jason answered her patiently, reaching out to tug one of the little girl's long brown curls. The deep murmur of his voice was at once soothing and exciting to Laura, flavored with the hint of a brogue that would never quite disappear. She listened to him and watched the sparkling scenery around them, the frozen ponds and snow-laden birch and pine that lined the sleighs' path.

The group in the lead sleigh began singing, and gradually the tune was picked up by the entire line of vehicles. Laura joined in with the others, smiling at Hale's enthusiastic rendition.

> *Over the river and through the wood,*
> *To grandfather's house we go;*
> *The horse knows the way to carry the sleigh,*
> *Through the white and drifted snow . . .*

Observing Hale and Prudence together, Laura decided her brother was truly smitten with her. She glanced at Jason to see if he had noticed Hale's unusual behavior. Jason read her thoughts exactly. He bent his head and whispered to her. "I expect your father would approve of a match between the Prescotts and the Warrens."

"Not entirely," she whispered back. "The Warrens are rich in respectability but poor in common sense. Their family fortune has shrunk to almost nothing. And Father has always wished for Hale to marry a girl with an impressive dowry."

"Hale could try working." They were both aware that Hale's position at a Boston bank was little more than a sham, designed to protect the Prescotts' interests. The genteel occupation was common among young men of Hale's position in society. It would have been slightly vulgar for him to be seen actively working to accumulate wealth, as if he were one of the immigrant nouveaus.

"A Prescott?" she asked doubtfully.

Jason grinned. "Not easy to imagine, I'll admit."

Hale interrupted them indignantly. "Here now, what are you two whispering about? I feel my ears burning!"

Before Laura could reply, the line of sleighs came to a stop. Jason half-rose from the seat and stared far ahead of them, using a gloved hand to shield his eyes from the glare of the snow. "Looks like a tree limb blocking the path," he said, jumping down. "I'll be back in a moment."

"I'll lend a hand," Hale said, and leapt after him.

Laura and Prudence were left with the curious, excited children. Wilfred, Sophia's small and bespectacled ten-year-old son, gazed at the inviting drifts of snow. "Aunt Laura, can I get out? Just for a minute?"

"I don't think that would be a good idea," she said cautiously. "I'm certain we'll be under way at any moment."

"Just for a minute," Wilfred wheedled, and Millicent took up the plea.

"Aunt Laura, can I go with him? Please, Aunt Laura—"

"I don't think—" Laura began, and Wilfred interrupted.

"Why, the others are all getting out!" the boy said hotly. "And they're . . . why, they're throwing snow b—"

Prudence shrieked as a soft white clump of snow flew past her ear. Suddenly the air was filled with happy shrieks and pelting snowballs. Wilfred leapt out of the sleigh and scampered to a nearby tree, scooping up a handful of fluffy snow on the way.

Laura set Millicent aside and stumbled after the boy. "Wilfred! Children, all of you behave! There is no—" She ducked with a gasp as a snowball came flying toward her and landed on the ground behind her. "Who threw that?" she demanded, trying to sound authoritative. The scene was chaos, men and women ducking and throwing, children screaming with delight.

Laura burst into laughter, running as fast as she was able to the protection of her own tree. Leaning against it, she tore off her mittens and began packing her own snowball. She felt like a little girl again, free and un-inhibited.

Jason made his way back to the last sleigh, keeping his head low. The vehicle was empty. He looked around quickly, wondering where the hell his wife had gone. It was certain that she was not participating in this free-for-all—she was probably hiding somewhere until it was over.

"Look here, Moran!" Hale's voice came from far ahead of him, and Jason turned quickly enough to evade a hurtling snowball. Jason returned the fire, hitting Hale squarely in the chest. Hale clutched the white splotch of snow on his coat and keeled over clownishly, causing a multitude of children to yelp happily and fall on top of him.

Jason chuckled and began to stride toward the squirming pile of youngsters. Suddenly he felt a solid *thump* between his shoulder blades. Spinning around in surprise, he saw the flap of a black cloak from behind a tree. His eyebrows drew together. Laura? No, his timid, docile wife would not have dared. Another snowball hurtled toward him, and he avoided it deftly, his eyes narrowed in curiosity. He saw a pair of discarded mittens on the ground. "Laura?" he said, perplexed.

His wife peeked at him from behind the tree, the plume on her hat dancing. Her eyes sparkled with merriment, but there was also an alert quality in her expression. It was clear that she had no idea if he would lose his temper or not.

With an effort Jason cleared the astonishment from his face. He felt a smile twitching at his mouth. "So you want to play . . ." He reached down to scoop up a handful of snow and began to stalk her.

Understanding what he intended, Laura shrieked and fled, gasping with laughter. "No, Jason! Remember, I'm your wife!"

Her skirts slowed her down, but she darted among the trees, venturing deeper into the woods. Hastily she flung clumps of snow behind her. She felt a small *thwack* on her posterior. His aim was deadly. "I surrender!" she called out, her voice quivering with laughter. "Jason, I surrender *wholeheartedly*!"

But Jason was nowhere to be seen. "Where are you?" she called, turning in circles. "I admit defeat!" She packed a snowball together as quickly as possible, in case he refused to be a gracious victor. "Jason?" There was a crunch of ice behind her. Whirling around, she saw Jason just before he pounced on her. She gave a short scream and tried to hit him with the snow, only to send them both falling to the plush white-blanketed ground.

Jason twisted to cushion the fall with his own body, then rolled over, pressing Laura into the snow. His husky laughter mingled with her giggles, and he raised himself on his elbows to stare into her face. "Surrendering wholeheartedly," he said, "means laying down your weapons."

"I didn't have a white flag to wave."

"Your aim is good," he said.

"You make a large target."

He grinned and picked up a large fistful of snow, brandishing it threateningly.

"I've already surrendered!" she squeaked, covering her face with her wet hands.

He dropped the snow and pulled her hands away, keeping hold of her wrists.

Her smile faded as she stared at his dark face and felt the weight of him between her thighs. He stopped smiling at the same instant, his gaze falling to her lips. She remembered the way he had kissed her in the breakfast room—the hot, wet interior of his mouth, the urgent hardness of his body. He was going to kiss her again . . .

"Has the tree limb been taken care of?" she asked.

"Yes. We should be leaving soon." Jason drank in the sight of her flushed cheeks, her half-closed eyes, the crystal-white puffs of her breath in the air. He wanted to take her right here, in the cold and the snow, wanted to sink into her slim, exquisite body and feel her mouth open and sweet underneath his.

He loosened his gloves finger by finger and pulled them off. With one fingertip he stroked a damp tendril of hair off her forehead. "Are you cold?" he murmured.

She shook her head blindly. The cloak kept her insulated from the dampness of the snow, and the length of her body pressed to his felt as if it was glowing with heat. His fingertips moved over the sides of her face like points of fire, trailing to her jaw and tilting her chin up. His breath was like steam against her skin.

She lifted her icy-wet fingers to his face, timidly exploring the line of his cheekbones, the tips of his slanting eyebrows. His head angled over hers, and his lips nudged hers in a velvet-soft kiss. With a small sound of pleasure, she slid her arms around his neck, and then the glittering white world around them seemed to fade away. He brushed another savoring kiss over her mouth, and then another, until her lips parted and she unconsciously pulled at his neck to bring his mouth harder against hers.

He gave it to her as strongly as she wanted it, allowing his hunger to dictate the movements of his lips, his tongue. Her slim fingers combed through his midnight-black hair and kneaded the back of his neck. Deliberately he tightened his knees on her thighs, and she arched into his body with astonishing fervor. The fact that she was responding to him at last made him as shaky as a boy with his first woman. The frightening truth was that he needed her as he had never needed anyone. She was his, and she alone could take away the loneliness and nameless hunger he had felt ever since he could remember. She was his, and he wanted her to acknowledge it with her body and her heart.

"Laura," he said, burying his mouth in her neck. "Laura—"

Hale's drawling voice was a shock to both of them. "You two are the most disgraceful pair of chaperones I've ever seen."

Laura started at the intrusion. Her eyes flew open and she tried to struggle wildly to a sitting position. The skirts and petticoats tangled around her legs, weighting her down.

"Easy—it's only Hale," Jason said, filling his lungs with a deep breath of cold air.

"Don't let him tease," she whispered, clutching the front of his coat. "Not about this."

"No," Jason said soothingly. "I'll kill him if he tries." He stood up and reached down for her. She took his hands and allowed him to pull her upright. Then she was utterly still, her crimson face averted as he reached around her to brush the snow from her cloak.

Hale regarded them both with a self-satisfied smile. His mustache twitched like a cat's whiskers. "A nice respectable married couple," he continued mischievously, "should be doing their utmost to preserve order and propriety, and instead I find you here rolling in the snow like some—"

"Enough, Hale," Jason said curtly.

He looked surprised. "Why, Laura, you aren't *embarrassed*, are you? I'm your brother, and besides—"

"Hale," Jason said in a voice of warning, and even Laura felt her spine tingle at the sound of it.

Hale sobered immediately. "The others are climbing

back into the sleighs. I came to find you before your absence became widely noticed.''

Jason regarded him sardonically. "Thanks.''

"No thanks necessary," Hale said, and gestured for them to accompany him. "I'll go back with you.''

"No.'' Jason shook his head, pulling Laura's unresisting form closer to his. "Go on ahead. We'll be there soon.''

"Don't take long.'' Hale looked at Jason over Laura's head, gave him a brilliant smile, and raised his hand in the gesture of a victorious prizefighter.

Jason scowled at him and pointed threateningly toward the sleighs. Hale left with all due haste.

Laura, who had missed the exchange, wedged her arms against Jason's chest to keep from being too close to him. She couldn't think when she was near him. He straightened her hat and pulled out the broken red plume, handing it to her apologetically. She accepted the bedraggled feather and looked at Jason with dismay.

"I've never seen such a blush," he said huskily, and hugged her to him.

Her arms crept around his back. "Shouldn't I blush?'' she asked, her voice muffled in the front of his coat.

"Not with me.'' He kissed her forehead, and she shivered at the masculine scrape of his jaw.

Laura could not fathom the reason for his sudden tenderness. Perhaps he had decided to play some sort of game with her. "Jason," she said bravely, "things cannot change between us, not in the course of a few days.''

"Yes, they can.'' His thumb stroked the side of her neck, lingering at her pulse. "For the past two months I've let my pride stand in the way of what I really wanted. That's going to change. We know as little about each other as we did on our wedding day. And that''—he kissed the side of her throat—"is damn well going to change.''

Laura was silent and troubled, wanting suddenly to cry. It was all happening too fast. How could she give herself to him when she knew all too well that he could turn cruel in one capricious moment?

Jason read her expression and experienced the taste of bitter regret. She was so young, and he had hurt her in ways he had not understood until now. "I won't hurt you, Laura," he said quietly. "Not anymore. And I'll have your trust no matter what it takes."

The evening was filled with games, amusing stories, and music at the piano. After dinner the guests gathered in the parlor, which originally had been two smaller rooms which Sophia had converted into one large one. Laura sat with Sophia and a group of married women while they laughed and discussed the latest happenings in Boston. The unmarried girls had formed their own group a short distance away, while the men congregated around the fireplace or puffed on cigars in Judge Marsh's smoking room down the hall.

Laura could not keep her eyes from her husband. As usual, Jason was dominating the group in his own charismatic way. What he lacked in sophistication he made up for with the spark of irreverence that was quintessentially Irish. Jason never seemed to be bored except when confronted by a particularly starchy Bostonian, and then he was capable of saying or doing something just outrageous enough to make everyone laugh. Because he made no pretenses about his background, no one guessed at his sensitivity about it. He was fully aware that there were many who enjoyed the appearance of friendship with him, but few who would have tolerated the idea of him marrying into their families.

Toward the end of the evening Laura noticed that Jason had become quieter than usual, his gaze frequently diverted toward her. She could feel him staring at her, and when she looked back there was an intent gleam in his eyes that made her flustered. She nervously declined when Sophia pushed her to play the piano, but her older sister was insistent.

"Do play something for us, Laura. Something lively."

"I can't. I'm sadly out of practice," Laura said.

"But why? You used to play all the time before . . ." Sophia stopped, but Laura knew she had been about to say *before you married Jason*.

Laura stiffened as she felt Jason's hand at her back. "Play something," he said quietly.

She felt a spark of indignation at what sounded very much like an order. She knew that Jason liked to show off his accomplished wife—he wanted her to play for the same reason he dressed her in fine clothes and jewels. Well, if he was determined to put her on display, he could share the limelight!

She turned her head to regard him challengingly. "If you turn the pages for me."

His dark gaze did not waver from hers. "All right."

"Splendid," Sophia exclaimed, rifling through pieces of music to find what she wanted. "It's a pity you cannot play, Jason, otherwise I would choose something you could do together. I suspect you never had the patience for lessons, hmmm?"

He smiled. He did not point out that pianos and music lessons had not been a great concern for a family that had scratched and clawed for every penny. "Page-turning is one of my more underappreciated talents," he said, guiding his wife to the piano bench and helping her sit. He arranged the music in front of her. "Now, Laura," he said silkily, and she knew he was enjoying her annoyance, "when it is time for me to turn, just nod your head."

She glared at him discreetly. "I'd rather kick your leg."

One corner of his mouth lifted in a half-smile. "You're full of surprises today," he said. "I'm beginning to wonder if my Irish temper hasn't rubbed off on you."

She began to enjoy being pert with him. "My temper is entirely my own."

"I didn't know Bostonians had tempers."

"They do," she said crisply. "The slow-burning kind."

"Better to let out their anger at once and have done with it."

"I doubt you'd enjoy having a wife who gave vent to explosions of temper whenever she felt inclined."

"You're wrong," Jason said, resting his weight on one leg and draping his forearm on the piano. A lock of black hair fell over his forehead as he stared down at her. "I'd enjoy having her very much."

Laura's cheeks turned apple-red. She touched her fingers to the keys and tried desperately to remember how to play. There was no possibility of getting through the piece without making countless blunders. Not when he was near—not when he was in the same *room* with her.

But somehow her hands moved, recalling the sprightly melody with ease, and she did not falter. His lean fingers turned the pages at just the right pace. And all the time she was so terribly aware of him. When he leaned close enough that his shoulder brushed hers, she felt an unfamiliar ache in her breasts.

She finished the piece with a short sigh of relief and graciously accepted compliments from Sophia and the others. Jason helped her up, his hand strong at her elbow, and someone else took her place at the piano.

"Well done," he said.

"Thank you." Laura wished he would take his hand from her arm. She could not help remembering what had happened earlier today, the weight of his body pressing hers into the snow, his demanding mouth teaching her things she had been innocent of.

"Why don't you play for me at home?" he asked.

"Because I don't wish to," she said bluntly.

He scowled, drawing her to the side, away from the others' observation. "Why the hell not?"

"Jason, your language—"

"Tell me why not."

Recklessly she cast aside her fear of his temper and told him. "Because I would not like having to perform at your command, whenever you wish to be entertained, or whenever we have guests you wish me to play for like some. . . . some trained monkey!"

"Dammit, Laura," he said softly, "I won't be blamed for depriving you of something you enjoy. If you don't feel like playing when I want you to, tell me to go to hell."

In spite of their quiet tones, the tension between them was perfectly apparent. Laura sensed the glances being directed their way, and she straightened her spine until it resembled a fireplace poker. "I won't be drawn into public arguments with you," she whispered sharply. "That may be done where you come from, but it's not done in Boston society!"

"It's done all the time in the North End," Jason said, relaxing a little, sliding his hands into his pockets. "And my grandparents thrived on it in County Wexford. Perhaps we should give it a try once in a while."

She looked scandalized. "Jason, the very idea—"

"I'll buy you an iron skillet to threaten me with. That will lend us a touch of authenticity."

In the midst of her anger Laura felt a smile tugging at her lips. "I do not want a skillet. And I do not want to play for you."

Jason looked at her with those disturbing black eyes, and although they were in a room filled with people, she felt as if they were alone.

As the hour grew late the guests became drowsy. They began to retire, the ladies gliding to their rooms, where maids waited to assist with the removal of bustles, petticoats, and corsets, and the brushing-out of intricate coiffures. Laura walked upstairs with Sophia while Jason remained with the men, who lingered over cigars, brandies, and unfinished conversations.

"Things seem to be going rather well," Sophia remarked as they neared Laura's room.

"You're referring to the guests?" Laura asked cautiously.

"Two in particular," came the airy reply. Sophia stopped and pressed her cheek to Laura's. "Good night, dear."

"Good night," Laura replied ruefully, and went to her room, where a small, cheerful fire was burning in the grate. The bedroom was decorated in bright floral chintz patterns of coral and green, the windows draped with cream lace curtains. A light netted canopy hung over the old high-post bedstead. But what most attracted her eye was the masculine trunk in the corner of the room, opened to reveal her husband's possessions.

She and Jason would be sharing the room. Laura remained still, while inside she felt a flurry of panic. Foolishly she had not considered the possibility until this moment. Of course they would be expected to share a bed . . . there were so many guests, and Sophia barely had enough rooms for all of them.

"Missus Moran?" The maid's quiet voice broke through her scattered thoughts. "Would ye like me to help wi' yer dress now, or—"

"Yes, do," Laura said, still staring at the trunk. She hardly felt the tugs at the hard-to-reach fastenings that trailed down the back of her gown.

Jason would want to stay the night with her. From the way he had been behaving lately, she had no doubt of that. But he had claimed he would not force her. If she pleaded with him to keep his distance, what would he do? Certainly he would be angry, but she did not think he would hurt her.

But *would* she ask him to leave? A mixture of fear and excitement nearly made her dizzy. What if she let it happen? What had Hale said . . . these matters were simple . . . just show Jason she was willing to accept his attentions.

Am I willing? she thought to herself. She could find no clear answer. It was up to Jason. If he approached her in a kind manner, if she could just let herself believe that he would not mock or hurt her, she would be willing.

She dressed in a white nightrail embellished with hundreds of tiny ruffles and tucks, the long sleeves and bodice ornamented with frothy lace. The white cambric wrapper she wore over the nightrail was even more elaborate, bordered with three deep lace ruffles at the hem and more lace from the wrists to the elbows.

Deciding to attend to her hair without assistance, Laura dismissed the maid with a smile of thanks. She sat at the walnut-veneered dressing table and stared into the small tilted looking glass. One by one she pulled the pins from her hair until the tangled chestnut waves fell down her back. Brushing it would take a long time, and the task was soothing in its monotony.

Laura was nearly finished with her hair when she heard a rap on the door, and her husband entered without waiting for permission. Their eyes met in the looking glass, his very dark, hers wide and green. Slowly she set the brush down. Still watching her, Jason pulled off his green-and-black-patterned waistcoat and narrow black necktie, and tossed them onto a chair.

The silence was heavy between them, the tension deepening until Laura could not bear it. With an incoherent murmur, she jerked up from the chair and strode rapidly to the door. She didn't know where she was headed, she only knew that she could not stay there alone with him another moment.

Jason caught her easily, his arm wrapping around her waist. He pulled her quaking form against his. "No, don't," he whispered against her ear, his hand sliding under her hair. His palm stroked up and down her narrow back.

"Not now. Please, not tonight," she managed to say.

"It all started with that damned wedding night," he murmured, fondling the back of her neck. "It was all my fault."

"No." She swallowed and shifted against him, and his hold tightened. "I behaved like a child," she ventured. "I—I turned you away."

"I didn't understand why, not at the time."

"I was . . . you were . . ." She flushed, overwhelmed by the memory . . .

Their wedding day had been long and nerve-wracking and tiresome, and by the time they had retired for the night Laura was exhausted. Jason had been emotionless and matter-of-fact throughout the wedding and reception, and she wondered if he had any feelings for her at all. After allowing her time to change into her nightgown, he appeared in her room with his shoulders squared as if for an unpleasant duty. Since that was precisely what her mother had informed her was soon to follow—an unpleasant duty—Laura regarded her husband with a mixture of reluctance and alarm.

Jason had never looked as tall and overpoweringly large as he did in that moment. In order to hide her fear, she kept silent and looked away from him, her heart thumping violently as she heard the sound of his breathing. He slid one hand behind her head and the other around her rigid back. His warm, hard mouth pressed against hers for a long time, and she squeezed her eyes shut, her body frozen with confusion. She knew that something was wrong, felt that he wanted something from her that she was not able to give. His hand moved over her back and then to her breast. It was when he touched her there that she pushed him away in a quick, nervous movement. "Don't," she said without thinking.

His eyes narrowed in anger, as if he had been expecting the rejection. "You'll have to get used to the idea of being my wife," he said, and reached for her again.

This time his mouth was hurtful, and his hand roamed over her body with insulting boldness. She tolerated it for as long as she could before jerking away with a tearful plea. "Don't touch me, I can't bear it!"

He looked as though she had slapped him. She covered her face with her hands, her whole body shaking. It was with relief and horror that she had heard him walk out of the room and slam the door . . .

The episode had been repeated a few times since then, until Jason had not approached her anymore. Until tonight.

"You were so strong," Laura whispered, "and you wanted so much. Things I didn't understand . . . things I still don't understand. I know now that you didn't intend to frighten me, but you did. There was such a look in your eyes . . ." She took a trembling breath.

It was fortunate she did not look up, for the same expression was in Jason's eyes right then, a hot glow of hunger.

"I didn't realize how innocent you were," he said, raising his hand to her head, stroking her flowing hair. "The mistake was mine. I was too damned impatient for you. When you stiffened and pulled away from me, I thought it was disgust you were feeling, not fear."

"Disgust?" she echoed in bewilderment.

"Because you knew I was so far beneath you. Because you'd been forced into marriage with someone whose ancestors were nothing but peasants in the poorest country in Europe. I knew what everyone had been telling you, that I was not fit to touch—''

''No!'' Impulsively she covered his mouth with her fingers. ''I was not forced into marrying you,'' she said in astonishment. ''Did you think I had no choice?''

His blank look was her answer.

''Oh, Jason, my father gave me every opportunity to refuse your proposal! Didn't you know that?'' She smiled tremulously as she saw the shock on his face. Had he been so accustomed to prejudice from others that he had expected it of his own wife? ''No wonder you made those remarks about buying me! But I was more than willing to marry you. The decision was mine to make.''

Jason pulled Laura's hand away from his lips. ''You don't have to say that.''

''I'm not lying, Jason. It's the truth.''

He shook his head stubbornly. ''I made the bargain with your father before I proposed to you.''

''And you thought he would have made such a bargain without my consent? You thought I was merely a pawn with no say of my own?''

He scowled at her. ''Yes.''

''You were wrong,'' she said with a touch of impatience. ''I *wanted* to marry you. For heaven's sake, I've wanted to be your wife since I was fifteen years old!''

Suddenly Laura realized what she had said, and she covered her mouth with her hand. The bald declaration seemed to echo in the small room. *Don't let him ask why*, she thought frantically, *please don't let him ask why*.

Mercifully he didn't.

But he stared at her strangely, his black eyes seeming to read her most private thoughts. Blindly she lowered her head, and was confronted with the broad, shirt-covered expanse of his chest. He spoke softly, his mouth against her hair. "I want to set aside the past, Laura. I want to share a bed with you tonight." The tip of his finger traced the delicate edge of her ear, causing her to shiver. "Most of all, I want you to trust me to be gentle with you."

She had imagined and dreaded this moment for so long. Jason had never been this way with her before, so tender and careful. The choice of surrender was suddenly made easy. Tears sprang to her eyes. "I don't know what to do," she faltered.

"I'll show you."

3

DEFTLY HIS FINGERS MOVED AMONG THE BUTTONS AND bows of Laura's wrapper until the garment slipped from her shoulders. Jason pushed the white cambric down her arms and over her wrists. She stood before him in her nightgown, her soft body unconstricted by stays and laces. He settled his hands on the natural curve of her waist, his senses enthralled by the scent and nearness of her.

Little by little he sank his hands into her loose hair until he was cradling her scalp. He bent his head and covered her mouth with his. Laura shivered at the masculine brandy-taste of him. The tip of his tongue coaxed her lips to part, and he kissed her as if he would never have enough, his hands easing her head back. Swaying dizzily, she reached for his waist to keep her knees from buckling. He wrapped his arms around her until her breasts flattened against his hard chest and her thighs were leaning into his. Her mouth twisted wildly, her tongue seeking his, her slim body molded to him like a second skin.

They broke the kiss at the same time, gasping roughly. Laura took advantage of his loosened arms and stepped back, clasping her hands to the center of her chest. Her heart thundered in a way she thought he must be able to hear. She glanced from Jason's flushed face to the thrusting outline at the front of his trousers. Hastily she looked away, but not before he had seen.

"Curious? Here, come closer." He drew her forward, tender and predatory. "Don't be afraid."

"No, Jason, I don't—" She stumbled against him, and he caught one of her hands, bringing it to his groin.

Heat radiated through the cloth of his trousers, seeming to scorch her hand. She blushed and tried to pull away. He covered her hand with his own and kept it pressed against his rigid flesh.

"Have you ever seen what a man looks like?" he murmured among the wisps of hair at her temple.

She turned her hot face into his shoulder, shaking her head.

"Never spied on Hale and his friends taking a swim, or—"

"No, never." She gave a choked laugh, still hiding her face.

A teasing note entered his voice. "You were a proper little girl." Slowly he let go of her hand. Her fingers remained against him for a scant second, then withdrew to the safer territory of his waist.

"My mother made certain that all of her daughters were proper."

"She wanted to keep you sheltered from men," he said without asking.

"Well, she . . . has never had a good opinion of them."

"Because of your father."

"Yes." Laura stared at him curiously. "Hale must have told you about that."

"Why don't you tell me?"

"My father is a good man, a kind one. But . . . there have always been other women. Sometimes his involvements are merely flirtations. Sometimes they are more than that." She shrugged helplessly. "He has always been discreet, but Mother has known for years. She says it's to be expected that a man will be faithful to a wife for only so long. She says that most husbands will stray because . . ." Abruptly Laura fell silent.

"Go on."

"I don't think—"

"Tell me."

She obeyed reluctantly. "Because they are creatures of a bestial nature." Her green eyes met his. "Mother also said that you were probably more bestial than most."

Jason grinned, knowing that of all the people who had disapproved of their marriage, Wilhemina had objected the most. "Her opinion of my character has never been a secret." He became serious, lifting her chin with his fingers. "Do you believe what she said about unfaithful husbands?"

Her gaze skidded away from his. "I don't know."

His voice was very quiet. "Do you think I've been unfaithful to you?"

Startled, she looked up at him. Her mouth went dry. "Things have not been right between us," she managed to whisper. "You've had cause to be."

There was a flash of something vibrant, perhaps anger, in his eyes. But his hand was still gentle on her chin. "By now you should know me well enough to be certain of a few things," he said, his gaze boring into hers. "I never lie. When I make a promise, I keep it." Laura wanted to shrink away, but she was mesmerized by his intensity. "I took you as my wife because I wanted you and no one else. I made a vow to forsake all others. It's been hell going to bed alone, knowing you were just a few doors away. More than once I thought about going to you and taking what was already mine."

"Why didn't you?" she whispered faintly.

"Pride. That and the desire for you to open your arms to me willingly." His smile had a self-mocking quality that made her uneasy. "And so I've waited. And since the day we were married I've been planning my revenge for all the times I couldn't have you."

Laura turned pale at his quiet tone. "What . . . what kind of revenge?"

He drew closer, his hard-planed face serious, his mouth nearly touching hers. "I'm going to give you such pleasure that you'll weep for each and every night we could have had together." He picked her up and carried her to the bed.

The firelight spread its wavering glow throughout the room as Jason lowered Laura to the mattress and stripped back the covers. Ferociously he tore off his shirt and bent over her, his hands framing her face as he kissed her. Instinctively she adjusted her mouth to his, answering the sweep of his tongue with delicate touches of her own.

Curiously she touched the hair on his chest, trailing her fingers through the thick, springy mass. She found a thin line of silken hair arrowing down to the waist of his trousers, and she rubbed the back of her knuckle across it in a questioning touch. To her surprise, she felt

Jason s breathing turn ragged.

He growled low in his throat and sought the peak of her breast through the bodice of her nightgown. Finding the hardening tip with his mouth, he nibbled gently. Laura gave a startled cry and twisted away from him, holding her hand to her breast.

"Did I hurt you?" he asked huskily.

Her cheeks pinkened, and she shook her head.

He pulled her protective hand away, replacing it with his own, his thumb circling the throbbing nipple. As he caressed her, he stared into her eyes, watching the green depths soften with pleasure. "You're so beautiful, Laura . . . I want to see the rest of you."

She didn't make a sound while he untied the bodice and took hold of the hem to draw it up her legs. She pressed her knees together modestly, feeling the cool air sweep over her legs . . . hips . . . waist . . . chest. Casting the garment aside, Jason gathered her slender body against his. When he pulled his head back to look at her, there was an absorbed expression on his face that she had never seen before. For him, too, time was suspended, and the outside world had disappeared. His kiss was relentless, flavored with desperation as he sought to make her understand how much he wanted her. Laura clasped her arms around his neck and sank her fingers into his black hair.

With a muffled groan, Jason let go of her just long enough to shed the last of his clothes. He pulled her to the mattress with him and slid his hands over her body with incredible gentleness. Her gaze wandered over him, and for a moment she couldn't breathe as she saw his naked, fully aroused body, primitive and golden in the firelight. Pinning her between his muscled arms, he lowered his head to her breasts. He covered the point of her nipple, his tongue gliding wetly across the aching bud. "Do you like it when I kiss you here?" he murmured.

"Yes . . . oh, yes . . ."

His mouth swept over her breasts, and he used only the lightest touches of his teeth and tongue. Wonderingly he stroked the length of her neck, the vulnerable hollow between her breasts, the downy smoothness of her stomach. Laura explored his body with the same sensitive lightness, bashfully touching the hair under his arms, the lines of his ribs, the lean surface of his flanks.

His palm ventured over her knees, his fingers tracing the line between her thighs. Her legs were still clenched together, resisting as he insinuated his hand between them. "Laura," he muttered, and she understood what he wanted. She felt the power and urgency contained in his body, the turgid length of him burning against her hip. "Laura, open to me."

She closed her eyes tightly and parted her knees enough to allow the gliding pressure of his hand. Jason kissed her breasts, her throat, whispering that she was safe, that he would take care of her. His lips brushed against hers, coaxing them apart, and his tongue reached for hers in skillful enticement that sent every hint of fear spinning out of reach.

His fingertips trailed over her stomach and dipped into the hollow of her navel. He paused at the triangle of soft chestnut hair at the top of her thighs, playing lightly through the curling strands. She began to breathe hard as his fingers slid deeper between her legs, stroking and withdrawing. Biting her lips, she tried to hold back a moan.

In spite of the desire that raged within him, Jason smiled triumphantly at the dazed, almost unwilling pleasure on Laura's face. He had brought that look to her eyes. He was the only man who would ever know her intimately. Watching her closely, he slid his teasing fingers inside her. She groaned with pleasure, her hands climbing up his back.

Although her caresses were unskilled, they stirred Jason to violent readiness. Wanting her too much to wait any longer, he pushed her thighs wider and lowered his body between them. He felt her tense, and he cupped her head in his hands, his lips brushing against hers. "Sweet darling . . . easy now, *mo stoir*. It will hurt, but only for tonight." He positioned himself and pressed forward, gritting his teeth with the effort to be careful.

Laura clung to him, moaning his name as he sheathed himself within her. There was pain, a white-hot burning that caused tears to spring to her eyes. She writhed and tried to push him away, but he rode her movements easily. His lips drifted through the tear tracks on her face. "Easy," he whispered. "*Gradh mo chroidhe* . . . you belong to me now."

She began to relax as he cradled her in his arms, the hard force of him buried inside her. His mouth moved to her breasts, pulling gently on her aching nipples. Her heartbeat roared in her ears, and her lips parted as she breathed his name. He slid deeper within her, his hands beginning a slow sojourn over her body. The steady thrust of his hips brought pain, but she felt an urge to push up against him, and the sensation was intensely sweet.

His body surged into hers, pulled back until he had almost withdrawn completely, then surged forward again. Laura gasped as she felt the inner tension increase. Her muscles tightened, and she gripped his upper arms until her fingers were numb. Half-frightened by the unfamiliar sensations, she tried to draw back from them, but it was too late. A burst of pleasure filled her body, causing her to strain against him with an incoherent sob. Jason smothered her cries with his mouth and pressed deep within her until her shuddering ceased and she was satiated and quiet beneath him. Only then did he release his own desire, thrusting one last time and groaning with violent satisfaction.

Laura was too exhausted to move or speak. Jason rolled to his side and pulled her with him. It took the last of her strength to lift her arm around his waist. For a long time they lay with their bodies entangled and their breath mingling.

Jason was the first to speak. "You'll never occupy a bed without me again, Laura Moran," he said lazily. His fingers brushed away the tendrils of hair that clung to her forehead and cheeks.

A shy smile stole over her face. "Jason?" she asked, shivering as he cupped her breast in his warm hand.

"Mmmm?"

"What did those words mean?"

"Which words?"

"The Gaelic words you were saying...before. It sounded something like..." She paused and wrinkled her brow thoughtfully. "*Masthore*. And then you said something like *grammacree*."

Jason was frowning. "Did I say that to you?"

"Yes." She looked at him expectantly. "What does it mean?" To her amazement, she saw a flush of color that went across his cheekbones and the bridge of his nose. "Jason?"

"It means nothing," he muttered. "Just...words of affection."

"But what *exactly*—"

He kissed her, and as he had intended, the question flew from her mind. "You're the most beautiful woman I've ever known," he said against her lips as his hands wandered from her breasts to her thighs. "I'm going to give you everything you've ever dreamed of."

She laughed unsteadily, for Jason had never said anything of the kind to her before. All at once he seemed younger, the usual harshness of his face softening in the darkness, his smile almost boyish. "There's nothing I want," she told him.

"A golden carriage, drawn by horses with diamond bridles," he mused, rolling to his back and swinging her above him.

Laura crossed her arms modestly over her breasts. Her long hair hung in a curtain around her. "That isn't necessary."

"Ruby rings for your toes . . . a castle with silver towers, a ship with moonlight sails to carry you across the sea—"

"Yes," she said. "I'll take the ship."

"Where would you like to go?"

"Everywhere."

Jason laced his fingers behind her neck. "Would ordinary sails do? We'll travel anywhere you wish—perhaps spend a few months in Europe. Or the Orient." He raised his brows suggestively. "Or the Mediterranean."

Laura stared at him in wonder. "Jason, you're not teasing, are you?"

"I'm being serious. We never took a wedding trip."

"You said you couldn't afford to leave your work."

"I can afford it now," he said dryly. "Where would you like to go?"

"Cairo," she said with dawning excitement. "I've always wanted to see the pyramids."

"And make an excursion up the Nile?"

She blinked in surprise. "How did you . . ." She frowned suspiciously. "Is there anything Hale *hasn't* told you?"

Jason chuckled. "No. But that's the last of your brother's meddling. And you have my promise for a trip in the spring."

A sweet smile curved her lips. "Thank you, Jason."

He stared at her as if spellbound. "You can thank me another way."

"How?"

He took hold of her wrists and pulled them away from

her body, his gaze lingering appreciatively on her round breasts before moving back to her face. "Lean down and kiss me."

She complied without hesitation, flattening her hands on his shoulders, lightly touching her lips to his. Beneath her she felt his body respond, desire flowing hot in his loins. Her eyes widened, and she tried to move away. He rolled to his side and slid his thigh between hers.

"Again?" she asked breathlessly.

"Again." His lips drifted over her neck in a moist, searing path. He murmured sweet beguilements in her ear, teased and fondled her until she was gasping and reaching for him hungrily. Laughing softly at her impatience, Jason slowed the pace even more, touching her as if she were as fragile as an orchid, as if more than the tenderest brush of his fingers would bruise her. He drove her past eagerness, past all reason, until all she could do was wait helplessly for him to release her from the silken prison. At last he slid into her, and she purred in exquisite relief, her green eyes half-closing.

Jason shuddered as he felt her arms closing around his back, her hips tilting to cradle his. He had never expected to find such fulfillment. All the bitterness, all the unspoken longings that had haunted him for so long, were quenched in the sweetness of her body.

The urgent rhythm of her hips pulled him into a flowing tide of pleasure, and he fought to keep his movements slow and easy. Laura muffled her moans of ecstasy against his shoulder, and Jason felt the shattering sensations sweep through him as well. He buried his face in the river of her hair, wrapped her in the shelter of his arms, held her tightly in the moments of darkness and bliss.

"Laura, dear. Laura." Sophia's voice called her from sleep.

She groaned, her face half-buried in the goose-down pillow. She squinted at her older sister, who stood by the bed. Sophia wore a velvet gown with an elegant knee scarf, a sash tied around the lower length of the skirt to gather it in at the knees. The curtains at the windows were tied back, letting in the white winter sunshine.

"What time is it?" Laura asked in a sleep-roughened voice.

"Eight o'clock, dear. I thought it best to wake you rather than allow you to sleep until a scandalous hour and become the subject of embarrassing speculation."

Laura began to sit up, then gathered the sheet to her breasts with a gasp as she realized she was naked. She blushed, throwing a cautious glance at her sister. Sophia seemed unperturbed.

"Is Jason downstairs?" Laura asked timidly.

"No, the men breakfasted early and went to hunt fowl," Sophia said.

"They went *hunting*?" Laura frowned in a befuddled way.

"The charm of the sport escapes me. I doubt they'll find a single thing to shoot. But after observing Horace's habits for years, I've come to the conclusion that men simply like to carry their guns through the woods, drink from their hunting flasks, and exchange ribald stories."

Laura tried to smile, but a quick, anxious frown followed. "How did Jason look at breakfast?" she asked.

"No different than usual, I suppose." Sophia's clear brown eyes rested on her steadily. "How should he have looked?"

"I don't know," Laura murmured, sitting up in bed. She winced, feeling battered and sore in every part of her body.

"I'll tell the maid to draw a hot bath for you," Sophia said considerately. "And I'll send up some cambric tea."

"Thank you." Laura continued to clutch the sheet

closely, her fists winding and twisting in the soft linen. Sophia left, and Laura stared at the closed door, struggling with a mixture of emotions. "Oh, Jason," she whispered, distressed at the prospect of seeing him this morning. In the light of day, the recollection of her behavior was mortifying—she had been shameless, foolish, and he was probably laughing secretly at her. No, she couldn't face him now, not to save her own life!

But there was no possibility of avoiding him. Sighing miserably, she crawled out of bed. She was refreshed by a hot bath that soothed her aches and pains. After much deliberation, she decided to wear a dress of shimmering olive-green faille that brightened her eyes to emerald. The maid came to assist her with the tightening of her corset laces, and spent a long time fastening the tiny loops and buttons on the back of her dress. The skirt was pulled tightly over her figure in front and gathered behind in a modest bustle topped by a huge bow. Painstakingly Laura twisted and re-twisted her hair into a perfect coiled chignon and anchored the chestnut mass with a gold comb.

Finally there was nothing left to do. She squared her shoulders and walked downstairs. She was relieved to discover that the men had not yet returned. Some women were attending to their needlework in the parlor, while others lingered in the breakfast room. The food was being kept in crested silver warming dishes, and Laura inspected the array with a smile.

Sophia knew how to serve the proper Bostonian breakfast, the heavy old-fashioned kind. The sideboards fairly groaned under the weight of fruit, oatmeal, preserves and molasses, waffles, biscuits, toasted bread, eggs, cheese, and custard. There was a variety of meats, including chicken with cream gravy, ham, and smoked fish. An empty plate held a few crumbs of what had once been an apple pie. As far as New Englanders were concerned, there was never an inappropriate time of day to serve apple pie.

"Everything will be cleared away soon," Sophia told her. "Come, have something to eat."

A plate was thrust in her hands, and Laura smiled, picking up a tidbit here and there. But she was too nervous to eat, and in spite of her sister's entreaties, she barely touched the food.

"More tea?" Sophia asked, hovering about her with maternal concern. "Chocolate?"

"No, thank you," Laura replied absently. She stood up. "I think I'll find something to read. Or perhaps I'll try my hand at the piano again. I have missed playing— I'd forgotten how soothing it is. I'll close the door so as not to disturb anyone."

"Yes, do whatever you like," Sophia said, regarding her with a touch of worry. "Laura, you don't seem quite yourself this morning."

"Don't I?" She felt her cheeks turn pink. "I'm perfectly well."

Sophia lowered her voice to a whisper. "Just set my fears to rest and I'll ask nothing else: Jason treated you kindly, didn't he?"

"Yes, he was kind," Laura whispered back. She leaned closer as if to impart a highly personal secret, and Sophia tilted her head obligingly. "I am going to the piano now."

Smiling wryly, Sophia waved her away.

Laura seated herself at the small rosewood piano with a sigh, her fingers running over the ivory keys as if waiting for inspiration to strike. Then they settled in a pattern she remembered from long ago, a melody that was melancholy and sweet. It suited her mood perfectly. She fumbled a few times, her touch uncertain from lack of practice. As she played, concentrating on the music, she sensed the parlor door opening. Her fingers slowed, then stilled. All she could hear was carpet-muffled footsteps, but she knew who the intruder was.

A pair of strong hands slid over her shoulders, up the sides of her neck, back down. The palms were warm, the fingertips cool. A low, vibrant voice sent a thrill down her spine. "Don't stop."

She pulled her hands from the keys and turned to face Jason as he sat on the small bench beside her. He had never looked so fresh and vital, his hair attractively tousled and his skin ruddy from the icy breezes outside.

For a moment they stared at each other, measuring, asking silent questions. Laura dropped her gaze, and it happened to fall on the muscled thigh pressed close to her own. She remembered that thigh wedged between hers, and embarrassment rushed over her.

"You left me this morning," she heard herself say.

Jason leaned over her downbent head, unable to resist nuzzling the nape of her neck. "I didn't want to wake you. You were sleeping so deeply."

She shivered at the heat of his breath and tried to stand up, only to have him catch her firmly around the waist and pull her back down. Automatically she braced her arms against his chest. "Look at me," he said quietly, "and tell me why you're skittish today."

Laura's fingers plucked nervously at his black-and-tan brocaded vest. "You know why."

"Yes, I know why."

She heard the trace of amusement in his tone. Her eyes flew to his, and she saw that the midnight depths were warm with laughter. Immediately she was horror-stricken. Oh, he was laughing at her, he was jeering at the way she had behaved last night, his chaste wife who had moaned and clung to him so wantonly.

"Let go of me," she said, pushing at him in earnest. "I know what you think, and I won't—"

"Do you?" His arms tightened until she was pinned

against his chest, and he smiled at her small scarlet face. "I think you're adorable." He dropped a kiss on her forehead while she struggled helplessly. "I think you need to be reminded of a few things." His mouth joined hers, pressing her lips apart. She could not keep from responding any more than she could stop her heart from beating. As her lips clung to his, he let her hands slip free, and her arms wrapped around his neck. Their tongues touched, circled, slid together languorously.

Gradually Jason released her mouth, and she gave a protesting moan. "I think," he said huskily, "you need to be taken back to bed."

Laura's eyes widened with alarm. "You would not embarrass me in front of the others that way."

He kissed her hungrily. "They'll understand."

"They will not! They're Bostonians."

"I think I'll carry you upstairs. Right now." He made a move as if to lift her, and she clutched at his shoulders.

"Jason, no, you can't . . ." Her voice trailed off as she saw that he was only teasing her. Her frown of worry dissolved into a scowl.

"Laura," he murmured with a smile, "do you need proof of how much I want you?" He drew her hand to his loins, and she caught her breath at the feel of him, hard and urgent, more than ready to take her. "I never thought it was possible to want a woman so much," he said against her ear. "And if it weren't for your blessed modesty, I *would* take you upstairs . . . or right here . . . anywhere . . ." He sought her lips, his mouth soft and coaxing, setting fire to every nerve.

"Jason," she whispered, leaning against him, "you would tell me if I displeased you last night, wouldn't you?"

"*Displeased* me . . ." he repeated in astonishment. "Laura, no one has ever pleased me *more*. Where did you come by such an idiotic notion?" Suddenly his dark eyes were stern. "If that's what you're fretting about, we really are going upstairs."

This time he was clearly *not* teasing. Alarmed, Laura tried to appease him. "No, I believe you, Jason, I do—"

"Convince me," he challenged, and choked off her words with a sultry kiss. She twisted to fit him more closely, her fingers sliding between his vest and shirt. The pounding of his heart was as wild as her own. She was lost in a wave of sweet madness, not caring what happened next, dimly aware that she would not object if Jason pulled her to the floor and took her right there.

They were interrupted by the harsh clanging of a tin drum and a shrill, metallic blast. The sounds seemed to pierce Laura's eardrums and sent a shock through her body. Jason let go of her with a muffled curse and nearly fell off the piano bench. Together they stared at the intruders.

A pair of giggling imps stood before them. It was Sophia's children, Wilfred and Millicent, holding tin instruments and banging them loudly.

"Lovely children," Jason remarked pleasantly, reaching up to rub the back of his neck, where every hair was standing up straight.

"You were kissing Aunt Laura!" Millicent cried in glee.

"So I was," Jason agreed.

Wilfred pushed up his glasses and squinted at them. "Uncle Hale said to come play for you."

Jason looked at Laura with a rueful grin. "Excuse me. I have two little elves to catch."

"What will you do when you catch them?" she asked in pretend worry.

He smiled darkly. "Bury them outside in the nearest snowdrift."

Wilfred and Millicent screamed in delighted terror and

scampered from the room as Jason chased them.

"Don't forget Hale," Laura called after him, and laughed.

In the days that followed Laura was unable to let go of the feeling that she was in a delightful dream that would end with cruel suddenness. Each morning she awakened with a sense of worry that dissolved only when she saw Jason's smile. It was miraculous to her that the husband she had come to dread was now the person she wanted to be with every minute.

Now that she was no longer afraid of his biting sarcasm being turned on her, she talked freely with him. He was an entertaining companion, sometimes thoughtful and quiet, sometimes roughly playful. He was a considerate lover, always sensitive to her pleasure, but with an earthiness that she found exciting.

To Laura's surprise, Jason seemed to relish the discovery that she was not the delicate, reserved creature he had thought her. One morning he swept her away from the others and took her on a ramble through the woods, teasing and flirting as if she were a maiden he was bent on seducing. Saucily she ducked away when he would have kissed her.

"No," she said, picking up her skirts and making her way to a fallen tree trunk. "I know what you intend, and I will not be taken advantage of in the snow."

He followed readily. "I could make you forget the cold."

"I don't think so." Primly she stepped over the tree trunk, and gave a little shriek as he made a grab for her.

"I never back down from a challenge," he said.

Swiftly she picked up a long birch stick and turned to face him, touching it to his chest as if it were a sword. "So this is the reason you brought me out here," she accused, "for an unseemly frolic in the middle of the woods."

"Exactly." With deliberate slowness he took the stick and broke it in half, tossing it aside. "And I'm going to have my way with you."

Backing up step by step, Laura considered the possibility of compromise. "One kiss," she offered.

He continued to stalk her. "You'll have to do better than that."

Her eyes sparkled with laughter, and she held out her arms to keep him at bay. "I will not bargain with you, Jason."

They eyed each other assessingly, each waiting for the other to make the first move. Suddenly Laura darted to the side, and found herself snatched up in a pair of strong arms. She laughed exuberantly while he lifted her by the waist as if she weighed nothing at all. Slowly he let her slide down until their faces were even, her feet still dangling above the ground. Without thinking, she twined her arms around his neck and fastened her mouth to his in a kiss so direct and natural that Jason staggered slightly, his senses electrified. He had to put her down before he sent them both tumbling in a heap. Spellbound, he stared at the woman in his arms and thought of what an arrogant fool he'd been. He'd assumed he knew her so well when he didn't know her at all.

"Jason," she asked wistfully, "do we really have to go back home tomorrow?"

"We can't stay here forever."

She sighed and nodded, wondering how long the truce between them would last once they were back in all-too-familiar territory.

It was with reluctance that they finally left the Marshes' Brookline home the next day and returned to their own Beacon Street address. Sophia had been able to guess at Laura's remaining worries and gave Laura an uncharacteristically long hug good-bye. "Everything will be all right," Sophia whispered, patting her on the back. "After seeing Jason with you the past few days, I've come to realize that there is no difficulty of yours that time will not solve."

Laura smiled and nodded, but she knew that in this matter Sophia wasn't right. Time meant very little. Two whole months of marriage had not accomplished for her and Jason what the past four days had. And there were problems that still faced them, problems that could not be resolved no matter how much time went by. She had to find some way of prying past Jason's deepest reserve, the barrier that kept them from reaching an intimacy beyond the physical pleasure they shared.

As he had promised, Jason took her to the site of his most recent building. It was the first time she had actually seen one of his projects under construction. Before now she been wary of showing too much interest in his business concerns. Now she inundated him with questions.

"What sort of people will be renting the apartments?" she asked. "Small families? Young men?"

"And young women, on a cooperative basis."

"Young women without chaperones?"

He laughed at her faintly censorious tone. "Yes, self-reliant women with their own careers, sharing an apartment together. Is that too radical a proposition for a Prescott to approve of?"

"Yes," she said. "But I suppose the Prescotts cannot hold back progress."

He grinned and drew her arm tighter through his. "We'll make a liberal of you yet."

As Jason walked her around the property, Laura was impressed, even a little awed, by the size of the undertaking. The air was thick with the noise of the steam shovel, the crew of men spreading gravel and swearing, the dust everywhere. Part of the property included a former rubbish dump, which was being covered with clean gravel.

The slight train of Laura's skirt dragged through the patches of muddy ground, and she paused every now and then to tug at it impatiently. She was outfitted in the most practical garments she owned, a wool and grosgrain walking dress of a deep plum color, a matching cape, and sealskin boots with double soles. The heavy draperies and tightly molded skirt prevented her from moving with Jason's ease, and he was forced to cut his strides to match hers.

Jason slowed their pace even more as they were approached by a thin, ragged figure from the street. Laura's eyes darkened with pity as she looked at the elderly man, who wore tattered clothes that were hardly adequate protection against the cold. His gray beard was thin and yellowed, his skin veined, and he reeked of gin. He spoke in a heavy Irish brogue that Laura could barely decipher.

"Here now, sir, d'ye have a coin t' spare for an ould man? The wind is sthrong an' could today."

Laura looked up at Jason, whose expression was unreadable. "Indeed it is," he said. He reached into his pocket and pulled out some coins, placing them in the outstretched hand.

The old man peered at him with watery eyes that suddenly brightened with interest. "Sure now, yer frae the ould sod."

Jason's slight accent became more pronounced than usual. "My grandfather left County Wexford during the first potato rot."

"Aye, ye have th' look o' Wexford, eyes an' hair black as coal. Meself, I come frae Cork." The man nodded in thanks, gesturing with the coins clutched tight in his bony fist. "God bless ye, sir, an' yer bonny wife."

Laura glanced back at him as they moved on; he was

scurrying furtively across the street, hands tucked underneath his arms. "Poor man," she said. "I hope he buys something to eat."

"He'll spend it on drink," Jason said flatly.

"How can you be certain?"

For a moment she thought he wasn't going to reply. "He can get whisky cheaper than bread," he finally said.

"Then why did you give the money to him if you knew . . ." Laura frowned and stared at the ground, feeling the tension in his arm, knowing that something had struck a raw nerve.

Jason felt a powerful urge to tell her what he was thinking, but his habit of privacy concerning his past warned him against saying anything. He opened and closed his mouth several times, feeling heat creep up from his collar as he fought an inner battle. There was no reason to confess anything to her, no need for her to know. And if Laura understood what his childhood had really been like, she would feel contempt for him. She would feel the same disgust that he felt whenever he remembered it. God knew why now of all times he felt driven to tell her what he had once vowed never to speak of.

Jason stopped walking and turned his gaze to the steam shovel as it bit into the hard ground.

"What is it?" she asked gently. "What did he remind you of?"

He spoke as if the words were being dragged out of him. "I knew men like that when I was young. Men driven from their home by poverty and disease, and most of all hunger. They didn't care where they went, so long as they escaped from Ireland. Often they landed in Boston with no money, no work, no relatives. They . . ." He stopped and took a short breath before continuing. "They used to beg for a warm place in my family's room at night, when the winter was bitter."

"Your family's room? Don't you mean your house?"

He didn't look at her. "We lived in one room of a basement. No plumbing or windows. No light except when the door to the sidewalk above was opened. Filth kept draining in from the street. It was little more than a gutter."

Laura was silent with amazement. That could not be true, she thought. He could not have come from that kind of poverty. She had known the Morans had not been a family of great means, but Jason was talking as if they had been slum-dwellers!

"But your father was a grocer, wasn't he?" she asked awkwardly. "He had enough money to send you to school."

"That was later, when his business began to succeed. Even then he had to trade his soul for the money. He managed to convince some local merchants and politicians that I would be a worthwhile investment." Jason's mouth twisted. "For the first several years my father ran his grocery in our cellar room. Until I was nine or ten, I remember eating nothing but scraps and foodstuffs gone bad, the worst of whatever he couldn't sell."

"But your education . . . How . . . ?"

"My father was one of the few who allowed—no, pushed—his sons into the free public schools. He couldn't read. He wanted at least one of us to be able to."

"Did you want to?"

"At first I didn't care. I was an uneducated brute who wanted nothing except food and what little comfort I could find. And there is an attitude in the North End, that a man isn't meant to rise above the life he's born to. The Irish are fatalistic about such things. I thought the only way to get something I wanted was to steal it." Jason smiled grimly. "When I couldn't find coal or wood to scavenge, the family had to stay in bed all day to keep warm. God knows I saw no use in learning to read.''

''What made you decide to try?''

He answered distantly, as if he were only half-aware of her presence. The memories were never far from his mind—they were what drove him—but until now he had never allowed himself to speak of them. ''I saw men laboring on the wharves until their backs were ruined. And the hostlers and stablers living in worse conditions than the horses they cared for. All the Irish laborers and domestics who will work for any wage—they call them 'green hands.' There was nothing I wouldn't have done to escape it.'' Jason looked at her then, his black eyes unnervingly intense. ''I worked all the time. On the docks, in saloons, anywhere there was a coin to be made. In school I studied hard, made the highest marks. I never lost at anything—baseball, footraces, public debates. Every man of means I crossed paths with became a mentor. But the admission into the Boston Latin School was nothing short of a miracle. I'll owe favors for that from now until kingdom come. That was when everything changed, when I finally knew what it was I really wanted.''

Laura did not ask what that was, for she was afraid of the answer. She suspected that what Jason really wanted was what he could never have, to assume a place in the most powerful circles of Boston society that would never be allowed to an Irishman. Such positions had been decided generations ago, and no intruders were admitted into the sacred circles. No matter how much money or power Jason acquired, he would always be considered an outsider.

''And then Boston Latin led to college,'' she prompted quietly.

''When it came time for that, some Irish businessmen helped to foot the bill. I eventually repaid their investments many times over.''

"Your family must be very proud of you," she said, and was puzzled when he didn't answer.

While she was still trying to absorb all of what he had told her, Jason took her by the shoulders, his gaze hunting for pity or revulsion. She felt neither, only a desire to comfort him. She thought of what he must have been like as a boy, hungry and too poor to hope or even to dream.

"Oh, Jason," she said softly. "I didn't suspect you had such desperate odds against you. You should have told me before."

She saw that whatever he had been expecting from her, it had not been that. His face was utterly still. She touched his lean cheek with her gloved hand.

"You should be repelled, knowing where I came from," he muttered.

Laura shook her head. "I admire you for it. I admire you for what you've made of yourself."

He gave no reply, staring at her in an almost calculating way, as if he wanted to believe her but could not. Her hand fell to her side, and she gave him an uncertain smile.

They were interrupted by the approach of the construction foreman, who had seen them from a distance. Eagerly he greeted them and conferred with Jason on some details of the project. Laura watched them, struck by how quickly the bitterness and memories on Jason's face had vanished, replaced by his usual calm authority. It dismayed her to see how easily he hid his feelings. She was afraid she would never fully understand him.

After bidding the foreman good-bye, they walked to the double barouche and Jason muttered to the driver that they were going home. Laura clambered into the velvet-lined carriage, arranging the mass of her bustle, petticoats, and heavily draped skirts in order to sit comfortably. Jason sat beside her, closed the door, and pulled the morocco blinds at the window shut. Obligingly he leaned over to help tug a fold of her skirt out from beneath her. The carriage started with a small jolt.

"Jason," she said in a low voice.

"Yes?"

"I hope you don't regret telling me about your past." Hesitantly she reached out to stroke his chest. "I know there is much more you've left unsaid. Someday I hope you will trust me enough to tell me the rest."

His hand closed in a fist over hers. Surprised, she darted a look at him, wondering if she had somehow made him angry. There was a dark blaze in his eyes— but it was not anger. He wrapped his other hand around the back of her neck. His thick black lashes lowered, and he looked at her with a narrowed gaze.

"Laura, why did you marry me?" he asked roughly.

She was startled, and turned a shade or two paler. Clumsily she tried to dodge the question by making light of it. "I believe this is called fishing for a compliment, Mr. Moran." She smiled, but he did not respond. His silence forced her to continue. "Why did I want to marry you . . . well, there were many reasons, I suppose. I . . . I knew you would be a good provider, and you were Hale's friend, and during those four years you spent Christmas with us, I became acquainted with you, and . . ." Her gaze dropped away. She tried to pry herself free, but she was held fast against one hundred and eighty pounds of obstinate male, and they both knew she would not be freed until she gave him what he wanted.

"The truth," he muttered.

"I can't tell you something I don't know."

"Try."

Helplessly she tugged at her trapped hand. "Why is it necessary?"

"Because I thought I'd forced you into marrying me. A few days ago you told me that you married me of your own free will. I have to know why.''

''I don't *know* why.'' Laura gasped as he twisted and dragged her across his lap. She was bound in a cocoon of skirts and stays, her head forced up by the pressure of his arm. ''Jason, please, I don't know what you want—''

''The hell you don't.''

''Let me go, you bully!''

He ignored her demand. ''Then we'll take another tack. If you had a choice, then tell me why you didn't marry someone from your own social rank. There were young men with good names and adequate means—you could have had any of them.''

''Oh, a prime selection,'' she agreed, glaring at him. ''Hordes of blue-blooded snobs reared to do nothing except preserve the money their grandfathers made. I could have married some dignified Brahmin who would insist on eating oatmeal every morning of his life, and tucking an umbrella under his arm even when it wasn't raining, and complaining until he was an old man about not being accepted into the Porcellian club at Harvard!''

''Why didn't you?''

''Jason, stop this!'' She writhed until her strength was exhausted.

''You told me you wanted to marry me since you were fifteen,'' he said ruthlessly. ''Why?''

She trembled with distress, her eyes glittering with sudden tears.

''No, don't cry,'' he said, his voice gentling. ''Laura, I've told you things I've never confessed to anyone. It can't be any more difficult for you than it was for me.''

His handsome face was so close to hers, and there was something pagan in the blackness of his eyes. Laura drew the tip of her tongue over her dry lips and swallowed. Her blood was rushing so fast it made her light-headed. ''The first time I met you,'' she managed to say, ''Hale had brought you home for the Christmas holidays. You kept watching me during that awful dinner . . . remember?''

He nodded slightly.

"You looked like a wolf in a cage," she said. "The room seemed too small for you. You didn't belong there, but I could see how badly you wanted to, how determined you were. And I knew I could help you."

"Dammit, you didn't marry me to be helpful!"

Futilely she tried to free her arms. "We'll be arriving home soon—"

"I won't let you go until I have the answer. Was it that you liked the idea of marrying a social inferior? So you could always have the whip hand?"

"No," she gasped.

"The money? You wanted to be the wife of a rich man, no matter how vulgar his bloodlines."

"Jason, you . . . you louse!" She struggled furiously. Had she been able to slap his face, she would have.

"Why did you marry me?"

"Because I was a fool, and I thought you needed me, and I—" She was so upset she was shaking, and she was terrified to realize she was on the verge of blurting out the truth.

"Why did you marry me?" came the relentless demand.

Her eyes stung sharply. "Jason, don't make me—"
"*Why?*"

"Because I love you," she choked, finally goaded into defeat. "I've loved you from the first moment I saw you. That was the only reason . . . the only one."

4

A TREMOR WENT THROUGH JASON'S BODY, AND HE pressed his lips to her forehead. He had never wanted anyone to love him before. There had never been room in his life for anything or anyone who would distract him from his ambition. Until his engagement, there had been affairs, but never without the mutual understanding that they were temporary. Laura was the only woman he had wanted for always.

"You're cruel," she sobbed, wondering what she had just done. It had been the mistake of her life to admit her feelings so soon. She should have waited, should have held her ground. "You're a bully, and selfish, and—"

"Yes, and a louse," he murmured, brushing her tears away. He kissed her wet eyelids. "Don't cry, *mo stoir*, don't."

Desperate to soothe her, he kissed her with all the gentleness he was capable of. He reached down and pulled her arms around his neck, while his tongue flickered in her mouth. His muscled arm was hard against her back. Slowly her tears ceased, and her trembling fingers slid into his hair.

At this sign of her response, Jason finished the kiss

with an infinitely soft stroke of his tongue and took his mouth from hers. He had to stop now, or he wouldn't be able to control himself. But her slim body molded to his, and her breasts shifted against his chest. He tried to move her off his lap. "We'll be home soon," he said gruffly, more to himself than to her. "We'll be home and then—"

Her red lips pressed against his, sweetly luring him away from sanity. Greedily Jason angled his mouth over hers, his tongue thrusting savagely. She writhed in response to the painful throb between her legs and returned his passion with equal force. His hand searched frantically through the mass of her skirts for her legs, her thighs, unable to reach any part of her through the tightly binding garments.

The carriage stopped, and Jason tensed with a muffled curse. Laura gasped incoherently, her fingers clenching into his coat. It took several seconds for her to understand that they were home. She looked at Jason, her gaze unfocused. Her hair was falling around her shoulders, pins dropping right and left, her hat dislodged, and her clothes disheveled.

Clumsily she raised her hands to her hair, flushing with mortification. She thought of the way the maids would giggle at the story of the cool, composed Mrs. Moran walking in with her clothes askew and her hair looking like a bird's nest.

The driver began to open the carriage door from the outside, and Jason caught at it easily. With a brief word to the driver, he pulled the door shut. Turning to Laura, he watched her twist handfuls of hair and jab pins in her chignon. "Can I help?"

"You have helped quite enough," she said in agitation. "How like you this is! When you want something you must have it regardless of time or place, and all other considerations be damned."

"When it comes to you," he said, "yes."

She glanced at him then, and found a caressing warmth in his eyes that caused her hands to falter. Painstakingly she rearranged her clothes, repositioned her hat, and gave him a nod when she was ready to leave the carriage.

After he walked her up the steps and into entrance hall, Laura stopped in the middle of the polished parquet floor. Quickly the housekeeper came to take her cape and Jason's coat. "Mrs. Ramsey," Laura murmured to the housekeeper, "I'll be down soon to discuss the plans for dinner. First I must change from my walking dress."

"Yes, Mrs. Moran. I shall send one of the maids to help you—"

"That won't be necessary," Jason interrupted matter-of-factly, taking Laura's elbow.

The housekeeper's face wore a mixture of speculation and delighted horror. Clearly she wondered what might take place upstairs. It was still broad daylight outside—an unthinkable time for a husband to lay with his wife. "Yes, sir," she said, and headed for the kitchen.

Laura tried to pull her elbow from his. "Jason, I don't know what you intend, but—"

"Don't you?" He guided her up the stairs without the slightest appearance of hurry.

"This can wait until evening," she whispered. "I know you must have many things to attend to—"

"Yes, important things."

As soon as they reached her room, he yanked her inside and closed the door with his foot. His mouth covered hers impatiently, his breath a scalding rush against her cheek. He pulled off her hat and worked at her hair, scattering pins until the long chestnut locks fell down to her waist.

"Jason, I need time to think about all that has happened—"

"You can think about everything to your heart's desire. Later." His hands moved restlessly from her breasts to her hips. "Did you mean what you said in the carriage?"

"About your being a bully?" She tilted her head back as his lips found the sensitive hollow beneath her ear. "Yes, I meant every word."

"About loving me."

It would be useless to deny it now. Laura swallowed and forced herself to meet his dark eyes. Jason looked almost stern, his mouth set with a firmness that made her want to cover it with enticing kisses. "Yes," she said huskily, "I meant that too."

Without another word he turned her around and unfastened the back of her dress. In his haste, his fingers were less agile than usual. The heavy dress collapsed along with masses of petticoats. Laura heaved a sigh of relief as her corset laces were untied and the contraption of stays and silk was tossed to the other side of the room. She heard the sound of cloth ripping and felt her torn cambric drawers slip to the floor.

Shivering, she leaned back against him, her head dropping on his shoulder. His palm rubbed in a circle over her abdomen. "Tell me again," he said against the perfumed softness of her neck.

"I love you . . . Jason . . ."

He turned her in his arms and hungrily sought her mouth with his, while he pulled the hem of her chemise up to her waist. Laura responded lovingly, her lips parting, her body arching to his. But as she felt the demanding pressure of his arousal against the inside of her thigh, she pulled away from him.

"No, we can't," she said. "I must get dressed and go downstairs. Mrs. Ramsey will be waiting—"

"Mrs. Ramsey be damned. Take off the chemise."

"I shouldn't," she said weakly.

"Don't you want to?" He approached her slowly, and

she backed away until her shoulders bumped against the wall. She was mesmerized by the darkness of his eyes. When he stared at her like that, she could refuse him nothing. Unsteadily she grasped the hem of the chemise and pulled it over her head.

Jason reached for her, his hands sliding over her back and buttocks. She wrapped her arms around his neck, every nerve kindling with the intense passion he aroused. Murmuring to her hoarsely, he lifted her against the wall, the muscles in his arms bulging. Her eyes widened, and she gasped in surprise as she felt him enter her in a hard, deep thrust. Obeying his whispered commands, she wrapped her silk-stockinged legs around his hips.

"You're so beautiful," he rasped, kissing her chin, her cheeks, her parted lips. "So sweet . . . Laura . . ."

Rhythmically he withdrew and thrust into her warm body, staring at her flushed face. Laura whimpered and tightened her legs, her heels digging into his muscled buttocks. She clung to him, her hands grasping frantically at his sweat-slick shoulders. Suddenly the exquisite tension coiled inside, tightening painfully. Gasping, she buried her face against his neck and felt herself burning slowly, slowly, her body consumed in a blaze of pleasure. Jason gritted his teeth as he strove to prolong the moment, but he was soon overtaken by his own release.

After a long time, Laura became aware that her toes were touching the floor. She was wrapped tightly in his arms. Hazily she thought that she had never felt so safe, so protected. She pressed her lips to his shoulder. "I've always loved you," she whispered, stroking the dark hair at the nape of his neck. "Even when you were cruel to me, even when you looked at me as though you hated me."

"I wanted to hate you."

"And did you?"

"Almost," he admitted gruffly. "When I saw you

with Perry Whitton. I couldn't stand the sight of another man's hands on you." He smiled ruefully. "I'd never felt jealousy before, and suddenly it was twisting at my guts. I wanted to strangle you only a little less than I did Whitton."

"There was no need to be jealous," she murmured, still stroking his hair. "I've never wanted anyone but you."

Laura hummed carols as she hung gilded eggshells on the Christmas tree, which was small enough that she could reach all but the top branches. It was a week before Christmas, and she had been busy for days with holiday baking and decorating the house. The scent of evergreens filled the parlor, bringing to mind many childhood memories. Since she had not had time to make more than a few simple ornaments, her mother and Sophia had each given her a few to begin her own collection, including the angel with glass wings that she had loved since childhood. Painstakingly she and one of the maids had strung cranberries to fill the empty spaces, and their fingers were reddened and sore after hours of work. The rest of the room was decorated with garlands of holly, wreaths of gilded lemon leaves, pinecone clusters, and gold velvet ribbons.

Idly Laura wondered how Jason's family would spend Christmas. They would probably gather relatives and friends at their home, sharing memories, talking and feasting together. Laura wished that she dared ask Jason about the Morans, and why they had not sent any invitations or cards. She had only seen a few of her in-laws once. Since Jason's father, Charles, had passed away a few years before, his mother Kate had attended the wedding with some of her children, two of her daughters and one of her young sons. They had not come to the reception afterward. The Morans had been nicely, if plainly dressed, and they'd seemed to be quietly awed by their surroundings. "Brogues you could have cut with a knife," her mother had said disdainfully.

In the past year Laura had exchanged short letters with Jason's mother Kate, but that was the limit of their interaction. She knew from those notes that Jason visited his family infrequently, always during his workday. He never invited Laura or mentioned the visits to her afterward—it was as if his family didn't exist, as if she and they occupied separate worlds that only Jason could traverse.

Deep in thought, Laura tapped her forefinger against her lips. She wished she could pay Kate Moran a visit. There were many questions about Jason that Kate could answer if she cared to. Laura wanted to know more about her husband, more about the past he found so difficult to talk about. Of course, if she asked for Jason's permission to visit the Morans, he would not allow it. And if she went without his knowledge, there was the chance that he would find out.

"I don't care," she muttered. "I have every right to see them." She squared her small jaw. "I *will* see them." Filled with a mixture of determination and guilt—for she disliked the idea of doing something behind Jason's back—she considered the best time to do it. Tomorrow morning, she decided, after Jason left for work.

The Moran home was located in a solidly middle-class section of Charlestown. The two- and three-family houses had once been inhabited by the well-to-do but were now occupied by the overflow of immigrants from the adjoining neighborhood. The street was well-kept, completely unlike the strings of crowded flats and garbage-filled passageways of the South End slum districts.

Laura emerged from the carriage and looked up and down the cobblestone street with interest. It was a dry, brisk day. Lines of work clothes, colored blue, gray, and brown, flapped in the breeze. The air was filled with the scent of stewing meat and vegetables. A young couple walked by her, their arms linked, their heads swathed in knitted caps and scarves. They threw her a few discreet glances but did not slow their pace. A few children interrupted their game of stickball to stand and stare at her and the elegant carriage.

After telling the driver to wait in front of the house, Laura went to the door unescorted. There was no brass knocker. She hesitated, then lifted her hand to rap on the scarred paneled wood.

A boy's voice came from behind her. "Yer knockin' at *my* house!"

Laura turned and was confronted by a small boy of eight or nine. A smile crossed her lips. He was a Moran, no question of it. He had black hair and dark eyes, fair skin, and ruddy cheeks that had not yet lost their childish roundness. His belligerent chin and aggressive nose pointed up at her.

"Donal?" she guessed, knowing that was the name of one of Jason's two brothers.

"Robbie," the boy corrected indignantly. "An who might ye be?"

"I'm Laura Moran." When that elicited no sign of recognition, she added, "Your brother Jason's wife."

"Ooohhh." Robbie regarded her wisely. "Ma says yer a foine lady. What d'ye want?"

"I would like to see your mother."

He grasped the door handle in both hands, tugged it open, and held it for her. "Ma!" he barked into the house, and gestured for Laura to go inside. "Ma, 'tis Jason's wife!"

He urged Laura to accompany him down a long, narrow hallway lined with garments hanging on hooks. The hall led to the kitchen, where she could see the side of the cast-iron stove. There was a graniteware pot on top of the stove, and the air smelled of stewing apples. "Er . . . Robbie, perhaps I should not come in unannounced," she said.

He was puzzled by the strange word. "Unan . . ."

"Perhaps you should tell your mother that I'm here."

"Sure now, I'm tellin' 'er," he interrupted, and called shrilly toward the kitchen. "Ma, 'tis Jason's wife!"

"Who is it, ye say?" came a woman's voice, and Robbie took hold of Laura's arm, triumphantly dragging her past the stove to the wooden table in the center of the kitchen.

Kate Moran, a sturdy, pleasant-faced woman in her mid forties, regarded Laura with round blue eyes. A wooden rolling pin dropped from her hands onto the piecrust in front of her. "God save us," she exclaimed. "Jason's wife!"

"I apologize for the unexpected intrusion," Laura began, but her voice was lost in the bustle that suddenly filled the room. Jason's sisters, both attractive girls in their teens, rushed in to see the visitor.

" 'Tis Jason?" Kate asked anxiously, her flour-coated hands pressed to her heavy bosom. "Och, somethin' has happened to me firstbarn, me precious boy—"

"No, no," Laura said, "Jason is fine. Perfectly fine. I've just come for . . ." She paused, conscious of the many curious gazes on her. "I've just come for a visit," she said lamely. "But I can see that you're busy. Perhaps some other time would be better?"

There was a moment of stillness. Kate recovered quickly, her worry replaced by curiosity. " 'Tis plaised we are that ye are here. P'raps a cup o' tea—Maggie, fetch the teapot, an' Polly, show the lady to the parlor—"

"I wouldn't mind staying in the kitchen," Laura ventured. She was conscious of the family's dumbfounded gazes as she eased herself into one of the wooden chairs at the table. The room was warm and cheerful, and she preferred its informal atmosphere.

Kate shrugged helplessly. " 'Tis here ye'll stay, then." She shooed the children from the room and gave Laura a measuring glance. "An' now tell me what yer about, me dear. To be sure, Jason knows nothin' of yer visit."

"No, he does not," Laura admitted, unconsciously resting her elbows on the flour-dusted oilcloth that covered the table. She hesitated before adding, "I've come to talk to you in the hopes that you would be able to explain some things about his past to me. Jason isn't an easy man to understand."

Kate gave a short laugh. "Nay, there's no understandin' that contrary, prideful boy, nor his fine notions. A hard head like his pa's."

Laura was barely aware of time passing as she sat in the kitchen with Jason's mother. The tea grew cold in their cups while the conversation lengthened. Kate's mood relaxed from careful politeness to amiability. It was clear that she liked to talk, and in Laura she found an encouraging listener. She brought out an old photograph of Charlie Moran so that Laura could see the resemblance between father and son. " 'Twas tuck the first day Charlie opened the store on Causeway," Kate said, beaming with pride.

"He was very handsome," Laura replied, struck by the similarity to her husband—except that Charlie Moran's face had been weathered and harshly lined by years of poverty and backbreaking labor. There was the hint of a smile in his eyes, however, and a vulnerable quality that was very different from Jason's dark, cynical gaze.

"I nivver showed this to Jason," Kate commented.

"Why not? I think he would like to see it."

"Nay, not after the way they left off."

"There was a falling-out?"

Kate nodded vigorously. "It started wi' that fancy school, that taught him that uppish talk an' them high-tone words. Och, the boys tuck it on themselves to tease. An' his pa told him not to spake so high-an-mighty.''

Laura thought of how isolated Jason must have been, caught between two worlds. "But his father must have been proud of him," she said. "It was remarkable for an Irish boy to attend Boston Latin, and then college—"

"Aye, Charlie near to burst his buttons." Kate paused. "But he fretted over it too, he did."

"Why?"

"Charlie said 'twas too much schoolin' by far. An' he was right, it tuck me Jason away fer good."

"Took him away?"

"Aye, 'twas plain as day. Jason would have none o' the girls in the neighborhood, foine girls though they were. He would have none o' his father's store, an' none o' his family. The local lads pressed him to take a position at the *Pilot*—'tis an Irish paper, dear. He could've gathered a followin' that would've led him to the state legislature. But Jason said he wanted nothin' but to mind his own affairs.'' Kate shook her head. "Ashamed he was to be Irish, an' to be the son o' Charlie Moran. 'Twas that they argued over the day before me poor Charlie died. Two stubborn divvils.''

"He passed away during Jason's first year of school, didn't he?" Laura asked.

Kate nodded. "When Jason made his money, he thought to buy me a grand house an' send his brothers an' sisters to school. I told him I'd not give up me home. Donal looks after the store, an' the girls hope to marry wi' good Irish lads—the rest o' me brood cares not a whit for schoolin'. Cut from a diff'runt cloth, Jason was.''

"But he needs his family," Laura said. "He does, although he may not realize how much."

Kate was about to reply when Robbie's high-pitched voice called down the hallway. "Ma! 'Tis Jason!"

Laura froze, staring in surprise at the kitchen doorway as her husband's broad-shouldered form appeared. Her heart thumped unpleasantly as she saw the ominous glint in his eyes. "Jason," she said feebly. She stood up and attempted a placating smile. "How did you know . . . ?"

His voice was cool. "I came home early. Mrs. Ramsey told me where you were."

Katie regarded her son placidly. "We've been havin' a nice visit, yer Laura an' me."

His expression didn't change, but he bent and kissed Kate's forehead. "Hello, Ma."

Laura winced as Jason took hold of her arm in a grip that was just short of being painful. "It's time to go home," he said softly, and she realized with a sinking heart that he was angrier than she had feared he would be.

After allowing her barely enough time to bid the Morans farewell, Jason rode back with her in the carriage. The tense silence between them sawed at Laura's nerves until they were shredded. "I wanted to tell you, Jason," she said hesitantly, "but I knew you wouldn't have allowed me to go."

He laughed shortly. "I hope you found the Morans entertaining."

"I—I didn't go to be entertained."

"I don't care why the hell you went. But it's damn well going to be the last time you set foot in Charlestown."

"For heaven's sake, it does no harm to anyone if I choose to see your family! I don't understand why you're taking on so."

"You don't have to understand, although you could

if you cared to look beyond the end of your nose. And wipe that wounded look off your face, or I—'' He clamped his teeth together, biting off his next words. His face was dark with fury.

"Why won't you let me have anything to do with your family? Why can't we include them in our lives?"

"Damn you!" he exploded. "My life with you has nothing to do with them! I don't want reminders—by God, I won't have you combing through my past for your own amusement! You don't belong in my family any more than I belong in yours. From now on you'll stay away from them." His lips curled in an ugly sneer. "And if you even think of defying me in this, I'll make you sorry in ways your soft little imagination couldn't begin to conceive."

Laura shrank back from his vicious tone, her green eyes alarmed. "Jason, don't threaten me—"

"Do you understand what I've just told you?"

"Jason, please—"

"Do you understand?"

"Yes," she said, hurt and intimidated. "I'll do as you say."

It was rare that Jason drank to excess, but that evening he closeted himself in the library with his whisky and stayed until well after Laura had retired to bed. He did not come to her room, and she tossed and turned restlessly, missing his warmth and his large, strong body to snuggle against. The next morning she awoke with dark-circled eyes and a sense of injustice. He was trying to punish her, she thought with annoyance. She would show him that she wasn't in the least affected by his withdrawal.

Sitting across the breakfast table from him, she saw with satisfaction that he was suffering from a fierce headache and his eyes were bloodshot. His temper was foul, but he was quiet, and he seemed to find it difficult to look at her. Slowly she realized that his anger was neither petty nor temporary, and that it had less to do with her than with the pain of old wounds. She thought about bringing up the matter of their argument—no, it might be better to keep her silence.

A few days passed, and it was time for them to attend the large Christmas Eve party that Sophia and Judge Marsh were giving. Laura had never felt less like laughing and pretending to be cheerful, but she was determined not to give her friends and family any reason to think she was having troubles with her husband. It took three hours and the help of both maids to dress and arrange her hair.

Her dress was made of deep rose satin, fitted so tightly to her body that there was not a quarter-inch of room to spare. It was embroidered from the square-cut bodice to the hem with thousands of crimson beads sewn in a flowered pattern. A ruffled satin train was draped from the small of her waist down to the floor, flowing gently out from her body as she walked. The sleeves were tight and banded at the wrists with more beads. Ruby combs glittered in the mass of braids and shining curls gathered at the back of her head.

Jason was waiting for her downstairs, his face expressionless. He was attired in flawless black and white, looking polished and astonishingly handsome. Something flickered in his eyes as he glanced over her, and when his gaze reached her face, she was aware of the feminine flutter of her senses.

An endless line of carriages blocked the street where the Marsh home blazed with light. Women in velvet mantles and furs were escorted to the entrance by men in greatcoats and tall hats. Groups of carolers strolled from house to house, filling the night with music. Hot run punch garnished with raisins and fruit slices lent its spicy aroma to the air, as did the pine wreaths and bayberry candles in every room.

Hale besieged them as soon as they entered the house, cheerfully kissing Laura and urging Jason to join him for a drink with some of the friends they had gone to college with. Dutifully Laura greeted her mother, who looked as stiffly displeased as usual. Wilhemina Prescott glanced at her youngest daughter assessingly. "And how is the situation between you and . . . that man?"

"You are referring to my husband, Mother?" Laura asked, and forced a bright smile to her face. "Splendid."

"I have been informed otherwise. You and he engaged in some kind of quarrel at the party you gave last month."

"It has been resolved, Mother."

Wilhemina frowned. "It is shockingly ill-bred to air one's grievances in public, Laura. I hope you are not taking on the coarse, vulgar habits that his sort of people indulge in—"

"Laura!" Sophia's light voice interrupted. "Dear, you must come and see how the children decorated the tree . . . absolutely charming . . . excuse us, Mother."

"Thank you," Laura said feelingly, trailing after her sister.

"She's in fine form tonight," Sophia muttered. "Father's not with her. She claims he is indisposed. My guess is they have had a row over his most recent fancy-friend."

Laura stayed at Sophia's side for much of the party, while the crowd grew lively with the dancing, music, and potent punch. Her gaze moved around the sea of familiar faces. She caught a glimpse of her husband as he talked with the people gathered around him. It was not difficult to pick Jason out from the crowd—his dark, vivid looks made everyone around him seem colorless in comparison. His manner was livelier and more intense than the cool crispness of the people around him.

Laura smiled slightly. It didn't matter to her if Jason was ever truly accepted by the Boston elite or not. She was glad of the differences between him and the rest of them, glad of his earthy vitality and even his exasperating pride. Impishly she decided to go to him to find some way of enticing him to a private corner. Surely he wouldn't mind a stolen kiss or two.

She made her way through the entrance hall, artfully sweeping up the folds of her train to keep it from being trampled by wayward feet. Hale and one of his friends walked past her to the front door, holding a third young man up by the shoulders. The man was obviously the worse for drink, and they were taking him outside to sober him up in the cold air. Such situations were always handled with dispatch, before the ladies could be offended by the sight of a gentleman in his cups. "Good evening, Mrs. Moran," Hale said wryly, grinning at her. "Step aside for Samuel Pierce Lindon, unfortunate victim of hot rum punch."

"Shall I fetch coffee from the kitchen?" she asked sympathetically.

Hale opened his mouth to answer, but he was interrupted by Samuel, whose head wobbled in Laura's direction. "Moran?" he slurred. "You're the sisshter . . . that one who m-married a m-m-mick."

"Yes, I'm that one," Laura said dryly, knowing that the boy would never have dreamed of saying such a thing were he sober.

Drunkenly Samuel lurched out of Hale's grasp and pinned Laura against the front door. "You're standin' under the mishletoe."

"I'm afraid you are mistaken," Laura muttered, shoving her elbows hard into his midriff. He wound his arms tightly around her and refused to let go.

"Here now!" Hale grunted in annoyance, trying to pry Samuel away. "Let go of my sister, half-wit. Sorry,

Laura . . . he's too foxed to know what he's doing—''

"You drather have a gennleman than a *mick* in your bed, wouldn' you?" Samuel asked, his liquor-pungent breath wafting in Laura's face. "I'll show you what you're missing . . . One li'l kiss, thas all . . . you green-horn wives don' usually mind sharing your fav—''

Suddenly Samuel was lifted and spun around as if by a tornado. Laura fell back against the door, aghast as she saw a brief scuffle between Samuel and her husband. Jason's face was white with rage, his black eyes blazing. Feebly Lindon swung and missed. A woman screamed while others swayed in ladylike faints. Jason drew back his fist and dropped the young man with one hard blow. He would have beaten him to a pulp had Hale not pounced on him and held him from behind. The crowd swarmed into the entrance hall, chattering excitedly.

"Easy, Moran," Hale hissed, struggling to keep hold of Jason. "No need to wipe the floor with him. He didn't hurt Laura—I was here."

Jason went still, struggling to control his temper. He shrugged off Hale's restraining arms and strode to his wife, taking her by the shoulders. He looked over her worriedly. "Laura—''

"Jason, I'm all right," she said shakily. "There was no need to make a scene. He's just a drunken boy. He didn't mean to—''

Her mother's icy voice cut through the hubbub. "How dare you," Wilhemina exclaimed, glaring at Jason. "How dare you turn a society gathering into a dockyard brawl! It may be common among the Irish to behave in such a manner, but it is not the way of decent people!" Her tall, thin body stiffened imperiously. "Your expensive clothes and pretend manners cannot conceal what you are, an ill-bred peasant—''

Laura interrupted, unable to stand any more. "Shut up, Mother."

Wilhemina's jaw dropped in astonishment. None of her children had ever dared to speak to her so rudely.

Hale snickered, throwing Laura a glance of surprised approval.

Sophia stepped forward and shook her finger at Samuel, who had managed to sit up and was holding his head bemusedly. "Young man, I do not appreciate having my guests accosted in my own home." She turned to her brother. "Please take your friend outside, Hale."

"Yes, ma'am," he replied dutifully.

"Sophia," Laura said in a low voice, slipping her arm through Jason's, "I believe we will be going home now."

Sophia looked from Jason's stony expression to Laura's distressed one. "I understand, dear."

Hale stopped them before they reached the door, clapping Jason on the back. "I . . . er, would like to apologize for Lindon. He'll be devilish sorry for all of this when he sobers up." He extended a hand and Jason shook it briefly, both of them exchanging rueful glances.

Laura was silent during the carriage ride home, wanting to let both their tempers settle. She was angry and upset by Jason's behavior. It had not been necessary for him to make such a scene! Samuel had been obnoxious but hardly dangerous. The problem could have been solved with a few brief words, and Jason knew it. He also knew that if two gentlemen ever found it necessary to come to blows, it was never done in the presence of ladies.

As soon as Jason escorted Laura into the house, Mrs. Ramsey appeared to welcome them. Laura waved the housekeeper away, and Mrs. Ramsey promptly disappeared, having read from their faces that all was not well. Jason turned and began to head toward the stairs.

"Jason, wait," Laura said, catching hold of his arm. "We must talk about what happened."

He shook off her hand. "There's nothing to talk about."

"Isn't there? You must admit that you overreacted."

"I don't call it an overreaction to stop some drunken fool from pawing my wife."

"There was no need to deal with him so harshly. He wasn't aware of what he was doing—"

"The hell he wasn't! Do you think he would have insulted you had you been someone else's wife? A Boston Brahmin's wife?" He sneered at her lack of response. "No. Because he and his peers are accustomed to giving the Irish housemaids a slap and tickle, or visiting the North End shanties for prostitutes, and in their eyes the fact that you're married to an Irishman makes you—"

"Jason, don't," she cried, throwing her arms around his neck and hugging herself to his rigid body. "Must you blame everything on the fact that you're Irish?" She pressed a beseeching kiss on the side of his neck. "Let's talk about this sensibly." She gave him another kiss, this time underneath his ear. "Come sit with me by the fire."

For a moment she thought he was going to refuse her, but then he agreed with a muffled curse and followed her into the parlor. While Laura drew up an overstuffed ottoman and seated herself, Jason stirred the coals in the grate. He threw on a handful of pine knots and a birch log, dusted off his hands, and sat on the floor, propping one knee up. The blaze of firelight played over his rumpled black hair and hard-edged face, turning his skin to copper.

Laura took a deep breath and groped for the right words to say. "Jason . . . that Lindon boy's remarks didn't upset me as much as your reaction did." She stared into the fire, picking at her beaded dress in agitation. "I'm afraid that you may have more in common with my mother and her prejudices than you think," she said. He gave her a forbidding stare, but she continued doggedly. "Deep down you seem to believe as she does, that a Brahmin should never have married an Irishman. You think the two worlds should be kept separate. But you can never erase your past . . . your family . . . your heritage. You can't turn your back and pretend they don't exist."

Jason was silent, motionless. Laura sighed with frustration, thinking that she may as well have been talking to a brick wall. "Oh, why must you be so stubborn?" After considering him for a moment, she stood up and went to the Christmas tree in the distant corner. "I have something for you," she said, picking up a small package wrapped in colored paper. "I'd rather give it to you now than wait until the morning."

"Laura, I'm not in the mood for this."

"Please," she entreated, bringing the gift to him. "Please, I want you to." Heedless of her fine dress, she knelt on the floor next to him and dropped the flat package into his lap.

He regarded it stonily. "I suppose this has some bearing on the conversation."

"Yes, I think so."

Slowly Jason ripped one side of the paper and pulled out a small photograph in a frame. He went still, his head bent over the sepia-toned albumen print. Laura had chosen a simple silver frame ornamented with a garnet in each corner.

The picture was of Charlie Moran in the doorway of his grocery store. It was a shock to Jason—he had not seen his father's face since the day before Charlie had died. He felt as if he'd received a hard blow to the chest. "Where did you get this?" he asked after a long time.

"Your mother showed it to me. I asked her if I could give it to you. She said you'd never seen it."

"No." He stared at the weathered face in the photograph, shaken by the memories it provoked.

Laura watched him with an almost maternal tenderness as he studied the faded image.

"Big, hard-drinking, blustering, hot-tempered Irishman," Jason said. "We could never talk without arguing. The last time I saw him was the worst. We nearly came to blows."

"Why?"

"He accused me of being ashamed of him and the family. I told him he was right. I . . ." Jason looked away from the picture, his jaw tensing. ". . . said things I never should have said. I wanted no part of his plans for me. God knows I was never meant to champion Irish causes, or go into ward politics, or take over his store—" He broke off abruptly. "It doesn't matter now."

"He died the next day, didn't he?" Laura asked.

Jason smiled bitterly. "That night, actually. It was quick, unexpected. Ma sent for me, but he was dead before I reached the house."

"You must have been devastated."

"I was angry because of all I'd said to him." Jason was too wrapped up in the memory to guard his words. "Because he'd gone before I could take any of it back."

"What would you have told him?" she whispered.

"I . . ." He swallowed hard and narrowed his eyes against the sudden glitter of tears. "Dammit." Roughly he rubbed his sleeve over his face, disgusted with his lack of control. "Hell, I don't know."

"Jason, you must forgive yourself," she said softly. "There is no one to blame. It wasn't your fault that you wanted a life different from his. It wasn't your fault that he died."

"I never . . ." Jason was surprised at how the memory could hurt after all these years. "I never made peace with him. He died thinking I hated him."

Finally she understood the burden of guilt he had carried for so long. She couldn't stop herself from reaching out to him. She curved her arm around his neck and laid her palm against his damp cheek. "No, Jason," she whispered. "That isn't true. He knew you loved him. And he was proud of you. Ask Kate and she'll tell you how much." She saw his fingers tighten on the silver frame, and she put her hands over his.

Jason stared at the photograph while the grief and guilt that had weighed on him for years began to ease. It would take time to let go completely, but he knew that Laura was right. The fault was not his—there was no one to blame.

Laura studied the picture along with him. "I want us to keep this on the mantel," she murmured, "for everyone to see. I want it to remind you of the past, and remind you that there is no shame in what he was and what you are."

"Perhaps not to you," he conceded gruffly, "but—"

"It doesn't matter what shallow-minded people think. I fell in love with you because of the man you are. And when we have children, I intend for them to know your family as well as mine. They're going to be proud of their Irish heritage." She smiled unsteadily. "And if you think I can't match your stubbornness, Jason Moran, then you have a thing or two to learn."

He was quiet, his brooding gaze fastened on the photograph, and then he set it aside. "Then we'll keep this damned thing wherever you want it," he muttered. "Hang it on the front door if you like."

A smile of pure gladness broke out over her face, and she knew then that everything would be all right. "Perhaps I will."

Jason pulled Laura into his arms, crushing her to his chest until she could hardly breathe. "I love you," he said hoarsely, burying his face against her hair. "I've always loved you."

"You had a fine way of showing it," she murmured,

nuzzling underneath his jaw. "Impatient, sarcastic—"

"Sassy little devil." He let out a long sigh. "I thought · if you knew how I felt you'd throw it back in my face. It was safer to let you and everyone else think I wanted you merely as an ornament, a trophy—"

"While I pretended that I married you out of a sense of duty to my family." She laughed softly. "We should have been honest with each other from the beginning."

He rubbed his cheek against her hair, holding her as if he would never let her go. He had never felt such peace. All his life had been directed toward this moment, this woman. The silence was unbroken by anything except the crackle of the fire. Its golden light glinted off the ornaments on the Christmas tree, the glass wings of the angel, the beads on Laura's satin dress.

Laura was suffused with a glow of happiness. She had always loved Christmas, but now more than ever because it was on this night that their marriage was finally beginning, and no greater gift could be given to her. How many holidays he had spent with the Prescotts, always an outsider. But she and Jason would spend a lifetime together and have their own family. And they would make every Christmas as magical as this one. She held him tightly.

"*Mo stoir*," he whispered, and dragged his mouth from her chin to the valley between her breasts.

Laura recognized the words he had said before. "Tell me what it means," she said, her eyes half-closing as his hand slipped inside her bodice.

"My treasure."

She caressed the back of his neck. "And the other thing you call me—"

"*Gradh mo chroidhe* . . . love of my heart."

She smiled in pleasure. "Is that what I am?"

"That's what you've always been," he said, and lowered his mouth to hers.

MERRY CHRISTMAS
from ...
LISA KLEYPAS

After graduating from Wellesley College, LISA KLEY-
PAS sold her first historical romance novel at the age of
twenty-one and decided to make writing her full-time
career. She has had four novels published and has been
featured in magazines such as *People* and *McCall's*. In
1987 she was given the *Romantic Times'* award for New
Historical Regency Author and in 1989 was awarded
Affaire de Coeur's Golden Unicorn for Best Time Travel
Romance. Lisa is a former Miss Massachusetts and com-
peted in the 1985 Miss America pageant. Her most recent
releases include *Then Came You* (June, 1993) and
Dreaming of You (May, 1994). She is currently a resident
of Texas and is hard at work on her next novel.

After Innocence

Brenda Joyce

Estranged from society, wealthy and beautiful artist Sofie O'Neil finds solace in her private world. She longs just once to taste a forbidden love—to follow the dangerous diamond smuggler Edward Delanza to paradise. But Edward wants far more from the innocent young heiress than a brief and passing encounter. For he is determined to heal her and possess her—now . . . and for all time.

"For Scorching Sensuality and Raw Passion, Brenda Joyce is Unrivaled."

Romantic Times

1

Newport Beach, 1901

It was a glorious day. Sofie no longer regretted leaving the city in order to attend her mother's weekend beach party.

A large sketchbook in one hand, charcoal in the other, Sofie paused on the crest of a dune to take in the view. The Atlantic ocean lapped the shore, dappled from the sun. Above, gulls wheeled. The sky was a nearly blinding shade of blue. Sofie smiled, lifting her face, shadowed by a straw hat, toward the sunlight. It was moments like these that made Sofie realize that there was life outside of her studio's four walls.

Then the throbbing of her ankle brought her back to her senses. She should not linger. Coming down to the beach could still prove to be a mistake. She did have a wonderful preliminary rendering of Newport's coast, which she would begin in oils as soon as she returned to the city; but an entire evening awaited her, and it would be even less pleasant for her if she were limping more than usual. Suzanne had a houseful of weekend guests, and Sofie could not help but feel some dread. In truth, if she had her choice, she would lock herself in her room and paint. But she did not

have her choice since she had promised Suzanne to
be her most sociable self, and Sofie intended to try
her best to please her mother.

Sighing, Sofie imagined the long evening ahead as
she began to descend the dune. She wondered if she
would know any of her mother's guests. She hoped
so. Immersed as she was in her world of art, Sofie
rarely ventured out into society and could not con-
verse with strangers and mere acquaintances with
the casual ease that seemed to be second-nature to
others. Her younger sister, Lisa, had once told her
that one conversed upon whatever topic was at hand
or in sight—such as the beautiful porcelain vase that
might be resting nearby. It sounded much easier than
it actually was. Sofie decided not to worry about the
impending evening. No one expected her to be the
belle of the ball.

Sofie moved awkwardly down the scrub-covered
dune in her uneven gait and, after several feet, paused
to rest. Trying to catch her breath, she glanced about,
and her eye caught a flash of bright white. Sofie looked
again. She glimpsed a man strolling down another
path in the dunes just below her. Like herself, he was
leaving the beach, but he had not seen her.

The sight of him was so arresting that Sofie froze,
completely forgetting herself and the rest of her surroundings. He was bareheaded, his thick black hair
a startling contrast to the stark white of his finely
tailored linen sack jacket. He wore it casually open,
its sides billowing in the breeze, and his hands were
shoved deep into the pockets of his pale cream-hued
trousers. He was a large man, Sofie could see that,
for he was tall and broad-shouldered. But he moved
with the grace of someone much smaller, seeming
as lithe and sleek as a black panther she had once
seen in the Bronx Zoo. Sofie was captivated. From

this distance she could just make out his tanned features, which seemed to be extraordinarily handsome. She imagined painting him. Abruptly she sat down, flipping open her notebook. Her heart thundering in excitement, she began to draw.

"Edward! Wait!"

Startled, Sofie's hand froze as she watched a woman flying up the path after the stranger. Sofie recognized her neighbor, Mrs. Hilary Stewart. Why on earth would Hilary be running after this man in such a fashion, with her skirts lifted high in one hand, shamelessly revealing long, white-stockinged legs? Then it dawned upon Sofie what this scene might be about, and she blanched, shocked.

Sofie sternly told herself that it was not her affair and that she should go. Quickly she tried to finish the study of the stranger, adding a few last strokes. Then the sound of his voice, low, silken, and baritone, made her hand still. Sofie lifted her head, finding herself helplessly ensnared by the masculine sound, involuntarily straining to hear.

Hilary was clutching his shoulders. She swayed a little, as if pushed by the breeze—or as if waiting for his kiss.

Sofie's eyes widened. Her heart beat doubletime. It was as she had thought—as she had feared. She dug her fingers into the warm sand, her sketch forgotten. She knew she must go before she saw something she had no right to see—but she was unable to move, absurdly paralyzed.

Hilary's throaty laughter sounded. And Sofie's eyes widened as she watched Hilary slowly unbutton her pinstriped jacket.

He wondered if he was growing old before his time—he was certainly too old for this. Africa had not been solely responsible for jading him, but it had certainly convinced him that life's comforts were worth waiting for. He had no intention of fornicating in the sand when cool clean sheets would be available at a later time. Besides, Hilary Stewart had only left his bed a few hours ago.

His smile was wry. He had met Hilary at a party a few weeks ago almost immediately upon his return to the city. He learned that she had married a much older man just a few years ago and was now newly widowed. Edward preferred widows; they tended to enjoy sinning without feeling guilt or making demands. The attraction between them had been mutual, and they had been carrying on ever since.

Now they were both guests at the Ralstons' summer home. Hilary was undoubtedly responsible for his invitation, but Edward did not mind. He liked her outside of bed as well as inside it, and the city was hell in the summertime. Suzanne Ralston, their hostess, had kindly given them adjoining rooms, and last night Hilary had kept him occupied from midnight until dawn. Yet apparently Hilary was far less sated than he.

Edward wondered when his enthusiasm, once boundless when it came to pretty, available women, had begun to die?

Still, he was a man, and his gaze flitted from her brown, bedroom eyes to her pale, white hands as they worked the buttons of her jacket free. Hilary was ravishing and voluptuous; despite his better intentions, knowing her as he did, his loins stirred.

"Darling, this might be indiscreet," Edward drawled.

Hilary's answered only with a coy smile as she pulled open her fitted jacket. She wore nothing underneath, not even a corset. Her breasts were large and milk-white, the nipples ruby-red.

Edward's mouth twisted and he sighed. Still, he slipped one hand around her waist, his other palm cupped her heavy weight. "I'll meet you later tonight," he told her in a low, somewhat husky voice.

She sighed, arching her neck back. His thumb moved over her nipple, methodic and skilled. She moaned. "Edward, I am so mad about you, I simply cannot wait."

Her skin was silk and for another moment he fondled her, his trousers becoming painfully tight, he was too much of a hedonist not to enjoy what he was doing. For a moment he was quite tempted and he debated; then he flashed his dimples. "We're both old enough to understand anticipation, darling," he said slowly, kissing one nipple lightly then pulling her jacket closed. Quickly and efficiently he slipped each black button into its frog.

She gripped his wrists. "Edward—I don't want to wait. I'm not sure I *can* wait."

"Of course you can wait," he murmured, his smile quick. "We both know it will be better if you do."

Her hand snaked out and she gripped his steel-hard erection. "How can *you* wait?" She whispered.

"Honey, rolling in the sand is *uncomfortable*."

She sighed with frustration, with resignation. "I'm afraid you'll go back to southern Africa and I'll lose you."

He laughed, prying her hand free—with more than a little reluctance. "Not a chance in hell," he said, meaning it. Edward put his arm around her shoulders to pull her forward for a quick, good-natured kiss. But a flash of movement caught his attention and he started.

His gaze swiftly sifted through the scrub-covered

dunes just above and beyond Hilary. His eyes widened. Crouched in the ridge of sand above them was a voyeur.

He swallowed his surprise, quickly looking away. But the sight of a pair of wide, avid eyes in a pretty oval face remained in his mind. The voyeur was a young lady with a blue-ribboned straw hat, apparently fascinated with them.

Hilary now gripped his wrists; he still had one arm around her, and his erection was suddenly the size of a cannon.

Edward was swept with a rush of excitement. He pulled Hilary close, wondering how much the observer had already seen and if she would go away now, when he kissed Hilary. It struck him that he was truly depraved. For he was far more excited by the thought of some young woman watching him make love than he was by the prospect of the actual act itself. Fornicating in a bed of sand no longer daunted him.

He kissed Hilary, acutely aware of being watched. He kissed her deep and open-mouthed, stroking her tongue with his, pressing her up against his rock-hard cock, until she was moaning loudly and clinging to him, her knees so weak he had to hold her up. When he broke apart he saw that the intruder was frozen and mesmerized. She had not moved from her crouched position behind the scrubby bush, but her hat had blown off and tawny golden hair blew around her face. Even from the distance separating them, he could feel *her* excitement, too. She hadn't realized that he had seen her.

His hand flicked down and quickly he worked the buttons of his trousers open, his breathing coming harsh and fast. His mind was disapproving even as his manhood sprang free. He heard a gasp and knew damn well that it had not come from Hilary, whose eyes were closed.

"C'mon, sweet," he whispered, nipping her neck even as his conscience sternly berated him for his appalling behavior. But he couldn't stop seeing the voyeuristic woman with his mind's eye, couldn't stop seeing what she must be witnessing. He closed Hilary's hand around him. He found her mouth again. He rained kisses down her throat to her collarbone and lower, working the frogs free as he did so, and finally taking one large red nipple deep into his mouth. Hilary collapsed, but Edward was prepared and he caught her, slowly sliding her down to the sand.

A moment later he dropped down to his knees, lifting Hilary's skirts and sliding deeply into her in one smooth and practiced thrust. As he moved inside her, fighting for self-control that should have been second nature after the previous night's excess, he was aware of the blood boiling inside his veins, expanding there. He felt as if there were two women lying beneath him. Suddenly he wanted to know who the stranger was. And then he could take it no more, and even as he was undone, he glanced up and glimpsed a wide-eyed face framed by golden hair. When he looked up again, sometime later, the voyeur was gone.

Edward closed his eyes. What had become of him? Suddenly he was ashamed and worse, he was frightened. It occurred to him that his black reputation was not as exaggerated as he liked to think.

Sofie tripped many times in her haste to get back to the house. There was a croquet game being played on the back lawn, but she did not want to be seen. She must not be seen. Not now, not like this, not after what *she* had seen. Her face was hot and flushed, and she could not breathe normally. Everyone, especially her mother, would instantly comprehend that something was wrong and demand to know just what.

Sofie avoided the back lawn even though it meant a much longer walk back to the house. Instead she hugged the dunes until she came to the tennis court, which was, thankfully, empty. She could no longer stand the pain in her right ankle, which had grown worse with every step. With a small cry, she collapsed in the sand just behind the court, covering her face with her hands.

She did not know how she could have done such a thing. When she realized that she had stumbled across two lovers—one of them her lifelong neighbor, dear god—she should have turned and fled. But she hadn't. She had lost all control of her body and her mind. She had stayed. She had stayed until the very end.

Sofie trembled wildly, reaching for her leg. *What was it like to be kissed like that? What was it like to be in the arms of such a man?*

Sofie shut off her wayward thoughts, gripping her ankle. That she had stayed to watch was horrible enough, but to be thinking in such terms was even worse. She had never before indulged in such speculation—now was not the time to start. She would never know what it was like, and that was that.

Sofie held her ankle, moaning, as tears filled her eyes; but whether from the anguish afflicting her lower leg or from something far more wrenching, she did not wish to know.

Sofie blinked back her tears resolutely. The couple hadn't seen her, so her terrible secret was safe. At least Hilary hadn't seen her. For one brief instant she thought the man had glimpsed her, at the end, but she knew that she must have imagined it in her distress. Otherwise he would have cried out in shock instead of passion and stopped what he was doing.

Sofie began to massage her aching ankle. She must not think about what he had been doing, or how he had looked while doing it. In truth, the stranger had been a glorious sight. Now Sofie understood why women were forbidden to attend classes using nude male models at the Academy.

She grimaced and slowly got to her feet. Pain shot through her ankle right up her thigh to her hip, finally distracting her. She bit her lip, refusing to cry out. Suzanne would say it was her own fault for going down to the beach unaided in the first place.

But sometimes Sofie grew so tired of being confined, of not being able to do what everyone else took for granted. And when she worked, she could not bear company, outside of that of an instructor or a model, if she were using one. And Sofie had spent the past two and a half months in the city, a fact that had made this day at the shore even more inviting, enough so that she had relinquished all of her customary caution and common sense. She so rarely found the opportunity to work *en plein air*, and so rarely at the beach. Foolishly, she thought she might make such a journey without mishap—how wrong she had been!

Sofie shook the sand from the ruffled cuffs of her white shirtwaste. At least she was breathing evenly now, and her hands no longer trembled quite so much. She wondered who the stranger on the beach was. His first name was Edward, which meant nothing to her. Sofie closed her eyes. "You fool," she whispered aloud. A man like that would never look twice at a woman both lame and eccentric like herself.

By the time Sofie arrived at the kitchen entrance of the house, she was not just exhausted from the painful aching of her ankle, she was distraught. She had left her sketchbook at the beach.

Sofie's work was the most important fact of her life, her *raison d'être*, and she had never before carelessly left her notebook behind. That she had done so now was just another indication of how agitated she was by having seen the two lovers together.

Her limp much more pronounced than usual, Sofie followed the hall to where it entered the house's central foyer and found her mother standing in the green and white salon, conversing with a young man.

"Sofie! There you are! We have been looking for you everywhere. Henry said you were at the beach. Is that true?" Suzanne's brows were raised as she took in her daughter's disheveled appearance.

Sofie paused as her mother moved toward her, the young man following closely behind. Suzanne was both an elegant and beautiful woman, her figure willowy and perfect, her hair dark, her skin as pale as ivory, and she was only thirty-six. Sofie had realized some time ago that she had been conceived when her mother was only sixteen. Often she had imagined how her beautiful mother had been swept off her feet by her handsome, charismatic father, Jake O'Neil. As often, she had imagined what their life would have been like if Jake had not been forced to flee New York fourteen years ago. How she missed him, and loved him, even to this day.

Sofie hoped her smile appeared genuine. "I am sorry, Mother. I was at the beach sketching."

Suzanne blinked. "Alone?"

Sofie nodded.

Suzanne turned toward the man, who seemed quite nervous. "Did I tell you that my daughter is also an artist? She studies by day at the Academy and often

paints all night in her studio at home. She is pursuing
a career in art."

Sofie blinked at her mother, who never spoke about
her professional intentions publicly. While almost a
quarter of her class at the Academy were other young
women, equally as dedicated as Sofie, it was still
considered very odd for a woman to be pursuing
art instead of a husband. She glanced at the young
man, who had managed to shake his head "no". She
realized why he was dismayed.

"Sofie is very talented," Suzanne said, smiling.
"Dear, show us what you have done today."

Sofie froze, recalling her sketchbook, left at the
beach, and why it had been left there, and her heart
skidded uncontrollably. "My notebook is in my room,"
she managed. "I would be glad to show it to you at
another time." But she stared at Suzanne, wondering
what she was about. Her mother did not approve at
all of her art, especially recently, and she would not
normally suggest showing it to her guests.

"I want you to meet Henry Marten, dear," Suzanne
said, guiding him forward. "He is a cousin of
Annette's. He has just graduated from law school
and will soon be opening up his own practice."

Sofie smiled, forcing her attention to the young
man, who appeared uncomfortable and ill at ease.
She extended her hand, guessing at the source of his
discomfort. He probably thought that Suzanne was
matchmaking, which she was not. Sofie had not even
debuted. How could she when she could not even
dance?

Sofie looked at Henry Marten, who could not know
that she was not interested in marriage, who was pale
facing her, thinking himself a prospective beau. Sofie
wished she were in her room, painting. But she took

a deep breath and smiled too brightly and said, "How do you do, Mr. Marten. And congratulations. Where did you graduate from?"

Henry took her hand, dropped it immediately. "Nice to meet you, Miss O'Neil. I . . . err . . . Harvard."

Suzanne excused herself with a smile, and Henry Marten appeared even more distraught once they were alone. Sofie felt her cheeks heating and wished her mother had not put her in this awkward spot. "That is a grand achievement, sir."

He stared at her and wet his lips. "Yes, thank you."

Sofie forced a smile again. "It is no easy feat to be accepted there, is it not?"

Still he stared. "No, it isn't."

"How proud you must be." She shifted her weight again to relieve her aching ankle. She did not suggest that they sit, because she wanted to leave, to find Lisa. Her notebook would still be at the beach, and she *must* recover her study of the dashing, dark stranger named Edward.

"Shall we . . . err . . . walk, Miss O'Neil?"

Sofie took a deep breath and smiled again, bravely. "Oh, ordinarily I would love to, but I am afraid that I must leave to rest in my room if I am to regain my appearance for this evening."

He hesitated, clearly relieved. "Of course, Miss O'Neil."

Sofie smiled, just as relieved, then quickly they separated, rushing off in opposite directions.

"Sofie—it is not there!" Lisa cried, closing Sofie's bedroom door behind her.

Sofie jerked. She was soaking her ankle in a salted footbath, clad only in a cotton wrapper. "But it must be! You did not look in the right place!"

Lisa, small and dark-haired and exquisitely beautiful, exclaimed, "I did! I took the path that starts near the tennis court, and I went all the way to where you can see the ocean from the crest of the last dune, just as you instructed—where you can see another path below. It was not there. I found your hat, though."

"Oh, dear," Sofie cried, dismayed and gripping her chair. "Someone has taken my study? But who? And why?"

"I really did look everywhere," Lisa said.

Sofie barely heard her. "How will I paint him now?"

Lisa touched Sofie's hand. "Paint him? Paint who?"

Sofie stared at her stepsister, at a loss.

Lisa gazed at her inquiringly.

Sofie realized what she had said. She took a deep, calming breath. "I saw this very debonair man walking on the lower path while I was on the dune sketching, and I did a rendering of him. He did not see me, of course." She knew she was blushing. The skin on her face was warm. She felt as if omitting the entire truth was akin to lying, which it was not. But she could never tell her younger sister what she had really seen.

"Who was he?" Lisa asked with real interest.

"I do not know. She called him Edward."

"She? He was not alone?"

Sofie wished she could take back her words. "No," she said, avoiding Lisa's gaze. How could she have let that fact slip?

But Lisa had sat down hard on the edge of Sofie's chair, crowding her. "You must mean Edward Delanza!" she cried in excitement.

Lisa's words stirred up a spark of both horror and anticipation. "Who is Edward Delanza?"

"I met him last night before supper—oh, how I wish you had been there! If only you had arrived yesterday instead of today!"

Sofie's insides began to curdle. "He is dark and handsome?"

Lisa gave her a look. "Far more than handsome. He is devastating! Dashing!" She lowered her voice and leaned toward Sophie. "*He is dangerous.*"

Sofie was ashen. No—Lisa could not be talking about the man she had seen on the beach. Surely he was not their houseguest this weekend. Surely not.

"He has the women in the house in an uproar," Lisa chattered on. "Every woman found him fascinating last night—our guests, the maids—even your mother looked at him more than once. His reputation is blacker than the night, Sofie," Lisa was now whispering, her tone conspiratorial. "They say he carries a small gun at all times—that he is a diamond smuggler—of stolen gems—*and* he is a *rake*."

Sofie picked up a novel she had been reading and vigorously began to fan herself with it. "I am certain the rumors are quite exaggerated. After all, why would Suzanne invite him if he were so despicable?" But she already half-believed the gossip, oh she did.

Lisa smiled. "Because he is hardly despicable, Sofie, despite what he does. They say he was wounded in Africa, and that makes him something of a hero! Several of the ladies here have set their caps for him, too; after all, he must be as rich as Croesus. I cannot wait for you to meet him, Sofie. This once, even *you* shall be smitten!"

"You're the one who sounds smitten," Sofie said, surprised that her tone was so calm.

"I am, but he is definitely not for me—Papa would never allow such a man to court me—and we both know it." But Lisa's dark eyes glowed. "Last night after everyone retired, he was with one of the women outside on the terrace. I saw them—it was shocking the way he held her! He was kissing her, Sofie!"

Sofie was frozen. "Who?" She croaked. "Who was he with?"

"You won't believe me—I didn't believe it either! It was Hilary Stewart!" Lisa leaned close. "I have heard that she wishes to marry him, too!"

Sofie could not respond. It had finally dawned upon her that the man she had spied on at the beach *was* Edward Delanza, and that in a very short time she would come face to face with him. Dear God, how could she possibly face him after what she had seen?

America Loves Lindsey!

The Timeless Romances
of #1 Bestselling Author

KEEPER OF THE HEART   77493-3/$5.99 US/$6.99 Can

THE MAGIC OF YOU   75629-3/$5.99 US/$6.99 Can

ANGEL   75628-5/$5.99 US/$6.99 Can

PRISONER OF MY DESIRE   75627-7/$5.99 US/$6.99 Can

ONCE A PRINCESS   75625-0/$5.99 US/$6.99 Can

WARRIOR'S WOMAN   75301-4/$5.99 US/$6.99 Can

MAN OF MY DREAMS   75626-9/$5.99 US/$6.99 Can

SURRENDER MY LOVE   76256-0/$6.50 US/$7.50 Can

Coming Soon

YOU BELONG TO ME   76258-7/$6.50 US/$7.50 Can

America Loves Lindsey!

The Timeless Romances
of #1 Bestselling Author

Johanna Lindsey

The WONDER of WOODIWISS

continues with the publication of
her newest novel in paperback—

FOREVER IN YOUR EMBRACE

☐ #77246-9
$6.50 U.S. ($7.50 Canada)

THE FLAME AND THE FLOWER

☐ #00525-5
$5.99 U.S. ($6.99 Canada)

THE WOLF AND THE DOVE

☐ #00778-9
$5.99 U.S. ($6.99 Canada)

SHANNA

☐ #38588-0
$5.99 U.S. ($6.99 Canada)

ASHES IN THE WIND

☐ #76984-0
$5.99 U.S. ($6.99 Canada)

A ROSE IN WINTER

☐ #84400-1
$5.99 U.S. ($6.99 Canada)

COME LOVE A STRANGER

☐ #89936-1
$5.99 U.S. ($6.99 Canada)

SO WORTHY MY LOVE

☐ #76148-3
$5.99 U.S. ($6.99 Canada)